MW01135150

NO
MORE
GAMES

NO MORE GAMES

A Story About Life, Love, and Baseball

MIKE GALLO

Copyright © 2021 by Mike Gallo.

Library of Congress Control Number:		2021904769
ISBN:	Hardcover	978-1-6641-6247-1
	Softcover	978-1-6641-6246-4
	eBook	978-1-6641-6245-7

All rights reserved. No part of this book may be reproduced or transmitted in any form or by any means, electronic or mechanical, including photocopying, recording, or by any information storage and retrieval system, without permission in writing from the copyright owner.

This is a work of fiction. Names, characters, places and incidents either are the product of the author's imagination or are used fictitiously, and any resemblance to any actual persons, living or dead, events, or locales is entirely coincidental.

Any people depicted in stock imagery provided by Getty Images are models, and such images are being used for illustrative purposes only.
Certain stock imagery © Getty Images.

Print information available on the last page.

Rev. date: 03/08/2021

To order additional copies of this book, contact:
Xlibris
844-714-8691
www.Xlibris.com
Orders@Xlibris.com
825607

NO MORE GAMES

The transition from childhood to young adult is never easy. When a man's young son asks him for help in overcoming his fears for an upcoming baseball game, it sends his father into his basement, where he revisits the summer that his friends, baseball, and a girl forced him to learn that he could no longer play games.

1 CHAPTER

As the sun leaked in through the drapes, David sat at his desk in his home office, poring through documents. To an outsider, these were the kinds of documents that every adult finds themselves shuffling through daily, the documents that kids just assume adults get handed to when they walk into and out of work each day. It's part of the standard procedure of being an adult that we all slowly come to accept. However, for David, these documents were for a presentation he had been preparing for over two weeks.

It wasn't unusual for him to be in his home office early in the morning, but this was a Sunday morning. This was the last chance he'd have to get everything just right before he met with his potential investors in about twenty-four hours. The thought of building a nice baseball complex and running his own baseball organization for young kids in tough neighborhoods made him beam with pride, a dream that seemed so far out of reach at one point in his life. Now he needed to make sure that he hadn't left any stone unturned. He had to make sure his budget and return on investment calculations were precise. Any mistakes or flaws could be a deal breaker.

Looking at him and his house, it was hard to imagine any sorts of flaws. He was the kind of man who looked like everything was always under control and came easy to him. The middle-class neighborhood oozed with comforts. Kids never had any wants in this neighborhood, and the biggest problem for adults was finding ways to hide the strain of wanting more for themselves while living within their means. His work office was a contrast between organization and a man who clearly spent a lot of time working there. The walls were lined with college degrees, family pictures, and books on the side his desk faced. At a glance, you would picture that this office belonged to a man who had it all—a beautiful wife with a degree in social work and one in psychology, his own bachelor's in business, and two healthy young kids.

The books were all neatly organized and covered a wide variety of topics from personal to professional. They lined both sides of his desk, which was covered in more books and papers that were somewhat orderly, but you could tell they had been recently run through and were not as carefully placed as the books on the shelf. There were lots of sticky notes lining the sides of his laptop, along with pictures of his family.

The family pictures were stunning. They seemed like the kinds of pictures you would find on display in the mall or when you purchased a new frame. David was a man in his late thirties but still looked like he could be in his late twenties. He had distinct features that more than hinted at the great athlete he once was. His jaw was still sharp and pointed, any wrinkles only slightly appeared when he was smiling, and in every picture, he was smiling. He had long lean, athletic muscles from his head to his toes on his over six-foot frame. His dark hair and skin accented his wife's blue eyes in the pictures they were in together. She, like him, looked like she could have been anywhere between the age of twenty-seven and forty. She also glowed in every picture. She showed little signs of being a mother of two and a person who dealt with others' problems all day every day, a woman who seemed to have it all with no cares in the world—the perfect husband and the perfect family.

Like most walls lined with pictures, this wall told a story. It showed how David and his wife had grown together, once young lovers from college and then with two young kids in their arms and now by their sides as they got older. A lot of people would look at these pictures and wish their life was this way. What amount of stress and adversity could these people had ever dealt with? They seemed so confident and reassured with themselves and their place in life in these pictures. The neighborhood suited them.

As he sat at his desk, his back faced two large French doors. Those doors were often closed when he was working. From a young age, the kids knew not to interrupt or to enter without permission when those doors were closed. David didn't want his kids to hear about the things he dealt with during his job or be stressed by the numbers of his sports management partnership. Yet today was a Sunday, and the doors were slightly ajar. It was early in the morning. It wasn't unusual for David to be in his office before everyone was up, but on Sundays, the doors were usually wide open. For this reason, his son, Jake, wasn't sure if he should enter or not.

Right as Jake was about to knock, David turned away from his desk and looked up from the documents he was shuffling through on his lap. It was a father's intuition, the kind that you don't understand when you're younger, but as you become a parent, you steadily sharpen. Kids don't have to make a sound for a parent to know when they are present and when they need you. David didn't have that when he was growing up, and he often wondered why his own parents didn't have these skills when he was a kid. How could he have developed this seemingly instinctive skill while his parents never did? Nobody trained him to sense when his kids were near or, more importantly, when they needed him.

David quickly slapped the documents he had been studying into an organized stack and placed them into a folder on his desk. Seemingly in the same motion, he turned completely around in his chair to face Jake, who seemed to still be trying to figure out how his dad had even known he was there and then managed to turn around so quickly. Just seconds ago, he saw his father as a grown man doing grown-up things that he didn't understand, but now he saw the face of a loving father who was giving him his whole attention.

Jake eased into the office, like he was still contemplating whether he should bother his dad. He couldn't quite bring himself to look right at his dad. Instead, he looked over to his right. This wall was lined with baseball memorabilia, from pictures to baseballs to plaques and awards. To an eight-year-old boy, that wall seemed like an endless maze of questions that he couldn't quite figure out how to ask, but he knew he wanted them on his own walls one day. He wanted to learn about the people in those pictures and the stories behind the awards. He didn't spend much time looking at that wall when he was a little boy, but now as his ninth birthday was approaching, he always looked at that wall first when he entered his dad's office.

As a young boy, he was always drawn to the wall on his left. That wall was lined with picture frames that held jerseys his father had worn during his playing days. There were a number of them from college and his minor-league days, but Jake liked how they all had his last name on the back, Collins. There were pictures of his dad on that wall from his playing days. His dad didn't look that much different now, which made it kind of intimidating to talk to him sometimes, especially when he was wearing a baseball cap like he was now.

Even though his dad never pitched in the big leagues, Jake viewed him as a big leaguer. With a hat on, he looked just like all the guys he saw on TV. He still had the muscles that his shirts always seemed to outline perfectly. Despite always being kind and funny, Jake knew his dad had the power in his body to get his way with others if needed. Jake had stared at those pictures countless times as a little kid. His dad was his hero, and he wanted to be just like him. He knew his dad had a job managing people, but more importantly, he knew his dad was once a really good baseball player. That was what mattered most to him now because he needed his dad to help him both personally and with baseball. Now as he was getting older and starting to play baseball like his father had, he was starting to develop self-doubt.

It was the same self-doubt that most eight- to nine-year-olds start to develop when they begin to realize that others are better at them in certain things or when they get called out by their friends for being better than them. It's the age where kids begin to branch out a bit but only because their parents make them. And by branching out, it means that they do the same sorts of activities that their parents enjoyed or excelled in when they were younger. It's part of the parenting handbook. Put your kids in the activities that you understand and enjoy while allowing yourself to recapture some of your past glory by living it through your kids and sharing stories with the other parents. This seems especially true with fathers and sons and sports. It only made sense for Jake to be playing baseball like his dad did. It was why his younger sister was in gymnastics and dance.

Jake was getting to that age where he was starting to sense some of that pressure of being the son of a former athlete. It wasn't coming from his father though; it was coming from the pictures on the wall. Jake wanted to be that guy. He wanted to be a picture of power and confidence. He wanted to stand on the mound, with everyone watching, and deliver. He wanted to be his dad, just like most kids at eight or nine.

All this was brewing in Jake's mind as he stood cautiously at the edge of David's office. David hadn't once pressured him. He loved going out in the backyard and playing catch with Jake or throwing him batting practice, but if Jake wasn't up for it, they didn't do it. He always smiled whether Jake did good or bad. He was never too busy with work to be bothered or to play with him. David seemed perfect to Jake, like every father should at that age. Jake assumed that David had grown up feeling the same way about his dad. He knew his grandpa played baseball as well from the stories he had shared, so Jake figured they must have bonded over that too. They must have spent hours playing catch and laughing together when David was growing up. Maybe even his dad got nervous when he played, like Jake was feeling now.

Jake bet he knew how much his own father would have never wanted to let down his grandpa when he was growing up. And he knew that there was no way his dad had ever failed. All he had to do was look at the walls of his office to know that his dad had never failed. There were artifacts everywhere to prove how successful his dad had been. His grandpa must have been so proud of him growing up.

Just as Jake was starting to think he had his dad and his childhood all figured out, his dad spoke up and broke his analytical thoughts and brought him to task. "What's up, stud?" David said like most adoring fathers do to their only son as he leaned forward in his chair, putting his hands on his massive quads.

Jake stood there for a second, looking at all the pictures and jerseys from his dad's playing days to his left. He was still lost in thought about how perfect his dad seemed and how perfect his life must have been when his dad interrupted his thoughts. Now that he had been addressed, he didn't remember why he had come in to speak to his father in the first place. He just kept staring off to his left, not really wanting to make eye contact with the man he had built up to be a legend.

"Nervous about the game?" David asked as he pressed upward onto his feet. There was a slight groan that hinted at his age, but once he was on his feet, he looked like one of the guys Jake idolized on the highlight reels.

Jake stood there, frozen by the fact that his father had somehow managed to analyze his inner thoughts in less than a few seconds. He fidgeted with his jersey while simultaneously pulling his cap farther down over his eyes so his father couldn't see them, yet he couldn't bring himself to speak.

David, now walking over to him, lovingly patted him on the head as he walked past, saying, "You'll do just fine."

Jake stood there looking down at the ground. He could hear his father making his way to the kitchen. He turned and saw him embrace his mother and give his little sister a kiss. He was a man who had it all—no worries, complete control.

Jake turned and walked slowly toward the kitchen. His mom urged him to grab a quick bite to eat as she turned to David. "Honey, is everything already loaded into the car?"

"Yeah, I took care of everything while you guys were sleeping," he replied. "I didn't want to have to rush out of the house this morning, and I wanted to make sure we were all prepared to watch Jake dominate." As he said this, he looked over toward Jake, flashed him a smile, and gave him a thumbs-up. While this would lift almost every other regular eight-year-old, it caused Jake to sink even further into the depths of his young mind and dilemma.

"I've got to check on the sprinklers, so I'll back the car out and see you guys in there in a couple of minutes," he said as he whisked through the door that led out to the garage.

"Jake, come on over and eat some toast," his mother urged. "You've got a big day, and we've got to get moving to get you to your game on time."

Jake kicked his feet at imaginary dust as he shuffled to the kitchen table, still looking down at the ground. His mother, like any mother in this situation, knew something was wrong. "Lauren, why don't you go outside and check on your father?" she asked in the way a mother does to one child when the other needs her attention.

"But I—" was all Lauren could get out before she got the look from her mother. It was the unspoken look that even a six-year-old could recognize, the look that begged, *Please do what I tell you because your brother needs my attention.* It was the same look her mother had given Jake many times before when Lauren needed her mother's undivided attention. She willingly but grudgingly got up from the kitchen table and made her way out through the door to the garage.

Now that his mother had Jake to herself, she could take him to task. Jake knew that he was going to have to spill the beans too. Fathers act like they are interested, but if you don't come out with it right away, you are dismissed. It's not that fathers don't care; it's just that they're different from mothers. A father always seems to have better things to do or doesn't always want to get caught up in the wash of a young kid's emotions, but mothers are seemingly built for this purpose. David really cared about Jake and his problem, but he knew that his wife would be the one better suited to get it out of Jake if he didn't come clean in ten seconds or less.

"So what's on your mind, sweetheart?" she asked as she eased next to him in his kitchen chair. As a mother, she knew to wait for a response. Fathers like to guess the answer as a means of avoiding or shortening a conversation, but mothers want to wait and hear everything on their baby's mind.

Jake paused, hoping that his mom would drop it, but was secretly happy that she wouldn't before he mumbled, "I'm scared."

"Scared of what?" his mom retorted, a bit taken aback.

"I'm scared I'm going to screw up and let you down," he replied with a little more timbre in his voice.

"Scared of letting me down? Sweetheart, you don't have to worry about letting me down. It's just a baseball game," she pleaded to her son.

"Yeah, but . . ." he trailed off, stopping short of spilling his thoughts.

"Yeah, but what?" his mother calmly pleaded.

"Yeah, but what if I screw up and let down the team? They'll all be mad at me and make fun of me," he mumbled as if he were melting back into his own world.

"I know your team and your teammates. They won't make fun of you," she urged, now slightly more aware of what was troubling him but also of the impending time constraints this conversation had because they had to drive to the fields. "Plus, your dad is the coach. He wouldn't let anyone tease you or get mad at you."

When those words came out, it seemed to be the trigger in both of their minds. Jake's mom realized she had tapped into the real issue, and he tried to hide it by taking a bite of his toast. In that moment, she was like a person who had been laboring over a puzzle to discover where the final pieces landed. She was keenly aware of her son's fears and anxieties but relieved to know that they were those of the average eight-year-old boy who was getting ready to pitch in his first championship game on a team coached by his dad, who happened to be a former minor-league pitcher.

"Oh, sweetheart, you don't have to worry about your dad. He'll never get mad at you or be disappointed in you," she began, right from the mother's playbook of standard answers.

"But let me tell you, I've seen your dad mess up plenty of times," she proclaimed in a slightly humorous tone as her voice raised.

Jake perked up a bit in disbelief. "Really?" he sheepishly responded.

"Yeah, really," she said as she nudged him out of the chair. "Your dad isn't Superman. I've seen him lose plenty of games. In fact, I remember when he was told he couldn't play baseball anymore."

"Couldn't play baseball anymore?" Jake repeated with raised curiosity and concern.

"Oh, don't worry, Jake, he can still play baseball, but every player at some point gets told that they can't play on a team anymore because they're not good enough," she said with growing confidence and certainty.

"So I could be told I'm not on the team anymore if I screw up?" Jake pondered out loud as he froze in place on their way to the car.

"No, no, no," his mother replied, dropping to her knees. She sensed she might have just caused a bigger problem right as she was on the verge of rectifying the original one.

"I mean, when guys get older," she said, searching for words. She studied Jake's face and knew that she had missed her mark. She was now getting desperate and knew she would hear the sound of the car honking from the driveway any second. Her son, one of the loves of her life, had his entire ego and identity melting before her. The man Jake loved and feared disappointing more than anyone in his world was going to be summoning them. Being late would only heighten both his and Jake's anxiety. She had to act swiftly, like all mothers do when balancing their professional lives, marriage, kids, and the emotions that encompass all those relationships.

"Jake, your father was a great ballplayer. I saw him do some great things, but I also saw him when he was down. He was just like you, except he was worried about letting me down. Your dad thought that every time he didn't do well, he was holding me back or letting me down. He didn't think he was any good and thought he was disappointing the people who loved him. He was scared all the time when he went to pitch, but there was one thing he used to help him get through those times."

"Really, what was it?" Jake asked, rejuvenated. He liked hearing that his dad was scared and was worried about letting people down.

"Well, would you like me to ask him to show you?" she responded with her heart beaming at her son's new demeanor and her restored confidence as a mother.

"Yeah, but do you think we'll have time?" Jake rushed out as he now straightened his hat and seemed to be acting like a normal eight-year-old again.

"I know he'll make time, so let's go ask him," she said resolutely.

Right as she finished up this statement, they both heard the horn summoning them to the family SUV. Jake shot a glance toward his mother. "Don't worry, sweetheart, he'll make time," she reassured.

Jake went hopping out to the car and got right into his normal spot behind the front driver's side seat. His baseball hat and uniform was all squared away. He smiled at Lauren, who was already playing with a combination of stuffed animals in preparation for their drive to the fields. "Well, that's more like it, little man," David said, smiling as he looked at him in the rearview mirror. "Where's your mom?" As soon as he finished his sentence, he looked back into the garage and saw her walking through with her arms full of snacks and accessories. She approached the passenger door with the window already rolled down and dropped her items through and onto the seat.

"Come on, get in. We've gotta get going," David tried to say as patiently as he possibly could, but he could see she wasn't about to get in as she motioned him out with her beautiful blue eyes. He knew this look, and he knew he shouldn't waste time negotiating. He quickly got out and maneuvered around the front of the vehicle to her side. Whatever she had to say was something she didn't necessarily want the kids to hear because she met him halfway on his journey to her side of the car.

"Babe, we've got to go," he whispered urgently in a feeble and desperate attempt that this would somehow resolve the situation and persuade her to either wait until after the game or find a way to speak in adult code in the car with the kids in the back seat.

She grabbed his hand, the same way she grabbed his right hand after the times when he had failed. She started with her left hand, running across the back on his hand to pull him in closer, and she then wrapped the fingers of her own right hand over his. It started as an intimate handshake as she pulled him in, keeping both hands wrapped around his. "Jake needs you," she implored as only a mother could. She made a soft, slow turn toward Jake, who was sitting at full attention in the back seat.

Those initial words and the way she said them caused David to lose his breath for a second. What could he need at this moment that caused his wife to grab him in that way? The way she would grab him when no words would help him? The way that always let David know that no matter what happened, she was going to be by his side? It didn't matter where his dreams took him; she was willing to visit him or live with him in any small apartment, in any random town, just to be with him while he pursued his dreams. It was the way that she would grab him when they were quietly watching their kids from a distance, and both knew that words couldn't describe the moment and their happiness. David knew that exact grip, and he knew it came at times when great comfort was needed or when there was a moment they wanted to remember. He knew he didn't need any comfort, so this had to be a big moment. He looked into the car at Jake, who was now staring back at his feet. She gave him a slight squeeze that drew his attention back to her beautiful face. He started to say something, but she beat him to it.

She started off almost apologetically because she knew what a great father David was and how much he loved his kids. Coaching Jake's team meant the world to him, and she was so proud that he was less than twenty-four hours away from pursuing another dream of sharing his love and passion for baseball with so many more kids and families who needed it. "Jake is scared of letting you down. He's scared of letting his teammates down."

David opened his mouth and was about to pull away when she stopped him and continued on, now speaking as a mother on behalf of the son she loved just as much as he did. She said what Jake couldn't. "This is the first championship game that Jake is pitching in, and he's scared. He doesn't want to let you down because he worships you. He sees all the baseball stuff in your office and wants to be just like you. You're his hero, and he doesn't want to disappoint you."

David now managed to get his hand free from her because he wanted to get back in the car and tell Jake how much he loved him and that he could never be disappointed in him, especially when he was just eight years old, but his wife grabbed him again, this time in a way that told him not to go into that vehicle before letting her finish.

"I told Jake about the thing that you had with you to remind you not to be scared when you pitched," she started. "I told him how it gave you courage. It made him smile to learn that you weren't always perfect, that you needed something to help you with your fears. I told him you would go get it for him."

David paused for a second, trying to process everything that his wife just told him. He looked again into the back seat of the car, but this time, he saw himself sitting back there, full of fears and uncertainties. He remembered those feelings well. He also remembered that they were cutting it close on time to begin with.

"Babe, don't you think I could talk to him after the game and give it to him then?" he pitifully asked as he shifted his posture back toward his side of the car.

"He's pitching because he's the best pitcher on our team. He's only eight, and he's blowing it by kids that are a full year older than him.

He'll do just fine," he declared in his last attempt to delay the inevitable and get to the ballpark on time. However, a quick glance at his wife told him that he wasn't getting out of this.

"Do you think the team will be okay if you're not there right when warm-ups start?" his wife said sarcastically as she knew she'd already won. "Go back into that house and give your son what he wants, what he needs." Victoriously, she smiled at Jake, who seemed to be hanging on their body language for clues about how the conversation had been progressing.

David looked into the vehicle at his two kids and gave them his million-dollar smile. As he started back into the garage and into the house, his wife tapped him on his butt. "I love you," she declared loud enough for anyone to hear as she gave him a wink. He winked back as he began a light jog back into the house.

As he descended into the basement to look for what had given him courage throughout his years in baseball and in life, he began to slow down as his heart started to race. How was he going to explain this to his son? Everyone has a past, and in the eyes of his son, he was perfect, a hero. He wanted to keep it that way as long as possible, even though he knew that every parent loses that status as their kids grow older.

When he hit the last step and opened the door to their storage area, he was overcome with a rush of emotions. He paused and looked around their finished basement. It was a cozy room that his kids had spent hours playing in. It was the type of room where he would shift from playing dolls with Lauren to Legos with Jake. They built things and broke things in that basement together. His wife had lined the walls with more pictures and memories of their perfect life together.

Stepping through that door, David was stepping back into his past—a past he had worked so hard to get beyond, a past that he had refused to let define him—but in so many ways, Jake's fears were a part of his past. The one thing his son needed and wanted was the one thing that took him back to that past. It was the one thing that would change his father from immortal to a human like everyone else.

David navigated his way toward the back of the storage area, where he had a handful of items from his playing days that he didn't have the room or desire to display in his office. Finally, he saw it from a few feet away, and he immediately felt guilty for having it tucked into a storage area where he rarely ventured into anymore. He glanced back out into his lovely basement and thought about his perfect house and family. His powerful body sagged as if all the confidence from this proud father and former athlete had been drained from him. Even though this item had been the life force behind so many great moments, it brought up a well of emotions and memories that he hadn't thought about since he had retired from baseball well over a decade ago.

The item had been sitting in that same spot since they had moved into this house a few years ago—his dream house, his dream family. David knew exactly where it was, and he remembered the guilt he felt when he left it in that spot in the basement. He knew he didn't need it anymore, and he remembered the mixed emotions he felt at that moment when he put it in the storage area and closed the door. It was like he had closed the door and turned off the lights on his guiding force. He had climbed the mountain and no longer needed this insensible source of strength.

He didn't know what he was going to say to Jake when he would give him this miniature stuffed lion, but at that moment, he remembered what it was like to be scared and full of doubt. He could see the tattered stuffed lion staring at him, and he looked into its eyes like he had a thousand times before. That lion always gave him comfort and strength, but at this particular moment, he felt weak. David wasn't sure if it was a weakness from the memories of his childhood or the strain of having to reveal that he was not always the man his son had envisioned. As he sat down on a bench and stared into the faded eyes of this stuffed lion that fit so comfortably in his hands, he forgot his time and place. David sat silently and squeezed that lion as a rush of memories suddenly overtook him.

2

It was the summer of 1991. Marky Mark was a flamboyant singer leading the Funky Bunch, not the bankable Hollywood actor. Michael Jordan just won his first NBA championship over Magic Johnson, who was still just a basketball player. AIDS was still scary as it had just taken Freddie Mercury. The year started off on a high note with the end of the Gulf War. American pride was swelling as we had quickly put a totalitarian leader back in his place with the might of our army. However, those good vibrations didn't last too long as the entire nation had its eyes opened to police brutality with the Rodney King tape. No woman felt safe being alone after *Silence of the Lambs* came out early that year, and soon afterward, police arrested a man in Wisconsin named Jeffrey Dahmer that made all Americans question the sanctity of our country's moral fiber.

Yet for fifteen-year-old David and his friends, most of that seemed worlds away. They were in no way sheltered from the world and its problems; in fact, their lives were riddled with them. But when you're in high school, the highs and lows of the country are typically projected onto you by some adult or teacher who thinks that kids want to discuss these things and need help in processing them. In reality, most high school kids can't really see beyond their own issues for more than five minutes. They didn't need an adult talking to them about the impacts of the recession when they can see it at home. High school kids were familiar with Freddie Mercury's music, but his death didn't affect them like it did the adults who were teaching them. The primary concern for David and his friends that summer was dealing with that awkward transition from kid to young adult.

This transition occurs at slightly different ages for most people, but for David, it happened during that summer of 1991, between his sophomore and junior years in high school. David was really young for his class, so despite getting ready to move into the upper levels of high school, he was still just fifteen years old and wouldn't turn sixteen until the fall. He was still a kid and wanted to be a kid despite the fact that all his friends were older than him, some by more than a couple of years.

He and his friends had spent their past summers playing baseball all day at the field adjacent to the town elementary school for as long as they could remember, but this summer was different. Some of the guys now had cars and other priorities, and a few of the older boys had jobs in some capacity. Gone were the timeless days of getting together and playing baseball all day. Now when they got together and played, it wasn't timeless because somebody had to go to work, or they had to schedule the days they could play around work. The excitement and joy they had as kids was now being replaced with a feeling of obligation to keep showing up despite there not being the same level of innocence and sense of endless possibilities. They didn't pretend to be MLB superstars anymore, just kids who liked playing baseball but didn't have parents who would commit to them playing for the local Legion team, kids who wanted the same opportunities as those in the neighboring town but didn't dare act like it because they knew they would quickly be put in their place by their friends.

Living in a lower-middle-class Midwestern town outside a city wasn't unique for many people. Riverview was a small town of a few thousand people that sat at the bottom of a large bluff that overlooked the city just a few miles away. It sat perfectly on the border of the urban ring, where low incomes and reality butted up against flourishing suburbs and privilege. Its inhabitants could clearly see the buildings and bright lights every day from the streets and their homes. The high and violent crime hadn't come to Riverview, but it was only a few wrong turns away. Even though the city was so close, few people had the means to enjoy any of its benefits. A handful of people in Riverview worked

15

in the city, but they weren't taking part in the high-paying jobs. Most people in town worked at the steel mill a few miles away or other blue-collar jobs that they spent their evenings complaining about at one of the many local taverns.

If there was one thing that Riverview had an abundance of, it was taverns. Each tavern was a fabric of the area it was surrounded by, and most people in town didn't venture past the one within a few blocks of their home unless it was one of the taverns that catered to the third-shift workers who would need to get some breakfast and a few drinks after their shift. David's parents could be found in those taverns every day. His mom was a waitress/bartender at the bar just down the street from his house, and his father was one of those guys who couldn't stomach going home from his third-shift job at the steel mill without being overserved in the morning.

Riverview wasn't a town that had a lot of violence or high crime, but its location adjacent to the interstate made for routine robberies of gas stations and convenience stores out that way. However, in town, the biggest issues for the police were dealing with bar fights and drunk drivers. It was pretty rare that people from Riverview actually fought one another. It was as if they had this unspoken loyalty that they knew they were bonded together. The fights usually occurred when people from outside of town would start something with the locals, mainly people from Fox Creek.

Fox Creek was just farther up the bluff from Riverview, and they had everything that Riverview didn't, minus the neighborhood taverns. People from Fox Creek were the ones who really had a view of the river, usually from their two-story houses and mansions. They were the ones who worked in and managed the businesses in the buildings downtown. Their town had the mall and all the chain businesses that wanted no part of setting up shop in Riverview.

In short, Fox Creek was the superior rival of the people of Riverview, except there really wasn't much to rival about. The people from both towns knew this, and while one group seemed to hate it, the other seemed to relish in the fact that no matter how rough things might get in their lives, they could always come to Riverview for a little while to feel better about themselves. Fox Creek had the nice new strip malls and new schools, while Riverview had small businesses that would go under and with signs that would never be replaced and schools that had been neglected due to insufficient tax revenue and community support.

When it came to sports, the town schools had stopped playing each other a few years back in football and basketball because the contests were so lopsided. Fox Creek was a booming community with schools that were expanding and people who only knew one another through the competition in appearance that they shared. Riverview was a town that looked like it never had booming days, and if they did, they were many years ago. Riverview was big enough that, while you didn't know everyone in town, it didn't take much to find someone who knew you or your family wherever you were.

Even the cops in town knew just about everyone. They knew who was weaving on the road and how far they had to go before they made it home to sleep off their troubles. They knew who acted like they wanted to fight versus who actually was going to fight. They knew that the locals loved nothing better than seeing someone from Fox Creek being pulled over, trying to speed through their town.

The officers were typically friendly with the kids. Since not much happened during the day in Riverview, the cops would often take lunch by the school where the boys played baseball and would comment on the games. The boys would talk about which cops they liked and which ones annoyed them, but the consensus was that Officer Smith was their favorite. He seemed to take a genuine interest in the boys and would give them a free ride home on days where it was really hot or when they just didn't feel like walking across town. He was quick with a smile and to chat up the boys, and it was hard to imagine him having a firm side to deal with the people fighting in the bars or holding up the convenience stores. He was middle aged with a fair complexion, sporting a thin mustache and fading muscles.

As kids, you're never fully aware of how your life compares to others. You assume that what you have and what you experience is normal, until you see something else that makes you think otherwise. However, by the summer of '91, David and his friends were fully aware of how their life compared to others, especially those who lived in Fox Creek. Even more so, David was aware of how different things were for him at home from his friends, and he spent many days and hours isolating himself, trying to figure out what he had done to cause these differences.

The summer of '91 would be the last summer David spent wondering about those differences, but leading up to then, it consumed him. He was a good-looking kid with thick dark hair and features. Even though he had just wrapped up his sophomore year of high school, he still hadn't quite gotten through the other side of puberty. It wasn't uncommon for people in Riverview to start school at a young age because their parents struggled with day care, and school was free; however, David—being born in late October—was unusually late.

He had always been a very bright kid, even from a very early age, so his parents didn't hesitate to put him in school despite the fact that he would be more than a year younger than some of his own classmates. So while he had the makings of a tall kid with plenty of lean muscle, he was always smaller than his classmates and the kids in the grade above him. This caused him to struggle a bit when it came to sports. He was a good athlete and could hold his own when they were younger, but through the middle school years and now into high school, David would routinely get outmuscled on the basketball court in the winter. During the fall when the boys would play football, he was forced to play wide receiver. He had the arm to play quarterback, but his body wasn't built for the pounding that position takes from neighborhood kids who had never heard of such a thing as a late hit.

This was why David gravitated toward baseball. Baseball was the one sport where it didn't seem to matter how tall you were or how much muscle you had. If you could hit and throw, there was a spot on the team for you, and David could throw. He knew he was pretty good based on how he performed throughout his days in Little League when it was rare for guys to put the ball in play against him, but he didn't use that as his measuring stick. He used his friends as his measuring stick, the guys he had spent his summers playing with in the lot next to their elementary school. He couldn't play with them in Little League because he was younger. On the basketball court or football field, they could use their age, size, and strength difference to bully him around. Because he was the youngest and the slightest of the group, most football games would end with someone tossing him the ball and everyone taking turns tackling him and pounding him into the ground. They likely did this for two reasons: he was the easiest target, and they spent all summer trying to hit off him in baseball and couldn't. The football field and basketball court was the place they could take out their revenge on him.

David loved being on the mound and watching his friends flail away ineptly when they faced him. His best friend, Dusty Scott, was the one who always caught him. Dusty was a loudmouthed stocky kid with light brown hair and freckles who would fight anyone to defend his friends or the town of Riverview. His name fit him perfectly. His freckles and raspy voice always made him seem . . . dusty. It's like some people, when they are babies and get their name, immediately are cast in life and spend the rest of their days fulfilling some sort of prophecy that goes along with the name they were bestowed with. That was Dusty Scott. He was scrappy with auburn hair and hated anyone who wasn't from Riverview. He had recently turned sixteen, and his parents had divorced a few years earlier, which Dusty wore as a Riverview badge of honor and rite of passage, but he couldn't stand his stepmother because of how much she treated him like a child and was always in his business. David loved Dusty's stepmom and was jealous of that. He couldn't figure out why it bothered Dusty so much that he had someone who was always checking on him and making him warm, fresh meals.

On paper, it didn't make much sense why David and Dusty were friends. David was quiet and shy, and Dusty was anything but. David would sit and dream about leaving Riverview for days on end, while Dusty's biggest ambition was to have his own stool at his neighborhood tavern one day. Dusty struggled in school and often spent his school days in the office because he had flustered his classroom teachers with his constant banter in class. Meanwhile, David got great grades and loved going to school. Dusty was stealing smokes from his elder sister and beers from his father ever since middle school. He would force David to join him in their passage to manhood despite David usually being much less enthused about these activities. If they hadn't been placed in the same kindergarten reading group, who knows if they would have become as close as they were?

However, there were some common bonds between the odd couple. Dusty was also young for his grade, having a summer birthday, and he also loved baseball and was good at it. The room oftentimes was only big enough to hold one personality like Dusty's, and he seemed to be aware of it and enjoyed it. It was likely what drew him to David. He knew that David wouldn't stand in his way. He also knew that David needed somebody to speak for him most times. Dusty had also always been David's teammate and catcher since they first started playing baseball together when they were seven years old. In this way, they were perfect for each other. They had been best friends since kindergarten, and the only thing that would change this was if one of them left Riverview.

David would always walk to Dusty's house every summer morning before the two would wander the town and eventually end up at the baseball field. David liked going over there because he knew Dusty's stepmom would always have some sort of breakfast around. Even though David didn't eat nearly as much as Dusty, she made two heaping plates of eggs, pancakes, and bacon for them. This morning was no different. David could smell the bacon long before he approached the stairs that led into their trailer. As David entered the trailer right into the kitchen area, he was greeted by Dusty's stepmother, Bonnie, and she looked genuinely thrilled to see him as she always did.

"Good morning, David!" she belted out as she was laying out her spread on the table for him. "How are you today?"

"Probably getting ready to complain about something!" Dusty belted out as he emerged from his room with a smile and a laugh that shook his whole body.

"Now, Dusty, be nice to David," Bonnie quickly snapped as if they were both her boys. "So what are you boys up to today?"

"Well, I thought we'd start off by throwing rocks through the school windows and then make our way to the dairy barn and beat up some little kids and steal their milkshakes. After that, we'll probably go rob Jay's convenience store for some booze and then find a couple of girls we can get pregnant," Dusty declared as an attempt to rattle his stepmother.

"But don't worry, I'll be home in time for dinner so we can talk about it together," he said with a lot more bite.

Bonnie never seemed to get rattled by any of Dusty's antics. She knew this was his way of testing her, and any sign of weakness would give Dusty all the leverage he needed. She didn't have any kids of her own, and Dusty's elder sister had pretty much moved out as she was moving in. Dusty was the only chance she had of being a mother to someone, and it didn't bother her how much he tried to hurt her. She had married Dusty's father, the Riverview fire chief, a year and a half earlier, not long after Dusty's mother had walked out on him and his father. David knew it ate at Dusty, and he really missed his mom, even though she had stopped calling not long after she had left. Dusty only had a slight idea of where she was now, and suddenly, he went from having a mom who didn't give a rat's ass about him to no mom at all to a supermom.

"Now, Dusty, you think you're funny, don't you?" she began. "It's a good thing you hang around David. I know he's too sweet and shy to do any of that."

Dusty looked up from his pile of eggs quick enough to give David a quick smile from the corner of his mouth. David knew he liked Bonnie, even if she was always there. Dusty had struggled for years to get the attention of his real mother, who bounced back and forth between waitressing and dancing. When she was dancing, Dusty would walk around, looking for fights. When she left, Dusty seemed to be his usual jovial self almost all the time. He ragged on Bonnie, but his demeanor and his belly told David how much he enjoyed her being there. David just appreciated how much cleaner their trailer was since Bonnie had arrived.

"So what are you boys up to today?" she persisted. "Hanging at the baseball field all day?"

"Most likely," Dusty replied with a mouthful of pancakes.

"We'll probably head to the Dairy Barn at some point, but I don't think I have much money," he sheepishly said, smiling to David through a half-eaten pancake.

"Well, here's five dollars," she lovingly replied while handing the money to David.

"Hey, wait! Why are you giving that to him?" Dusty fired back as he choked down the pancake he'd been working on.

"Because I want to make sure that you both get something," she cheerfully replied as she gently nudged one of Dusty's chubby cheeks. This made David laugh, which in turn brought the death stare from

Dusty. David knew it didn't matter. Dusty would force David to give him the money the second they left the trailer anyways.

Besides, they both had their own money. They had gotten part-time jobs in town that paid them cash, Dusty washing dishes and occasionally cooking in the kitchen at his neighborhood bar and David unloading trucks and stocking the shelves at Jay's convenience store and pharmacy. Yet Dusty knew that Bonnie would always give him money when he asked. She would do anything to win him over, and she already had despite the fact he would never publicly acknowledge it. Every boy needs a mother, and Dusty had finally gotten one who cared about him. It bothered David that Dusty seemingly had a real relationship with a mom of any sort, but he loved to watch how they interacted.

The boys quickly finished up breakfast—well, Dusty did, while David picked at a piece of bacon. Dusty grabbed his baseball bag that held his catcher's gear, and they started out the door into the already humid and hot sun. David stopped for a second to help Bonnie with the dishes, but she only smiled at him and whispered, "Go ahead, David. I'll take care of this. I appreciate you offering."

She brushed his hair in a way that made him want to stay in that kitchen all day until he heard Dusty behind him from the bottom of the steps boom, "Hey, Romeo, let's bounce!" Bonnie winked at David, and off they went. David could never quite figure out why Dusty couldn't say "thank you" or let Bonnie know how appreciated she was, but there were a lot of things he couldn't figure out.

Since it was going to be a muggy day, the boys had decided the day before that they would get an early start to their baseball game that day. It was about a half a mile from Dusty's trailer to the school field. There were plenty of shortcuts through alleys and ditches along the way, weaving through trailer lots and ranch-style homes that had been largely neglected when it came to exterior maintenance. However, the shortcuts were for the way home. On the way to the field, the boys had to gather up the rest of their gang.

Not too far down from Dusty's trailer lived Ricky Rogers. He was a trash-talking fiend who was always in and out of trouble with someone's parents growing up. He had a smile that could convince any mom that he was sweet and innocent and tell a kid that he was going to kick their ass if he didn't do what he wanted. David hated him because he was always picking on him. Even though he was a grade older and had already just turned seventeen, he wasn't much bigger than David. Ricky was as wiry as his mouth, and David knew he didn't have to shut it because Dusty would and had on several occasions. Even his sandy blond hair seemed wiry and stringy. Both boys didn't care for Ricky, but he was always around and liked to play baseball. Even as he was approaching his senior year and had stopped playing for the high school, Ricky was always to be counted on for a pickup game of any sport, although lately he'd been running with a different crowd of people who lived much closer to the city. Everyone in their group was getting concerned about Ricky, but anytime they would bring it up, he would brush it off with his award-winning ear-to-ear smile. That kid was all teeth and all talk. Ricky must have seen the boys walking down the street from the bedroom window of his trailer because he started walking toward them before they reached his place.

Next on the route was Gary Shannon. Gary was the oldest and most mature of the group who looked like an athlete on and off the field. He had dark hair like David but was much taller with thick shoulders and an unusually soft voice. He fit both parts of a smooth talker with the ladies and someone you didn't want to run into on the streets of Riverview if you were a stranger. His parents had a little bit of money, so he lived in a ranch that was relatively well maintained just outside the trailer park. He had a car that occasionally worked, which was about the same as Gary himself. When his car did work, he was notorious for taking David and Dusty for rides and then making them walk home when he met up with a girl. Even though he has just graduated from high school, he still hung around the younger kids. He didn't seem to know what he wanted to do, but his parents told him that if he went to college, he wouldn't have to get a steady job; therefore, he decided to go to the local junior college and walk on to the baseball team. He definitely had the ability, but like his car, he didn't have the consistent drive. You could tell when he had a steady girlfriend because he would be difficult to get down to the field for baseball in the summer of football in the fall, but in the summer of '91, he was single.

He picked on David too but not on the personal level that Ricky did, more like a big brother whom David didn't have. Gary recognized that David was pretty talented when it came to baseball, so he limited his taunting to athletics mainly to keep David in his place. The entire baseball season for the high school, Gary made David carry his stuff to and from the bus despite the fact that the coach told Gary he didn't want David putting extra weight on his throwing arm.

David really liked Gary though. He liked the way he looked and carried himself with a certain swagger that athletes do. He loved how he could just approach any girl and start a conversation and seemingly get a phone number whenever he wanted. Things always seemed to come easy for Gary, and David was envious of that. Everyone in their little gang looked up to him, and Gary knew it. He didn't take advantage of it too much, but he had no problem making David and Dusty feel like little kids when he needed to. David wouldn't say anything, but Dusty always would. They would usually squabble before Ricky would come in and break them up. Ricky desperately wanted to be Gary's right-hand man, but as laid back as Gary was, he too was starting to distance himself a bit from Ricky because of some of the choices he was making.

On the days that Gary wanted to play baseball, he would usually be waiting in his driveway for people to start showing up. He'd typically be messing around with his car, trying to get it to work, and trying to act like he knew what he was doing. Today was no different. Before David and Dusty could engage him, he smirked. "What's up, chumps?"

Ricky, smiling like a dog who had just heard his name called by his owner, was the first to respond. "Hey, Gary! Whatcha up to?"

"Just trying to get this thing to run. I've got a couple of girls who want to meet up tonight and catch a movie. Then they both said they were up for hanging down at the creek in the park afterward," he boasted with his prized smile.

"Well, that's great, but you wouldn't know what to do with one girl, let alone two," Dusty chirped. "Besides, it's not like you've got a car that can get them there or money to get into the movie anyways."

Obviously bothered and eager to put Dusty in his place, Gary fired back, "Well, at least I can get one girl to even give me the time of day, tubby. Well, at least one that's not my stepmom."

Gary knew that would get Dusty going, and it did, but before he could come back with a clever retort or a barrel-chested shove, Ricky chimed in, "I've got more than enough cash." He was smiling from ear to ear with those thirty or forty teeth while thumbing through a wad of cash in his pocket. This made everyone uneasy and got the focus away from Dusty's stepmom.

"Yeah, I'm good, but thanks," Gary answered out of obligation and trailing off.

"Oh, come on, it'll be a blast. Plus, Joey has a car. We can all go. I can even score us some beers, no problem." Ricky had suddenly come to life as everyone else was fading in the midmorning sun.

Sensing that nobody was really all that enthused about his plan, Ricky turned to the person he figured he could bully into compliance. "David, you're in, right?" he said in a hopeful but directive tone.

David looked down and kicked some of the gravel in Gary's driveway. "Well, I don't really think you or the girls want me around. Besides, I need to be at home."

"Bullshit!" Ricky barked back. "Everybody in this driveway knows you're the one person that never has to be home. You can come and go as you please, so what's your problem? Are you scared? Afraid you might have to talk to a girl? Afraid she might find out that you don't have any hair on your balls?"

Just as Ricky was getting going, Dusty jumped in. "Listen, he said he didn't want to go, and he needed to be home!" Dusty barked as he walked up on Ricky.

"Do you need him there to get laid?" he continued on as he now was on the offensive.

Ricky knew it was wise to back down off David at this point because Dusty was coming. He was already piqued by the comment Gary had made, even though this was how they talked to each other every day. "Hey, whatever, guys. It'll be your loss anyways. Besides, I'll get Joey to come with me. At least he's got a car that works," he said as he started off toward the school baseball field. From Gary's house, it was only down the block and around the corner. The other three guys stood there watching their friend stroll away. In some ways, they were all thinking the same thing without anyone having to say a word.

Just as Ricky had gotten about twenty yards from the driveway, they heard a car come screaming up the street from behind him. They didn't have to turn and look to know who it was. Joey Logan was the last one of the boys who regularly ran in their group. He was going to be a senior, but he had been held back in school and was already eighteen. He lived at the far end of the trailer park, and nobody bothered going out of their way to walk by his place. It didn't matter because he had a car, a 1980 burgundy Chevy Caprice with a loud stereo and tears in the interior lining of the roof. Joey was somewhat reserved, but that was mainly because he didn't have an original thought in his head. He was your classic follower, and he was following Ricky, which had them all worried.

Joey came roaring down the street, ignoring the 25 mph sign or more likely oblivious to anything related to the road and safety of others. Getting in a car with Joey was literally taking a ride on the wild side, and one was never sure if they'd live to see it through. He drove fast because people told him to drive fast. He hung out with questionable people because Ricky was hanging out with questionable people. He was a huge kid who stood over six feet three and weighed well over 250 pounds. The weight fit his body frame well. He had been a good football player but never really took good care of himself. He had a premature smoker's laugh that came to him naturally since he'd been smoking regularly for over four years. It was the kind of booming, deep, lingering laugh that they all loved. Every group needs a guy who just doesn't care and is there to lighten the mood, and that was Joey. He had shaggy brown hair and a voice that was deep, aged by smoking and drinking, but distinctive. Although he looked the most rugged in the group, he was typically polite and well mannered. He enjoyed still being a kid and playing baseball at the lot.

"Hey, boys," he said barely over the blaring music. "I see you must have already pissed off Ricky." He chuckled with his smoker's cough following as he looked down the street toward Ricky, who had now stopped walking. "Well, I have no doubt he deserved it." He motioned his head toward the vagabond and continued to chuckle.

"I'll make him come with me for a couple of minutes, and we'll pick up some drinks and meet you at the school in a few minutes," he said as if he was asking a question.

"Sounds good," Gary said as he thumped the car door twice. With that, Joey nudged ahead and picked up Ricky, and they steamed down the rest of the street. As they turned right to head to Jay's to pick up some drinks, Ricky made sure to clearly extend his arm and flip off his group of admirers.

"I worry about that guy sometimes," Gary said half-heartedly.

"I worry about both of them," David said both sincerely and straight faced.

"Yeah, well, don't give it too much thought," Dusty said as he slapped him across the back. "They ain't worth it, and you ain't got enough room up there with everything else you've got going on anyways." He now ran his hand up to the back of David's head and shoved him forward. David just smiled and started walking up the street to the field, with Dusty and Gary immediately behind.

As the three boys turned left at the end of the street to head to the school baseball field, they could already see the rest of the baseball crew assembling. There were four other kids from across town who would routinely show up for their pickup games. Dallas, Eric, Jason, and Brooks lived on the other side of town out by the high school/middle school, so they ran together. The Riverview Little League fields were out that way as well, but they weren't big enough to handle the boys as they got older and into high school, so they would ride their bikes to the elementary school to meet up with David and his friends to play "real" games. They were going to be freshmen and sophomores in high school, so they didn't pose much of a threat but were needed to play. Even though David was the same age as the sophomores or not much older than the freshmen, he considered himself to be much older when he was with his friends. They almost always beat David's group to the field because they were younger and seemingly had even less to do than them.

Dallas, Eric, Jason, and Brooks had a very important job that was essential to the ability to play any sort of game. It was the kind of job that was passed down to them from David's gang as they became the elders of the school baseball field and the job that they would eventually pass down to the middle school kids who would occasionally want to play with them. It was a sort of rite of passage to get to be a part of these regular games. Each boy was responsible for stealing one newspaper from someone's driveway on their way to the lot. There were no permanent bases on the field, and the yellow weather-protective sleeve made for easy-to-spot bases in the all-grass infield and a suitable pitching rubber.

The field itself wasn't really a baseball field. It was only called a baseball field because it had a chain-link backstop that had weeds and ivy growing all over it and a circular dirt area with an embedded plate. The rest of the baseball field looked more like a football field. There was nothing to suggest baselines or an infield besides a pitcher's mound. The grass was thick and long, like what you'd expect to find in a pasture, mixed with crabgrass and clover. The infield area was especially clumpy because of all the high traffic and lack of maintenance. Most ground balls stayed true or died in the thick throngs of green, but every now and then, you'd get one hit hard enough to remind you that it was best to work off to the side of the ball than dare stay in front of it.

The outfield seemed to consist of more clover and dandelions than the infield area, but when it was mowed down, it looked decent from a distance. There really wasn't much of a right field. Starting about 225 feet away from home plate down the right field line was a row of huge elm trees that looked like they had been there for hundreds of years. They protected the elementary school from any ball that may be headed its way and also provided much-needed shade on the brutal summer days. The row of trees extended the length of the entire lot and rarely came into play except on plays right down the line or when a ball was tossed into right-center field. They extended in a perfect row from one street to another. The school and the field sat perfectly sandwiched between two quiet side streets.

Left field ran about 450 feet from home plate to the street. Unlike right and center fields, it didn't get any shade during the day; so by midsummer, the crabgrass would take over, and the ground would feel like concrete. In the middle of the summer, when the ground was particularly parched, it wasn't uncommon for the older boys to rope a ball that would bounce beyond anyone playing the outfield and keep rolling all the way into and across the street. It was strictly in a residential area of their small town, so there were barely any cars up and down those streets during the summer days anyways.

Debates would rage on every day over balls that would get up into the trees or roll across the street. Would the ball in the tree have been caught; was it a double, a homerun? "There was no way a ball that rolled across the street should be considered a home run!"

"If that ball was hit to the shaded side of the field, it would have died in the grass!"

"You can't keep intentionally hitting the ball to the opposite field and into the trees!" Those were all common arguments that had bonded the kids of Riverview on that field for years.

David remembered when he was in middle school, watching an all-out brawl occur between the older kids in town over a ball that was lofted into the row of elm trees one day. The cops had to be called out, and a few kids got hours of community service. He also remembered Officer Smith coming up with a resolution that turned their lot into a real baseball field in his eyes. For their community service, those boys spent their hours constructing a baseball mound under the watchful eye of Officer Smith. David remembered all the dirt, sand, and clay those boys had to haul and shape. It wasn't perfect, the pitching rubber was eventually stolen, and the mound was not very well maintained since that summer, but at least there was something he could throw off.

The older boys always hated when the younger kids would show up, but they also remembered what they felt like when they were little. The guys who played on that field were the ones you looked up to as a kid, and it was a rite of passage for them to put you in your place. The younger guys had to play the positions nobody else wanted, like third base and left field in the baking sun. You had to bide your time until you could pitch, play shortstop or center field, and you had better not screw up. There was nothing more terrifying than stepping into the batter's box when you were one of the middle school kids trying to prove your worth. There was an unspoken guarantee that you were going to be thrown at, and everyone was going to watch your reaction. If you showed that you were scared or intimidated, you might as well not even bother coming back. If you stood in there like a man and eventually learned to make hard contact, you were gradually accepted into the group and the game.

David had worked his way into that group as a sixth grader. He was mocked and laughed at, and if it weren't for Dusty's mouth and Gary's elder brother vouching for him, he wouldn't have been given a shot. His first time at bat, he was drilled right in the ribs by a kid who was now working at the Shell station out by the interstate and stood about six feet two inches. The next time at bat, he struck out but fouled a couple off. His third time at bat, he lined a base hit over second base that drew a glare and some cursing from the to-be senior on the mound. It also helped that he showed off his arm by throwing someone out going to third from left field. He was allowed to stay as long as he understood his place in the pecking order.

Ever since that day, David viewed that field as his second home—well, third home if you counted Dusty's trailer. The games and conversations were epic and the bonds everlasting. It didn't matter how hot it was or how beat up the field was. School maintenance mowed it once a week in the summer, and that field was heaven. The beat-up backstop didn't snag nearly enough foul balls, so the neighbors who had weathering ranch-style homes with cars in their driveways took a beating. Nobody seemed to care too much, though, because a baseball dent wasn't going to cause any appreciable or noticeable damage, relatively speaking. The boys would chip in to buy baseballs and then throw them in Dusty's equipment bag with his catcher's gear.

The only people who watched the games were the Riverview police officers on their lunch break. Their biggest concern was making sure no windows were broken and that the newspaper bases were returned to their owners before they got home from work that evening. The boys didn't always play actual games. A number of days, they would play "five hundred," which was a ground ball and fly ball game that consisted in anything short of murder to catch a ball and earn the right to hit. They also played home run derby, using the trees as their green monster. During those games, the officers would sometimes participate or offer to throw batting practice.

David couldn't remember having to go through a lengthy or arduous process of trying to find guys to play when he was in middle school. When you showed up at around ten thirty, you could almost guarantee there would be enough guys there to play some sort of game almost every day. The summer between his sophomore and junior year was a bit different. He and his friends were taking on more responsibilities, and the middle school kids were showing up less frequently. Even the police officers seemed to have less time to drop by and partake in the games or cheer the boys on. There were a lot of things changing that summer of 1991, including another fan who was taking more interest in their games, and all the boys were taking interest in her as well.

Becky Reeves lived in the house right down the third baseline between home plate and third base. Her house was one of the rare two-story houses in town, but that was about the only thing that made it unique. There were usually at least three vehicles parked in the driveway, only two of which were ever used or ran. The driveway itself was a smattering of asphalt chunks and gravel with weeds growing through everywhere. The siding was light gray wood that was covered in moss and neglect. The backyard had a walkout deck that led to an inflatable swimming pool. Adjacent to the pool was a fishing boat that hadn't been put in water in years. The front of the house was shaded by a couple of trees that killed enough sunlight to prevent grass from growing, but the thick moss gave the appearance of green growth. The backyard featured thick grass in the spring, but because it was neglected and fried by the sun in the summer months, by mid-June, it was a patch of weeds and dandelions. In the back corner farthest away from the field, there was a dog kennel that was home to two large dogs of no particular breed with a sizable thicket that divided their property from the house behind them. There were a couple of tie-ups with circular patterns worn into what remained of the lawn, where the dogs had been allowed to roam during the day to enjoy the shade cast from the trees in the thicket during the day. The two first-floor windows facing the baseball field were always closed, and outsiders were prevented from seeing inside, thanks to a throw blanket in each window that served as blinds. If someone didn't know better, there was no reason to give a second look at the property.

If you were to walk or drive by the property when there wasn't a baseball game going on that summer, you wouldn't think twice about another neglectful Riverview property owner. But when there was a game going on, Becky Reeves made sure to come out and watch and bring everything to life. She was sixteen, soon to be seventeen, and a senior. Like David, she had a late birthday and was young for her class, but she looked mature for her age. She was a slender five feet eight inches and had long hair that was naturally gold, that sweet color between blond and brunette. It flowed without flaw just below her shoulders. It was a genuine moment for a young man to watch her flip her hair or manipulate it into a bun in ways that boys never understood but girls made look so effortless and sexy. Her skin almost perfectly matched the color of her golden hair in its lack of flaw and tone. She had legs for days that she loved to show off and a smile that was readily available to light up a room and the soul. Her blue eyes seemed to explode from the golden backdrop of her skin and hair. While they weren't a dominant feature that defined her, they drew you in. She wore makeup in just the right way, never too much and only to accentuate her eyes and keep everything in the golden and simple tone of her skin.

Simply, she was a beauty. It appeared that she was from a different mold from the rest of the women from Riverview. She looked like she belonged in Fox Creek. Her mother was relatively young and attractive, but endless shifts working as a medical assistant at the senior living center seemed to have drawn any life and radiance out of her early forties. Maybe most women in Riverview looked like Becky before they were exposed to the endless smoke and drafts at the local taverns, but she was like none of the other girls their age, especially in the eyes of the boys.

Becky had grown up in Riverview at that same house, yet as a kid, she didn't come outside much during the day to watch the games. Her dad worked first shift at the steel mill, so if he came home and the boys were still playing, he'd sit outside on the deck with a few cold beers and watch them play. It wasn't until the past summer and this one that Becky came outside to torment the boys figuratively and literally. She most likely didn't want to deal with older boys harassing her when she was younger, but now that she was just as old or older than just about everyone on that field, she had no reservations about being seen and heard from the field. Another factor was that her dad had left her mother a couple of summers ago, and her stepdad was a gruff alcoholic whom she tried to avoid at all costs.

She had gone to school with David throughout the years, but since they were in separate grades, they had limited interactions. David wasn't the type of guy to initiate a conversation with anyone, especially someone like Becky, who seemingly had no problem talking to anyone. Quite frankly, she intimidated the hell out of him when they were younger. He would always watch her from a distance on the playground, cafeteria, or bus when she wasn't paying attention. He wasn't even sure if she knew who he was. The Riverview schools were small, so they had some interactions but nothing lasting. David always thought she was cute, but she always looked young and innocent. When they were younger, he was drawn to her magnetic personality and seemingly fearless ways. It wasn't until the past year that she really blossomed, and everyone seemed to take notice of her physical attributes. David had gone from admirer to luster in a short period. He knew that she knew his name and would be friendly, but beyond that, he figured he didn't stand a chance with her.

Becky was a sort of late bloomer like David. Growing up, she never really stood out from a looks standpoint, so she used her flamboyant personality to fit in with just about everybody. It seemed like most boys in the school had dated her at one point, but those relationships never lasted very long. Their school in town was too small to really have a traditional popular clique; plus, everyone in town was basically on the same economic grounds, so being popular didn't really come with many benefits. She flowed back and forth seamlessly from hanging with groups of boys or girls. However, when you got to high school and your world got a little bigger, being popular might get you access to friends in Fox Creek. As Becky's looks and body blossomed, so did her social interactions with the boys from the next town over. Everyone was taking notice, including David.

David had never had a serious girlfriend before. There were a couple of girls who called him their boyfriend for a while, but he just wasn't interested in everything that having a girlfriend entailed. He didn't like talking to people all that much, so having a girl who wanted to speak on the phone every night was not anything that appealed to him. He liked wearing Umbro shorts and a T-shirt everywhere, so he wasn't interested in being told he had to dress a certain way. He had gotten serious enough to kiss a girl in the past, but when she wanted him to start styling his hair like Zack Morris, he just stopped talking to her until she got the hint and moved on.

A lot of things were different that summer of 1991 though. David started to catch himself staring at and thinking about girls a lot more often. He still felt inadequate and that he looked much younger than other boys his age, but he was definitely taking an interest in the opposite sex, and that interest was squarely focused on Becky Reeves. The only problem for the introvert was that everyone's eyes and interest were focused on Becky that summer.

"Hey, guys, what do you say we call it a day? We've been out here for a couple of hours now," Ricky asked, trying to get the approval of Gary as they both had sweat streaks between their breasts and shoulders.

"Nah, just a little while longer," Gary replied, motioning over toward Becky's house.

She had left a little earlier to walk over to the Dairy Barn. The Dairy Barn was the local ice cream stand that people from all over flocked to. Even people from the city would come over for their special ice cream and milkshakes. It really annoyed the locals in the summer when they'd have to wait fifteen minutes just to get served in their own hometown. It was like they couldn't even enjoy the one thing that brought others to Riverview, and as they were waiting, they were forced to watch others roll in and out of town with their nice cars.

Becky went to the Dairy Barn every day. The Dairy Barn was Riverview's one and only attraction. It was a walk-up and drive-through ice cream place that literally operated out of what looked like an overgrown shed or barn. It was famous across the entire region for its ice cream twists and milkshakes. It had a large parking lot and area where people could enjoy their summertime treats and socialize.

Keeping with the Riverview theme, it was cash only and ridiculously cheap, which was probably why it drew large crowds at all hours every day during the summer months. She'd go there almost every day to draw the attention of people she'd never seen before or the boys from Fox Creek. She'd go there and mingle like she was the princess of Riverview, and she would spend time getting to know her suitors on the swing set that was there mainly for little kids but usually overrun by older kids. But for the boys on the baseball field, the best part was when she'd come back. She'd usually come back with a good-sized ice cream cone that she'd eat while sitting outside on her deck.

Today was no exception. The Dairy Barn was about a mile from their field, but Becky would usually persuade one of her suitors to buy her ice cream and give her a ride home. That quick trip back was enough to prevent the ice cream from melting. When Becky got home was when she really went to work.

She casually slid out of the passenger seat of a brand-new red Ford Escort that was driven by some guy nobody on that field recognized. She closed the door and bent over the frame and into the car to say goodbye. While the driver thought he was getting the prize, the boys on the field were the lucky ones. They all stared, and nobody said a word as they took in the most perfect pair of tanned legs they had seen. Those legs ran all the way up to her Daisy Duke shorts, and as she was bending over that door frame, there really wasn't much left to the imagination.

After giving some sort of phony line to the driver, she quickly pivoted and headed for her backyard. The boys tried to quickly resume their game, but they were all busted. Becky knew it and loved it. She took her time walking over to her deck, glancing at her onlookers as she slowly took her position on her throne, the sun chair.

Before she sat down and ate her ice cream cone, she had to put the boys through one more torturous ritual. She couldn't possibly eat her ice cream with a good T-shirt on. Also, these were prime hours in the day for getting a golden tan. She would have to get out of those clothes and reveal the bikini she was wearing underneath while holding that ice cream cone.

Watching any woman undress was a mixture of excitement and torture for teenage boys, but watching Becky Reeves do it was on another level. To make the seduction and process even more torturous, she would have to do it with one hand. Something about that ice cream cone made her have to move and contort her body in all sorts of ways that only enhanced the fantasy these boys were living out—the swivel of the hips as she wiggled off her short jean shorts, the raise and arc of her body as she worked her T-shirt off with one hand to reveal her voluminous chest. In raising her shirt over her head, Becky's hair was tousled, which forced her to have to throw it around in a seductive way to get it out of her face. Once her pink bikini was fully revealed and she was seated on her sunning chair, the next torturous ritual began; she would actually lick and eat the ice cream cone, usually while harassing the boys.

"Hey, Romeo, let's see what you've got left." Gary smirked as he dug in from the right side of the plate with his back to Becky. David had lost all sense of where he was. Becky was the only thing that could make him do that on the baseball field. "Hey, lover boy! You gonna keep playing or what?" Gary was now getting impatient.

Everyone was getting impatient. They had been out there for about four hours, with a couple breaks, for this moment. This was everyone's opportunity to impress the goddess in the bikini who was eating an ice cream cone. During those moments, every boy on the field wanted to play like a big leaguer. They all secretly felt in some way that if they did something impressive, it would somehow catch the eye and, more importantly, the interest of Becky Reeves.

"Come on, David, show her what you've got," Dusty said while smiling from his catcher's crouch. The comment was directed at both David and Gary. Gary laughed at his buddy's humor, but David was pissed that his friend had called him out like that in front of Becky. They weren't in middle school anymore, but David still wasn't comfortable with a girl knowing he liked her.

As he stepped back on top of the mound and tried to regain his focus, he heard a voice coming from beyond the third baseline. "Yeah, let's see what you've got, Romeo," Becky sarcastically said as she crossed her legs and wiggled her toes.

David felt a strange sensation run through his body. He didn't know if it was anger or adrenaline, but he knew she was watching.

He also knew he was facing the best player on that field. They had faced each other hundreds of times before, but suddenly, this was the most important out of his life. It didn't matter that Gary was two years older. The princess was looking at her suitors, and whoever won this confrontation was going to leapfrog to the front of the line in David's mind.

The boys in the field all chose their sides as this epic confrontation was about to begin. Most of the guys were cheering on Gary for a couple of reasons. First, he was the oldest and could make life hell on them at that field for the rest of the summer if he wanted; and second, most of them personally didn't have a chance when they faced David. It was as if this moment was their opportunity to experience what it was like to get a hit off him while the princess was watching. Maybe if they were lucky, Gary would hit a ball their way, and they could make an incredible catch that would suddenly thrust them into the spotlight. Either way, they were all glad to be out in the field because they could watch Becky lick that ice cream until there was no more.

"Come on, Gary, you've got this," Ricky said from shortstop. David could see his teeth glaring with that huge smile out of the corner of his eye. The other boys started up their banter as well, supporting Gary.

"You've got this, David," Dusty said in the same tone he addressed his foes just before he fought and pummeled them.

David took a deep breath, trying to focus on Dusty and not Becky and her ice cream cone. He knew Gary would be expecting a fastball first pitch; so did Dusty. He put down two fingers for a curveball just in case they weren't on the same page, but David was already starting his windup when those fingers went down. Strike one, a knee buckler that even had Gary smiling.

"Attaboy," Dusty encouraged as he lobbed the ball back to the mound.

"Don't worry about that, Gary," Joey said in his lowbrow way from third base. David didn't hear either one of them as he was completely locked in.

"Oooh, nice pitch." It came from the same direction as Joey but from a voice that wasn't on the field. Becky was indeed watching. She had spoken those words while uncrossing her legs so she could sit up in her lounge chair.

Don't worry about her. Don't worry about her. Don't worry about her, David kept repeating in his head. He had to focus on his next pitch. This was the pitch that would get Gary even or tip the at bat heavily in his favor. He wanted to double up on his curveball, and Dusty was right along with him. He smiled as he put down those same two fingers. David nodded in agreement. The one-strike pitch was on its way home.

Gary managed to swing and foul this one off. It was a dribbler that was well foul down the third baseline. Gary was way out in front and had just gotten a piece of it. The ball rolled about sixty feet. Joey was more than happy to go and retrieve it as he got a much closer and better view of Becky. The count was now 0–2, and everyone seemed to perk up a bit more.

Ricky was the first to speak up. "Don't let this twerp strike you out!"

"One more, David," Dusty said with the pride of a father or big brother. The other kids began chirping in the outfield as well. David knew he was way ahead, but he wanted to end this at bat on this next pitch. He took the throw from Joey, who was in full support of Gary, and snatched it with his glove.

He was going to blow his best fastball right by Gary right in front of Becky. There was going to be a new king on this field, and he would make sure to remind everyone about it afterward who was cheering on Gary. His entire focus was on this next pitch.

As he bent over and looked to make sure he and Dusty were still on the same page, he heard the voice of Becky. "Come on, David, you've got this." It was as if those words had caused everything to pause for a moment. Gary stepped out and looked over his left shoulder at her. He gave her that smile that athletes do when they know they're going to prevail. He dug back in and gave David that same smile.

David, on the other hand, backed off the newspaper that served as their pitching rubber. For a moment, he had forgotten she was there. His entire focus had been on Dusty and his glove; however, now he was fully aware of her and her interest. She folded her hands around the ice cream cone and placed them on her knees. She leaned forward in her chair, enhancing what she had been blessed with and what every guy on that field was staring at.

As he got back on that pitching rubber, he had a perfect view of her. One eye was on Dusty while one eye was firmly on her. He didn't care if she noticed. Dusty sensed this and patted his glove. "One more, kid," he declared as he put down two fingers.

David shook him off. Dusty put down two fingers again and motioned his glove toward the ground. He wanted David to bounce a curveball in the dirt to see if Gary would chase. David knew this was the right pitch. He was way ahead in the count, and this was where you tried to make good hitters get themselves out. However, this wasn't a normal situation in front of a handful of people in a high school game against some kids from another town you didn't know. This wasn't just an at bat to entertain the local cops on their lunch break. This was an at bat against the guy who had made him carry his bags at practice for two years, against the guy who had been king of this diamond for the past two summers, against the guy who thought he could make a run at Becky Reeves if he got a hit. He wasn't going to get him to chase a ball in the dirt or ground out; David was going to blow a fastball by him and prove a point.

After he shook him off for the second time, Dusty obliged David and put down one finger and clenched his body a bit in anticipation of what he knew was about to happen. David nodded and took one last peak at Becky, who looked like a fan watching the seventh game of the World Series. This was going to be the pitch that gave them both cause to celebrate.

David rocked and fired. As soon as the ball left his hand, he knew it was a mistake. Instead of running up and away, the ball started cutting back in over the plate. David's only hope was that Gary would foul it off or hit it on the ground. Neither one of those things happened. Instead, Gary hit a ball way up into one of the elm trees in right-center field. Nobody even moved or questioned the legitimacy of whether or not it was a hit or an out. In fact, they had never seen a ball hit that high up into that particular tree before.

Before David noticed the cheering of Joey and Ricky and all the younger boys who hoped this victory would save them from being harassed for a couple of weeks, he noticed Becky. When Gary hit the ball, her shoulders had slumped. It was as if her team had lost. While it should have made David feel better, he felt like he had let her down and blown any chance he might have had to impress her.

He started to pick up the newspaper from the mound as he knew the game was over for the day, but he was rushed by Ricky and Joey. Instead of celebrating Gary's hit, they were celebrating David's failure. While a fire burned inside him, he knew that he just had to take it.

As the celebration eventually calmed and everyone began gathering their things, Gary enjoyed the victor of his spoils by sauntering toward Becky's backyard. They had a brief conversation that nobody could hear before he came jogging back over to join the group as Becky walked inside her house. "What'd she say?" Eric eagerly asked.

"She said that people should know their place," Gary sarcastically replied as he looked at David. Normally, this was Gary's way of trying to keep the peace and lighten things up, but David wasn't having it. He simply nodded with his mouth firmly closed and his head down as he started walking down the street on his way back to Dusty's house.

"We good for tomorrow?" Dallas asked as the group was starting to break up.

"We adults have to work, but you kiddies can play with yourselves—I mean, by yourselves for the next couple of days." Dusty chuckled as the group retired for the day.

Gary hopped into the car with Ricky and Joey, and they were off to go celebrate at the Dairy Barn. Normally, they would all go, but Dusty knew that David wanted no part of that car ride, so they walked silently back to his trailer for a minute or two until they reached the end of the street.

"Hey, I can't have you over tonight," Dusty began as if he was starting off a eulogy. "I picked up an extra shift in the kitchen. Do you want me to call when I'm done?"

David heard him but didn't really acknowledge him.

"Look, you've got to stop always thinking about yourself," Dusty responded in a sharp tone after it was clear David wasn't going to say anything. "You're not perfect, and quite honestly, when you act like this, it's amazing you have any friends at all."

David shot him a look, but Dusty wasn't going to let him speak until he was finished.

"Did you ever once think that I might be right? You knew Gary was waiting for a fastball. We both knew it, but your arrogant ass wanted to show off your arm. You think Becky gave a shit about whether you struck him out or got him to ground out? Instead, you think you're better than all of us and have some damn point to prove. Maybe if you took the time to listen to or care about anybody but yourself, you'd see that."

David stopped after that last sentence because he wasn't sure what to say or how to react. Dusty was pretty much his only real friend, but he was tapping into a level of their friendship they hadn't quite explored. Dusty sensed that maybe he had crossed a line and knew how fragile that David could be, especially when he had to go home.

"Look, man, I'm sorry," Dusty began as he grabbed David's shoulder and prevented him from walking home thinking he had no friends. "It's just that sometimes you act like you're better than the rest of us, and on the baseball field, you are most of the time. So while you're over there pouting about giving up that hit to Gary and constantly thinking about yourself, it might be nice if you would acknowledge to me that I'm not a moron. Maybe if you had listened to me or been willing to believe that you don't have all the answers, you'd be the hero, and we'd be talking with Becky right now, not that I would have expected you to give me any credit anyways." He was starting to trail off a bit.

David wasn't sure how he was supposed to begin, but he knew that he had to say something. "I'm sorry," he began. "You're right, you're always right. I just wanted to show you and the guys that I could blow it by Gary."

"And Becky too," Dusty chimed in as if he was suddenly back to himself.

"Yeah . . . Becky," David said as he kicked the road and seemed to start reliving his failure all over again. "Pretty stupid to even get wrapped up with her, huh?"

Dusty gave his familiar belly laugh. "Dude, you don't even know!"

But the way he had said that piqued David's brain. "Why did you say it like that?" David responded with a slight lift in his spirits.

"Open up your eyes a bit, man," Dusty started. "That girl has got more going on than just her body."

David started to think about the steady number of guys who came and went from her driveway or who hit on her at the Dairy Barn. He knew he didn't stack up with them and that she was probably just messing with him when she seemed interested in him on that baseball field earlier. He was probably just another pawn in her flirtatious games that she played all day every day. "Yeah, you're right," David said, assuring himself.

"You'll figure it all out one day," Dusty said as he smiled and started off toward his house to clean up for work. "Just remember, even though you're better than us as at most things, you aren't better than us. We've all got it bad in some ways, but you don't have it worse than the rest of us, so don't sit in your room all night feeling sorry for yourself. I'll come check in on you tomorrow at work." With that, Dusty picked up his gait and made for home.

It was coming up on three thirty in the afternoon. The early summer heat was in full bloom, and David wanted to cool off, but he didn't have anywhere to go besides his own house. He lived on the side of town closest to the interstate, about a mile away from the elementary school and the trailer parks and surrounding neighborhoods. He could cut through some fields to avoid walking along the main road, but he wasn't in any hurry to get home. His life there was far from ideal, and this was the worst time for him to go home.

On his way home, David decided to take the long way. He replayed the at bat with Gary over in his head, but he couldn't let go of the conversation he had with Dusty. Maybe he was right; maybe he shouldn't feel so bad for himself. Maybe others had it worse than him. Maybe he didn't pay attention to other people like he should have. Maybe Dusty was right. David was lucky to have him as a friend. He always called him out when needed, but he hadn't cut as deep in the past as he had after their game today. Plus, throwing in his emotions about Becky, he needed to take the long way home. He knew he was better off not trying to get involved with her, but he couldn't stop thinking about how beautiful she was and how she had been cheering for him.

All these thoughts consumed him so much that he barely noticed he was almost home. He figured it had to be close to four o'clock, which was the absolute worst time for him to come home. He did everything possible to avoid his house at that precise hour, but today he had no choice but to go to his own place to get out of the heat.

On the outside, David's house was a lot nicer than most of his friends. For one, it was a house and not a trailer. It was a split-level brick house that was built into the side of a steep hill surrounded by woods in the rear that overlooked the city. David's room was above the garage, so it gave him a perfect view of the skyline. Most of his friends didn't venture out his way on foot too often since he was closer to the interstate and a lot closer to the higher crime areas that overflowed from most cities. His friends knew his house because they had often driven past it on the way out to the interstate, but very few had been inside. In fact, the rumor was that his house had an elevator because it was a split level with both levels visible from the road as you passed by.

While most of his friends longed to live in a house like that, it was usually the last place David wanted to be. In a way, when David went home, he retreated to his own world. Living off the main road into town, there was always constant traffic buzzing by. There was a residential street that went up the bluff from his house that was winding and rose at a steep incline until it dead-ended. There were a few houses on the road that were all shaded by thick trees, and most were inhabited by older couples. Yards were impossible to play in because they were severely slanted, and once a ball got rolling, it was a long way before they would stop. David really didn't have any other kids around whom he would play with, and even if he did, there wasn't much of an area to play in except running around and hiding in the woods.

He was an only child, a mistake. His mother had gotten pregnant while his parents were in high school, but that didn't seem to be their biggest mistake. To David, it seemed like the bigger mistake was staying together all the years since, trying to make it appear as if they were a family.

David's father was a tall and slender man, just like him. He had really high cheekbones that made him appear a bit wiry. He had been a baseball player in high school like his son and looked like he could still walk out there and play if he wanted to. He appeared to be in good shape, thanks mainly to genetics and the fact that he was only thirty-three years old. His hair was dark brown and fell off both sides of his face like it hadn't been combed for weeks. He usually had a few days' worth of stubble that made his youthful face appear dirtier than it really was. His father usually wore flannel shirts throughout the winter and sleeveless shirts in the summer months. He had gone to work at the steel mill right out of high school from necessity and had worked his way up into a decent position. However, as the youngest shift manager at the mill, he was stuck working third shift. This meant he would leave the house around nine each night to get to work early and get briefed by the second-shift managers. He would get off work at six in the morning and then go grab breakfast and a number of beers before coming home and going straight to bed. The number of beers depended heavily on how stressful his night at work had been or how rough things had been at home. Lately, he had been drinking a lot of beers. However, he would wake up each day at around four so he and David's mom could spend a little time together, or argue, before she went off to work.

David's mother had just turned thirty-two years, and she was a knockout. David knew it; worse off, his friends knew and harassed him about it, and his father knew it too. This was often the source of most of the fighting in the house. David's mom worked down the street at the local tavern as a waitress and bartender. She got hit on all the time, and her job required her to be out late and away on the weekends. She would usually sleep in until around noon each day after she worked, so David was free to come and go as he pleased for the most part. She was tall and fit with curves that hadn't faded with age. She had dark hair and dark eyes that really stood out on her long face. Her makeup always looked good, and she liked to wear tight clothes. She said it helped her earn extra tips, but she also liked the attention from other men. She was far more outspoken than David's father, and she always smelled good. David's father was always worried about her having an affair.

They had David when his father was a senior and his mother was a junior. David's father had finished high school, but despite having the grades to go to college, he used some connections to get a good job at the steel mill right out of high school and provide for his new family. His mother tried to finish up high school but couldn't manage it because her parents both worked steady jobs and couldn't watch him while she was in school. His father's grandparents worked jobs with odd hours, so they couldn't help out much either. His mother had been an honor roll student but eventually had to settle for getting her GED in her midtwenties. She had been using her looks and personality to earn money as a waitress and bartender ever since she had David.

In spite of having a child in their teens, they both managed to make a decent living together financially. The house was not upscale by middle-class standards, but it was nice and well maintained. His mom had planted flowers along the driveway, and his father did a nice job with the landscaping around the house. David even had a large area under an oak tree where they had put in a dirt basketball court for him. On the outside, this house had everything that most other homes in Riverview did not; but on the inside, it was as loveless and divided as most others.

As he made his way up the driveway, he could tell that his father was already awake because the blinds to his room were drawn up. He hoped that this would be a rare day where his parents weren't fighting with each other before his mom went off to work, but his wishes faded as he walked up the stairs to his front door. He could already hear his father lecturing his mom in their bedroom. His dad didn't really say too much to anyone; it was as if he saved it all up for her before she went to work.

When he reached the kitchen to grab a drink, his only wish was to be able to make it down the hallway to his room before his parents had noticed that he was home. His bedroom stood almost exactly halfway from the refrigerator to their bedroom. His room was on the opposite side of the hallway from theirs. Their room sat at the end of the hallway, with the home's only bathroom right across from David's room. On good days, they would contain their disputes to their bedroom or the living room; but other days, it would rest in the bathroom outside his room. Today was not a good day.

David grabbed a soda from the refrigerator and nabbed a quick snack from the pantry as he overheard his dad barking to his mom about her not needing to go above and beyond for tips. He could hear his mom talking from the back of her room and thought he might make it to his room unnoticed as he was gliding down the hallway, but as he was about three steps shy, his parents' door suddenly burst open, and his dad started to bolt down the hallway. He and David met almost simultaneously outside his door. David's father gave him a look that said, *If you say a word, I'll unload on you,* and kept marching down the hallway to the kitchen.

His mom, who always had to have the last word, started out of her room, yelling out at him, but noticed David standing outside his door. Like she had done for years, she treated David as if he was a child who didn't know what was going on and stopped midsentence and tried to act like everything was fine and they hadn't been fighting. "Hey, sweetie, how was your day?" she said in as motherly a tone as she was capable of.

Before David could even shrug and try to ignore the question, his father came storming back out from the kitchen with the checkbook in his hand. He was demanding to know what she had written two checks for earlier that day. His mother slid into the bathroom and went about getting ready for work as if he hadn't even asked the question. Neither one seemed to care or notice that David closed the door behind him.

They continued to banter about finances for another five minutes or so until he could hear his mom tell his father on her way out the door, "Have fun thinking about me at the bar earning extra tips while you're at work tonight." With that, she closed the door and began her walk to the bar across the main road about three minutes from their house. David could hear his dad mumbling from the kitchen back to his room. Once he heard his dad flip on the TV in his room, he knew he was clear and wouldn't be bothered by either one until he happened to be around at the wrong time again.

This fight was a good one but not one of their worst. David could gauge when they had a particularly bad fight because they would usually buy him a gift of some sort as a sign of peace or to say they were sorry for acting like kids. The gifts from his father usually weren't anything that he wanted or needed, further proof in David's eyes that his dad didn't know him or care about him. His mom was equally bad about expressing her emotions to him as his father, but she was much better at giving gifts. When David was younger, he loved getting baseball cards, posters, or sports apparel from his mom for no reason. He thought this was what all moms did, but as he got older and had his own problems he needed to talk about, he came to resent the gifts. He had a closet and dresser full of clothes he didn't even wear. He didn't want to give his mom the satisfaction that her gifts made his life any better or fulfilled any voids in his life. Since this fight was a good one and his dad was the agitator, he figured he'd come home to a thoughtless gift from his father in a day or two.

The only person who really served as a traditional family figure for David was his grandfather. His maternal grandfather had moved out of Riverview when David was just a few years old, most likely from a broken heart. He had seen his only child get knocked up in high school. Her once promising future abruptly halted, just like so many other girls in Riverview. He tried to help David's father, but they seemed to have equal resentment for each other. Eventually, he moved about forty-five minutes from Riverview. His wife had died a couple of years afterward, and he constantly seemed in search of things to do to keep his mind off her. He loved David and knew he needed a real father figure. He was around as much as possible, oftentimes avoiding David's father. In recent years as David had gotten older, he would often avoid coming around when either of David's parents was around.

Since his only child had gotten pregnant in high school, for David, he was the cool grandpa who didn't have gray hair and could still get around like a younger man. He drove a new car every couple of years and dressed better than his father did. He loved sports, particularly baseball, and would always be the one to take and pick up David from his practices and games. For most of his life, David had become accustomed to his grandpa being the only family he had in the stands for any of his games. His father seemed uninterested and blamed work as did his mother. It seemed to be the only thing they had in common.

The best thing about David's grandpa was that, once school was out, he would pick David up a couple of times a month and take him to the professional baseball games downtown. Going to those games was like therapy for both of them. His grandpa was recently retired and on full pension from working over thirty years at the same company, so he needed something to keep him busy and away from his empty house. David wasn't retired, but he needed something to keep him occupied and away from his house as well. They both knew why those games meant so much to each other, but they never really talked about it directly.

David's grandfather had lived the typical Riverview life. He had grown up without much in life, fallen in love in high school, gotten married, and started a family at a young age. Because of complications at birth, David's mother would be the only child they would be able to have. Being born in 1938, he had managed to avoid going off to fight in any foreign wars, so he hooked into a national logistics and shipping company. He worked his way up from the docks into an upper management position and was wise with his money and investments. He would never reveal where all his money was coming from, but he had plenty of it and frequently talked to David about the importance of investing money wisely. As a kid, David would love looking up the stock reports in the paper and highlighting them for his grandpa. In fact, he'd even do it at his own house when his grandpa wasn't around.

When his grandpa left Riverview, he found some land out in the country and settled there. It was close enough where he could come and get David and take him there on the weekends when he was little. David remembered how much fun he had fishing and going out to eat with his grandparents. It was completely foreign and surreal being away from the city and neighborhoods, but David loved it. He felt like a real family when he was with his grandparents, but everything changed when his grandmother was diagnosed with cancer.

Her battle didn't last long, and everyone dealt with things differently. David's grandpa didn't talk much about it, but after she died, he didn't take David to his house much after that. It seemed he didn't want anyone in that house that he was once so proud of, including himself. His grandpa would hang out with his friends, take trips to new places, or take David to countless baseball games—anything to avoid spending time around his house. For David, it was the first time he had lost anyone close to him. He was twelve years old and didn't quite grasp everything. Nobody talked to him about it, so he figured that when someone you were close to died, you just didn't talk about it and moved on.

His mother had seemed the most angered and bottled up by her death. Things had never been too great at home, but there wasn't the constant fighting and arguing like there was after her mother had died. It was as if her death triggered something in her. She became more distant to David and his father. She would lash out at both of them seemingly out of nowhere. She and David's grandpa rarely did things together anymore. They were broken, and nobody knew how to fix it. Far be it from David's father to say anything or to offer any sort of emotional support, so they all just moved forward in their own ways.

The benefit for David was that his grandpa was now there for all his baseball games. He'd tell David how good he had done, like all grandfathers are supposed to do regardless of the outcome or performance. He would take David to the Dairy Barn, and they'd sit on the hood of the car and rehash his game and then talk about the major-league teams. In high school, his grandpa got more analytical about David's performances. The offer for ice cream was still there, but after a tough loss, they usually didn't go. He'd tell David that he had a lot of potential and that he felt David could play beyond high school. For kids from Riverview, that seemed like a pipe dream. His grandpa told him that he had been offered a class B contract with the White Sox organization out of high school, but he was in love and wanted to get married. He wouldn't be able to provide on what they were offering, so he went to work.

He didn't seem to regret it at all. David regretted it because he wanted to brag that someone in his family had played professional baseball, regardless of the level. The closest thing to a town hero was Randy Black. He had been drafted in the late rounds out of high school by the Pirates and made it up to Double-A as a pitcher. He ran into arm problems and never rose above those ranks, but that didn't stop him from telling his stories about how he would have made it.

Randy Black had traveled and played in numerous towns across America, but like most who were born in Riverview, he found his way back. You could find him in one of the local taverns any night of the week, telling someone about the good ole days and how he would have made it if his arm hadn't gone out on him. People would ask him to retell stories from high school and the state quarterfinals game that they lost 2–1. It was the farthest any Riverview team had advanced in the state playoffs in their history.

David had heard all these stories and pretty much had them memorized at this point in his life from all the times when he was younger and his dad had taken him to get something to eat at the local taverns. He hated these stories. All David saw was a man in his midforties who looked like he couldn't run across the room without having a heart attack or throw a ball straight if his life depended on it. How was this guy some sort of hero? His dad worshipped him and talked about how all the guys on the baseball teams after him wanted to be the next Randy Black. It only made David resent him more. These stories made David want to be better than he ever was so Randy would stop waddling around town, telling stories about his not-so-glorious glory days. He wished his grandfather had signed that contract, and he could go toe to toe with Randy Black on stories about his grandfather, who still looked like he actually could play the game, not like a washed-up has-been with baggy pants, a stained trucker hat, and an endless supply of dirty sweatshirts.

When David's grandpa would take him to the professional games downtown, David would often stare at the big buildings and stadium as they drove in without saying a word. Even though he could see the skyline and lights of the stadium from his house five miles away, the colors and size of everything exploded up close. David would dream about what it would be like to be a professional athlete and spend all your time in big cities. He loved the buzz and energy. Despite living just less than ten miles away, most of his friends rarely got to go to games—or downtown for that matter. This made David feel even more special. He'd tell his grandpa how he was going to live in a city one day, and then his grandpa would remind him how much he had enjoyed fishing when he was younger. David would agree and then say that he would live in a really nice area outside a city, kind of like Fox Creek, so he could enjoy the best of both worlds.

David's grandpa would point out various players during the game and tell David to watch their actions before each pitch. He would guess which pitch the pitcher was going to throw and then explain to David how he knew what pitch was coming. He explained to David that the great pitchers were the ones who could get batters out even when they knew what pitch was coming. David was getting baptized in baseball by his grandfather and loved it. He loved it when his grandpa would talk about his playing days and which players reminded him of himself when he was younger. He wished every day could be like the ones where his grandpa took him to the games. David always kept score and kept the scorecards in a box in his room at home. He would take them out and look at them during tough times or when he hadn't seen his grandpa in a while. Tonight was one of those nights.

David lay low in his room until around seven o'clock, trying not to think about Becky and thinking about what Dusty had said. He replayed his parents' fight in his head and how nobody had said anything to him since. He wondered if anybody had any idea what it was like to be a prisoner in your own room. Then he looked around his room and noticed he had quite a few nice things, from posters to books, from clothes to an aquarium, from a nice stereo to a color TV; from the outside, it didn't look all that bad. But for David, he looked at those items as incentives to stay in his room. He thought about his grandpa and how lucky he was to have him in his life, but then he got mad because he lived so far away. He walked over to his window and looked out at the skyline of the city, and he could see the lights of the stadium as the sun was hinting at beginning its gradual descent and thought of the good memories they had, but he was angry because his closest friends lived closer to town, and they were all working or celebrating Gary's triumph without him.

David twisted and bent Dusty's words over and over in his mind, and he became more and more upset. How could Dusty think he was selfish? Dusty had a stepmom who made him whatever he wanted and was always supportive of him. She had replaced a woman who could care less about him. Dusty's dad would take him to the drag strip most Friday nights and hang out with him like most fathers should. He didn't know what it was like to feel alone in your own house. Almost as a way to prove a point to Dusty, David ventured out into the living room, where he knew his dad would be getting ready to watch the baseball game before he had to go to work.

David sat down on the couch that was positioned slightly behind his father's recliner. This way, he could see his dad, but his dad would have to make an effort to turn around and look at him. They both sat and watched the top half of the first inning in complete silence, and the entire time, David thought how his grandpa would have been analyzing away and explaining things to him if they were there together. As the game wore on, David's anger at his father's dismissiveness turned into a game. He wanted to see if his dad could go the entire time without saying a word before he left for work. Right as David seemed to be finding joy in his own game, it was as if his father sensed his enjoyment. After nearly an hour and a half in complete silence, his dad finally uttered something to David.

"Bring home some eggs and milk after work tomorrow," he grumbled as he rose from his recliner and started down the hallway to get dressed for work.

David didn't respond. He couldn't respond. His father had sat in that chair watching the same baseball game as him for almost two hours, their favorite team nonetheless, after he had come home from being gone all day and walked in on his parents fighting with each other, and that was all he had to say? Why couldn't he or his mom get those things? Yeah, he worked at a convenience store, but he'd have to carry those things home. It was almost as if his dad had sat in that chair the entire time thinking of the one thing to say that would piss him off the most. David wished Dusty could have been there to witness it.

A few minutes later, his father emerged from his room and made the slow walk down the hallway to the kitchen, down the basement stairs, and out through the garage in his car. He was kind enough to give David a slight flick of the hand as he passed through his line of vision. It was subtle as if he was shooing a fly away from his front pocket.

Once he was gone, David took the transistor radio from the kitchen counter and walked outside. He slung it over his right arm as he grabbed the ladder from their three-season porch. He climbed up on this roof and lay on his back where he could get a better view of the city and the lights of the ballpark. He tuned the radio to the local baseball broadcast as he did most nights when he had the house to himself. He would let the local broadcaster bring the sights and sounds of the game he loved to him. In a way, he was the father he never had. He stepped in for his grandfather on the nights they weren't at the games.

As he lay on that roof, his mind wandered from topic to topic. He had a shitty day, and nobody seemed to care about it. Every now and then, the doors from the tavern where his mom worked would open, and the music would blare, or he'd hear people laughing. It made him angry. He felt bad for his dad, who was off to work a job he found no joy in while his wife was getting hit on by the town drunks. He hated the fact his mom worked there, especially so close where David could hear all the shenanigans taking place or the fights that would spill into the parking lot. He understood why his father was so mad at her. She seemed to be playing a game with his dad, just like Becky had been with him earlier.

He laid there until the game was over, and he was starting to get sleepy. He knew he eventually had to go into his empty house and his room filled with all the nicest things a kid his age in Riverview could want. He set his alarm so he'd be up on time for work tomorrow, and he wrote himself a note as a reminder to make sure he brought home milk and eggs.

5
CHAPTER

The next morning, David's alarm went off at six o'clock. He gently turned it off, took inventory of himself, and listened for any other signs of life in the house. The only light in his room was from the small aquarium on top of his dresser across the room. He didn't mind getting up early, but he didn't like the thought of going to work.

He worked at Jay's convenience store just up the street from the elementary school where they played baseball. It was where they went to get refreshments most days when they were taking a break. Jay's was an all-in-one-type store that every town seemed to have in years past that have now been replaced by chains. There was a pharmacy in the back and a magazine rack along the entire front wall as you walked in on the left. They sold everything from baseball cards to deodorant and grooming products to basic auto parts to frozen and dairy products. The floors were covered in a green and white tile flooring that could survive a bombing, but the lighting left a lot to be desired. The shelves stood tall in the narrow aisles, which made it rather easy for kids to shoplift. This was why the boys loved going there to cool off in the summer months and why David hated working there.

A friend of his grandparents was the manager of the store, so he had gotten David the job there as a favor to his grandpa. He told David it would be good for him to start learning the value of money and that, one day, he could buy his grandpa a milkshake with his work money, even though he would never allow it. He made it impossible for David to say no. The manager was a woman in her midfifties who had inherited the business from her parents, and she seemed as miserable as David was to be working there. The biggest difference was that this was David's first job as he was starting out in life; this was her first and her only job. She was a short stocky woman who looked closer to her midsixties. She wore large glasses with red rims that covered most of her face. There was no official dress code for employees, but she always wore odd-colored slacks and long-sleeved faded button-down shirts, usually with stripes or polka dots of some sort. David had no idea how his grandparents had been friends with someone like this, but as much as he didn't like going to work, he did enjoy having his own money in his pocket.

Since he was still just fifteen, he and the manager had a deal. He would come in on Monday, Thursday, and Friday mornings to help unload the trucks and stock the shelves with the heavier items. There wasn't much of a working crew outside the pharmacy and a cashier, so David was pretty much free to leave whenever everything had been stocked and straightened. In exchange for his services, she would pay him cash under the table tax-free. It was a pretty fair deal. David was in by seven and out by one or two at the latest. He still could play baseball with his friends, and it didn't interfere with his weekends or evenings. Plus, since he was so quiet and the shelves were so tall, he often got to overhear all the good town gossip. For the most part, he found his job tolerable, and it gave him some financial freedom and responsibility. He also could drink up to two sodas a day for free, something he wished he never told his friends because they assumed that applied to them as well. The worst part of his work experience was when they would pop in while he was working.

David walked to work each morning along the main road through town. It was about a mile from his house. He had a bike that he used to ride all the time when he was younger, but there was something a little degrading about being in high school and riding a bike around. Even though it took longer, he and his friends decided it was a better look to be seen walking around town. The morning walks were good for him to clear his head anyways. His mom would be sleeping after working into the wee hours of the morning, and his father was getting breakfast and beers with coworkers at their favorite bar on the far side of town out by the high school. He enjoyed the quiet walks before the summer sun felt like a furnace. Everything about this day was a normal Thursday, including the visit from his friends at around noon.

David was making sure that all the labels were facing forward and all items pushed to the front of the shelf in the feminine hygiene section when he heard Joey's car roar into the parking lot. The combination of screeching tires and loud music was a dead giveaway. Of course, they had to show up at this exact moment. Before he could even think about taking the few remaining boxes he had left to open and stock to the back room, Ricky sprung through the door like a gangster in a Western movie. He quickly scanned the place and spotted David.

"Hey, looks like we caught you red-handed." Ricky chuckled at his own joke as David tried tossing the rest of the maxi pads he was stocking back onto the cart before anyone would see. It was too late though; just as Ricky had spoken, the rest of the gang came strolling through the door.

"Glad to see you didn't hurt yourself last night." Gary beamed as he gave David a good ole boys wink and a smile.

Dusty approached David and put his hand on his shoulder as if he was a big brother. "You doing all right?" he asked with sincere concern.

"Yeah, I'm fine. I'm over it," David said with an unforced smile and look to Dusty to let him know that he also had thought about what he'd said yesterday and that they were still cool. "My parents had another blowout, though, yesterday, right when I walked in the door."

"Oh yeah?" Dusty replied back with earnest.

"Yeah, seems to be just about every day anymore," David responded as he tossed a box of maxi pads onto the shelf.

Dusty could tell that this had been wearing on David. "Well, you think you'll get anything good from it?" Dusty knew that when his parents got into it pretty good, they would usually buy him something to say they were sorry.

"I got a shopping list out of it so far," David said with disgust as he started to pull the note from his pocket.

"You boys going over the scouting report for your next failure?" Ricky quipped as he turned the corner with an armful of drinks and a couple of bags of chips. The question didn't irritate David as much as what was in Ricky's arms. He knew what the next thing to come out of his mouth was going to be. "So you think you can hook us up?"

"I can't hook you up with all that. You've got to pay like everyone else," David chirped back at him.

"Since when do we have to start paying for things around here?" Joey chimed in as he emerged holding more in his arms than Ricky.

"Since you guys started coming into your own flow of cash. I've got an honest job, and I'm not about to lose it," David replied, raising his voice. His tone and direct implication that they were involved in things they shouldn't be set them off. It was probably the sharpest thing that David had ever said to them over the course of their lives. Dusty's eyes even popped when he heard David mouth off.

"Listen, you arrogant little asshole, keep your mouth shut about things you don't know." Ricky sneered as he put his loot down to show David he was willing to make him pay with fists if he didn't dial down his tone.

Dusty sensed this and stepped in between them. "David says one thing you don't like over the course of your life, and now you wanna act tough? If you're that upset about it, maybe you should grab one of these." Dusty chuckled as he tossed Ricky a box of maxi pads. This only made Ricky more upset. "I wouldn't take that next step if I were you," Dusty said as he pushed Ricky back.

Right at that moment, Gary came around the other end of the aisle and saw what was going on. "Hey, what the hell are you guys doing?" Ricky started to explain what David and Dusty had said, but Gary cut him off. "I don't care what they said or did. You're not making David pay for things that you've got the money to buy yourself, either of you," he stated it firmly as he looked at both Ricky and Joey.

That was what David admired about Gary. Even though he was older, he looked out for him and Dusty when needed. He could be a jerk like Ricky at times, but he liked to keep him and Joey both in their place on the field and in their little group; however, David knew Gary would always have his back if needed. It was a Riverview thing. Even though he had a hard time tolerating Ricky and Joey, he knew they'd have his back if needed and likewise.

As the five boys stood among the feminine hygiene products bickering like a bunch of girls, arguing over who was going to pay for what they wanted, the bell above the front door rattled to remind them that they didn't have the store all to themselves. They could all see out the front picture window beyond the cashier into the parking lot. Two cars full of Fox Creek kids had rolled into the parking lot, and they were walking into Jay's.

"Well, isn't this a Kodak moment?" were the first words to greet them from the mouth of Ryan Harding. He was Mr. Smooth. He had everything. He was tall with broad shoulders, a rigid jawline, dark complexion, and black hair that was thick and plush. He would pull it back to show off his symmetric features given to him from years of privileged families interacting with one another and forming families, but he could also let it down and flow to appear as if there was a wave he had to catch at any minute. He was a hell of a ballplayer and was going into his senior year. The biggest problem in his life was trying to figure out which car to drive each day and which scholarship offer to take.

Nobody in their group liked Ryan, especially Gary. Gary saw him as the person he wanted to be but knew he couldn't. While Gary was the king of Riverview, Ryan was the king of Fox Creek, and there was a big difference between the two. They all viewed Ryan as an arrogant prick who only came to Riverview to put them down and show off to people who might actually be impressed, much like the adults from Fox Creek who came into the local bars and caused fights.

"What are you doing in here?" Gary sniped back, trying to wipe the smile off Ryan's face from a distance.

"Oh, not much, just heading downtown to catch the ball game today. Our dads gave us their season tickets since they're working." Ryan flashed the tickets as he motioned over his shoulder to show that he had equal numbers of support as a few more guys from Fox Creek flowed through the door.

"Yeah, real tough guy," Dusty sarcastically interjected what everyone was thinking.

Ryan didn't change his demeanor one bit, but he did have a question for one person in particular. "David, we didn't know if you wanted to come with us. We've got an extra ticket and knew you liked baseball."

David couldn't believe what he had just heard. He would have loved to have gone to the game, and if his friends weren't there, he might have even considered it, but he knew what he had to say while they were standing there. "Sorry, man, but I've got work," David said as he nudged one of the boxes on the floor in front of him.

Ryan tried to sound sincere. "Yeah, no problem. I get it."

David thought how he could possibly get it. This kid hadn't worked a day in his life. He didn't know what it was like to not just do whatever he wanted whenever he felt like it. Besides, why was he asking him to go with them anyways? Outside of playing baseball against each other a few times over the years, they really didn't know each other that well.

"You sure you can't get outa here early?" another kid from Fox Creek asked with sincerity and directness.

"Yeah, blow this dump off," another instigator blurted out.

"Hey, what are you calling a dump?" Dusty blared out as he stepped forward from behind Gary and David. David smiled because it was what he should have said and wanted to say, but Dusty usually did the talking for him anyways.

The Fox Creek boys all started in on Dusty, and David was sure this was going to lead into an altercation in the parking lot or even the store. The manager or cashier weren't going to jump in and stop them, so somebody needed to before the fists started flying.

Ryan, who was the unquestioned leader, turned to the four guys who had pressed in behind him in the narrow aisle, put his hand squarely on the chest of the kid who called this place a dump, and calmly shoved him back a few feet. He then turned to the other kid who had engaged David and said, "Listen, if he said he has to work and can't come, he can't come. I respect that, and so should you."

As things were beginning to settle a bit, Ricky—who had just been willing to throw down to defend David and the rest of the town—threw his hat in the ring. "Why the hell would you want to go to a game with this kid? I'll go with you, guys. Look, the first round of dogs is on me," he said as he pulled a wad of cash from his pocket.

"We're good," Ryan said as he started backing down the aisle.

Gary, seeing Ricky pull the money from his pocket, slapped him on the back of the head. "Really? You were going to make David steal or pay for your shit, but you'll buy them hot dogs?"

"Man, I don't get it," Ricky declared as he shoved the money back into his pocket.

"What do they want with you?" he asked pointedly as he looked directly at David with a sneer.

Gary wrapped his arm around Ricky like he was a younger brother who would never quite be able to figure something out. "They're recruiting him."

"Recruiting him?" Joey bellowed out as if there was an echo.

"Yeah," Gary said as he started to pick up the items Ricky had set down earlier when he wanted to fight David. "They want him to join up with them on their Legion team this summer." As Gary said those words, you could hear the disappointment in his voice—not for David but because he had not been asked.

"Recruiting?" Ricky muttered. He then shot a look at David and down the aisle to the boys, who were almost gone. From there, he gave his great speech as his eyes bounced wildly from David to Gary to Ryan. "He ain't never gonna play for you, arrogant pricks. He ain't even the best baseball player in this aisle. All you Fox Creek assholes only come to this town when you want something or when you need to feel better about your own pathetic lives. You guys can all rot in hell, and I'm willing to send you there right now." He started to charge after them down the aisle, but Gary and Dusty caught him.

Hearing this speech and having been called out, the Fox Creek gang did an about-face and asked Ricky to repeat himself again, which Ricky was more than willing to oblige. Gary handed Ricky off to Joey to hold as he and Ryan tried to hold back their gangs from brawling in the middle of the convenience store aisle. At that point, it seemed inevitable, but the bell above the front entrance rattled again, and the person who walked through was the only one who could have prevented what was about to happen at that moment.

Becky Reeves came in to see what had been taking the Fox Creek boys so long inside the store, and when she walked in, she immediately followed the sound of all the commotion. Ryan and his crew were at the front of an aisle off to her right, and she ran over and tried to push her way to the front of the pack. However, as she was pushing her way forward, everyone else was moving backward toward the exit and parking lot. As the group moved into the open area between the aisles and the front counter area, Becky seized her opportunity to jump in between everyone. "Hey! Hey! Knock it off!" she shouted. "What is all this about?" The sight of her de-escalated everything. Nobody wanted to look like a complete jerk in front of her, except Ricky.

"These pricks came in here looking to start trouble, so we're ready to give them what they came looking for," he said as he raised his chin in an effort to seem unfazed by Becky's presence.

Becky looked over at Ryan to confirm if this was indeed true or not and in the hopes that he could say something that would calm things down. Being the suave guy that he was, he did just that. "We don't want any trouble with you, guys. We're on our way out of here," he declared in a calm voice. This brought everyone and everything to a standstill. Whatever solution Becky had been hoping for seemed to work.

As wise and well timed as she had been upon her entrance, her exit nearly blew the entire thing up again. Before she made her way out, she asked two questions that drew the ire of the Riverview boys. First, she asked one of the Fox Creek boys if they were going to have time to stop by the Dairy Barn for ice cream before going to the game, to which one boy shrugged. Then she turned to David, who was standing in the back of the pack and wanted no part of the fighting, especially while at work, and asked, "So are you coming with us?"

Everyone seemed to be shocked by the question, but for once, nobody jumped in to answer for David or repeat the question. This was squarely on David to answer for himself and the Riverview group. Normally, David took time to choose his words wisely, but he knew exactly how he wanted to respond to that question. "Us? You're with these guys? What are you doing hanging around with these guys? Why would I want to hang out with you or them?"

This response drew immediate favor from the Riverview boys, and all eyes from both groups fell on her. "Well, I know how much you love baseball and figured you'd want to go," she replied in the sweetest and most straightforward way imaginable. David couldn't help but feel alive inside and ready to jump in the car with her and tell her about all the games he'd gone to with his grandpa, but as those feelings swelled inside him, he saw the guys standing behind her, the guys who had insulted him and his friends.

His response was as straightforward as hers. "Thanks, but I don't want to go with those guys, and I can't believe you would." With that, he turned to head back down the aisle to finish stocking the shelf that seemed like a lifetime ago that he had been quietly working on.

Becky's shoulders dropped, and she stood there disappointed. She went from looking like a young woman filled with confidence to a girl who didn't have any answers in life, but as Ryan tapped her on the hip to get her to turn around and leave, she made sure to throw her right arm around his waist on the way out the door in front of the Riverview boys. She made sure to look back with a sad look in her eyes, but David had already disappeared down the aisle.

As they were all leaving, the most arrogant of the Fox Creek boys grabbed a handful of candy, threw a twenty-dollar bill on the counter, and told the cashier, "That's for these and whatever these bums were going to try and steal." He looked right at Ricky and laughed, but the boys knew the moment was over. Even Ricky didn't have anything to say and seemed to feel bad about being called out.

It was statements like those that really cut deep into the people of Riverview. They knew that no matter what, the people of Fox Creek always seemed to have the upper hand. Not only had they come into a store in their town and embarrassed them but they also did so with the best-looking girl in town.

They all looked out into the parking lot through the picture window and saw Becky hop into the passenger seat of Ryan Harding's red Mustang convertible. They seethed with envy, but nobody could blame her. They all knew they'd never have a car like that or season tickets to the baseball games. They all stood and watched her pull away, off to get ice cream and then soak in the good life.

Ricky went back to the aisle, grabbed the items he and Joey once had in their arms, and defeatedly dropped them on the front counter. He shot David another look on his way back up front but didn't say a word. At the register, he told the lady working to keep the twenty-dollar bill because they had caused a commotion and that he was paying for the candy and everything else on the counter. Joey made sure to shoot David a disapproving look from Ricky's side as he started digging into his pocket.

Gary had kind of been standing in the same spot the entire time at the front of the store. He didn't raise his head but turned it slightly to David with his lips pursed. It was a look of both contempt and disappointment. David wasn't sure if he was angry about Becky, who seemed to have forgotten about his triumph yesterday, or if he was angry that David had been the target of Ryan's offer and not him. Either way, David knew he hoped Gary didn't say anything because he didn't want to talk about it.

As the other three boys began to head out the door, Dusty flashed a finger to them to let them know he needed a second with David. He walked down the aisle and straightened a couple of boxes that had been knocked cockeyed on one of the shelves in the scuffling. Once straightened, he walked right up to David with a big smile on his face. Dusty loved mixing it up, so this had been a good time for him.

"Well, at least now we know why they came into this place," he started as he punched David on the arm. David stood there confused and speechless. "You don't get it, do you, dummy?" David had no clue what Dusty was getting at, so Dusty connected the dots for him. "They came in here because she told them where you were." David stood there trying to catch up with Dusty.

"How did she know?" David managed to get out.

"Oh my god! For a smart kid, you don't have a lot going on up there most of the time," Dusty said as he tried to flick David on the side of his head. "It's a good thing we were here because I bet if we weren't, you would have gotten in that car with them."

David managed to avoid the knock to his head, but he couldn't get what Dusty was saying. Dusty could read David perfectly, and he knew his friends weren't going to wait for him forever, so he kicked a box off the bottom shelf and smiled. "Don't think too hard about it, even though I know it will keep you up all night. I've got to work the next couple of nights, but Gary said we're going to play at the field Saturday around ten. See you then?"

"Yeah," David said in a way that suggested he had more to say. He needed his friend to explain things to him. He needed him to help get him out of his house. He needed him to explain Becky to him.

Sensing all this and seeing his best friend standing there, staring at a box of maxi pads, Dusty chuckled as he backed out of the aisle. "Don't worry, man, if you don't have it figured out by Saturday, we can hang out at my place, and I'll explain it to you." With that, he disappeared around the corner and was heading to the parking lot to join the rest of the group.

Before he could exit the store, David called out to him. Dusty popped his head around the corner and looked at him with concern because it wasn't like David to ask for another word. "Do you really think I would have gone with them?"

Dusty seemed a bit surprised by the question and moved the rest of his body around the corner of the aisle. He paused for a second, which wasn't like him. "I don't know, man, but I don't think anybody would blame you if you did." He stood there awkwardly for a long moment before snapping back to his usual self. "I liked your speech though." He gave David a wink and then bolted out toward the exit.

David heard them screech away in Joey's car and was glad everything was over, but he couldn't stop thinking about Dusty's answer and Becky. Saturday couldn't come soon enough so he could see them both again.

6 CHAPTER

Weekend games at the school field weren't the same as those played during the week. The town had a little more energy and traffic during the weekend summer days, but the boys were the opposite. Not everyone was available to play on the weekends, so it was usually a continual game of home run derby or five hundred. Those who did play usually trickled in later than their usual times and came and went throughout the day. This Saturday was a bit different, though, as the weather was a little bit cooler than a typical June day. Also, after the showdown earlier in the week between David and Gary and then the run-in at Jay's, the boys were chomping a bit to get back on the field.

David walked straight to the field on the weekends. He didn't like going to Dusty's house on the weekends like he did on the weekdays because he felt like he was intruding on their family when they were all there for breakfast on the weekends. As he turned the corner and the field came into sight, he was relieved to see that Dusty was already there and the older boys weren't. He glanced at the deck beyond the third baseline and noticed that it was unoccupied. He felt a sense of calm come over him. It was a relief for him to be there without anything that was going to stress him out.

Dusty extended his arm out to David and pulled him in for a hug instead of a handshake when he got to the backstop. "How you been?" he asked.

"You know, the usual. Parents really got into it again last night. My mom didn't get home until after five this morning. Pretty sure my dad was waiting up for her because I could hear them arguing in the living room. I've been up pretty much ever since," David confessed in a matter-of-fact tone.

"So in other words, it's Saturday and time to play a little ball," Dusty said, trying to change the topic and lighten the mood. He knew the weekends were especially rough for David because his parents typically fought more. His mom worked really late each night, and his dad was off, so he would usually go out and tie one on pretty good both nights. The result was usually either a drunken argument that left little regard for David's sleep and welfare or a lovefest that did the same. David preferred the arguing, and Dusty knew that.

"Yeah, let's play," David said as he began stretching.

Dallas, Eric, Jason, Brooks, and a few other younger kids were already out in the field playing catch. The younger kids loved the weekends because they knew they would typically be given more opportunities to join in, and whatever games they were playing were to be taken as seriously, so on Saturdays, there were always quite a few more younger guys out there. David remembered those days well and how much he used to look forward to Saturdays. Today was no different as there were a number of middle school kids out there he wasn't all that familiar with.

"So I heard you guys almost got into it with some guys from Fox Creek the other day," Jason said to Dusty as they started playing catch. Jason was going to be a freshman and looked up to Dusty because they were pretty similar.

"Nah, nothing to brag too much about," Dusty rebutted.

"Well, I heard that Ricky was about to go off," Brooks interjected. He was also a freshman-to-be and a good ballplayer. He wasn't sure if he wanted to earn his stripes with the group more with his baseball skills or his toughness off the field.

"That toothy fool was the problem and was lucky we were there to keep him from getting his ass kicked," Dusty chirped back. All the younger kids liked Dusty and looked up to him, so they were satisfied with his answers.

It was going to be a good Saturday. The sun was out, but there were little humidity and nice clouds to help shade them. Everyone was in a good mood, and nobody was around to take things too seriously. "So you guys wanna play five hundred or home run derby?" Dusty asked the group.

"How about we run things back again from the other day?" came a voice booming from the street along the first baseline. Ricky, Joey, and Gary had decided to walk over from Gary's house, and nobody had noticed them coming. Ricky and Joey looked hungover, and Gary just looked agitated. Ricky liked stirring the pot, and apparently, getting people's emotions charged up was the remedy for what he had done last night.

"We were thinking about just taking it easy today, guys," Dusty said, trying to keep the peace and sensing the tension.

"I've got no problem with that, unless you guys have something to prove," Gary responded while looking at David half-smiling and half-provoking.

"Yeah, let's play some ball today," Dallas eagerly blurted out.

"Let's play some ones versus ones," Brooks chipped in, looking to get Ricky's approval.

"I've got no problem with that," James said as he slapped Brooks on the back.

For the younger guys this was their chance to step up and show that they belonged. Ones versus ones was a challenge where somebody called you out, and you had to go on the mound and face them. A lot of times, it was the younger guys' chance to call out an older guy they thought they were better than. Since there were so many younger guys around today, they were all about it; but for Gary, today was all about putting David back in his place.

Dusty looked over at David and saw that he wasn't feeling as enthusiastic about things as the younger guys and tried to call it off. "Hey, you guys know that weekends are a little more laid back. Why don't we save it for next week?"

"Is your boy scared?" Ricky said to Dusty while looking at David. "Ain't got the guts, Collins? Afraid Gary's gonna rope another one off you? Afraid you're going to have to tuck tail in front of Becky again?"

David was getting so upset that he didn't notice Becky had come out in a pair of short white denim shorts and a light blue belly shirt that didn't have any sleeves and left little to the imagination. He had no interest in giving in to Ricky's demands, but as the boys began to squabble with one another loud enough to be heard across the entire field, Becky became more interested. "So what are you guys arguing about? Are you going to play or what?" Becky asked with playful interest that would only further incite and divide the boys.

"Well, we're trying to play ones, but your hero, David, doesn't want any part of facing Gary again," Ricky boasted as he was intent on restoring Gary's confidence and reminding David of his place in the group. He also wanted to remind Becky that David didn't belong with the Fox Creek boys either.

"Well, I was just hoping to watch some baseball, and that was fun the other day," she replied, looking at the boys as if they were her flock and she was guiding them to the slaughter. This was all they needed to convince them that it was game on.

"I'm in if you're in, David," Gary said, somewhat embarrassed. He appreciated what Ricky was trying to do for him, but he liked David as well. He liked keeping him in his place, but he didn't want things to get so confrontational with the group. However, he was pissed at Becky for hanging with the Fox Creek boys and leading them to David, so this contest would be his way of getting back at all of them.

"Sure, let's do it." David sighed as he flipped a ball up over his head and into his glove without looking. He took a deep breath, turned his back to Becky, and started walking out to center field. He knew that he and Gary were the main event, so the younger guys would face off against the person of their choosing first. Nobody would pick him since they all wanted to see him face Gary. Dusty trotted out to quickly join his friend.

"You okay with this?" he asked as if he were David's keeper.

"Look, it's fine. Everybody will get what they want out of this. Plus, after this, Becky will leave me alone too. Maybe we'll get back to normal," David sarcastically droned, but he was also filled with a hint of hope.

Dusty tapped him on the butt and went to start putting on the catcher's gear. As he started off back toward his equipment bag, David patronized him by saying, "And don't worry, I won't shake you off today either. You can take all the credit."

Dusty didn't like the tone of his friend's voice, but he knew they would talk about things later. He got his gear on, and the younger kids started calling out their combatants. Becky hopped on her bike to run up to the Dairy Barn for some ice cream. While the younger boys cared about her, she didn't care about them. By the time she returned with a large cone that was halfway eaten in one hand, it was just about time for the main event.

"So did I miss anything big?" she asked as if she were a sixth-grade student returning to school after she had missed a few days.

"Well, you missed—" Brooks began eagerly from shortstop. He was beaming from his success earlier in the day and the fact that he was playing shortstop, but before he could continue, he was cut off by Ricky, who was walking out to left field with his hat shoved so far down his face that it almost hid his acne and teeth.

"Not a damn thing!" he rumbled as he continued his march to the outfield.

Joey chimed in to fill in the gaps. When he was excited and laughing, it was hard to tell if he was speaking a sentence or coughing it out. "Well, David darn near took off Ricky's head with a line drive. Twice!" He continued to laugh as he looked back out to Ricky, who had stopped and heard what he said.

Becky tilted her head a bit and tightened her lips to show her satisfaction. She didn't care much for Ricky either, so she smiled at David, who had been listening to the entire exchange. That smile made David feel good, but he didn't acknowledge it.

Ricky responded like a villain. "He's going to get what he's got coming here in a few minutes anyways."

"Yeah, when is the main event anyways?" Becky asked as she slowly and torturously began to work over her ice cream cone.

"Right now," Gary declared as he slapped David on the back.

"You ready to get this over with?" he asked as if he knew that neither one really felt like being there at that moment.

"Nice! Well, good luck, Gary. Think you can hit another one like you did the other day?" she inquired midlick. Hearing those words, Gary's demeanor changed a little bit.

He glanced out at his friend who was sulking in the outfield and made sure to say loud enough for him to hear, "David's not as good as he thinks he is, and I'll keep reminding him of that as long as we're playing on this field." With that, he flipped his glove in the air to show his confidence and looked out toward left field to make sure Ricky had heard him. The beaming teeth from the shadows of the hat confirmed that he had.

Becky liked the fact that things seemed to be getting a bit chippy and that she was right in the middle of it. "Well, we all need to be put in our place from time to time," she said flirtatiously to Gary. Her tone suggested that if he came through, he might be getting more than a short conversation afterward.

David just shook his head and wanted to get this over with as soon as possible. He got on the mound to take some warm-up throws, but he noticed that the attention had shifted from the field squarely onto Becky.

Her flirtatious comment drew the ire of Ricky. He didn't hesitate to start speaking his mind toward Becky. "Speaking of being put in our place from time to time," he began, "what the hell was that the other day at Jay's?"

"What do you mean?" she responded, trying to sound innocent.

"You know damn well what I mean!" he fired back. "You show up with a car full of guys from Fox Creek who were looking to start something. You have them invite David to go to the baseball game and sit in their field-level seats, and then you throw your arm around Ryan Harding as you make your grand exit. Can't believe you had to ride your bike up to the Dairy Barn today and didn't have one of your boyfriends come give you a ride in a shiny new car instead. So maybe *you* shouldn't forget *your* place." He made sure to emphasize the *you* and *your.* "Whatever you do or try, you're still going to be the same piece of trash from this town like the rest of us."

As he had said all that, he had walked closer to her but raised his voice and began pointing his finger. While most of the boys might have agreed with what Ricky had said, he had put a sudden black cloud over their beautiful day. Becky was clearly taken aback and rattled by his words. She wasn't going to cry or give him the satisfaction of getting upset though. She leaned forward in her chair, suddenly conscious of her outfit and trying to cover her stomach with her arms.

"Oh, now you realize it's just us Riverview boys here, so you want to cover up?" Ricky continued. Sensing that Ricky was about to go too far, Gary started walking down the third baseline to intercept his friend. Gary called out Ricky's name, but that wasn't going to stop him. Only one voice on that field could stop him.

"Shut the hell up and leave her alone, Ricky!" David barked from the mound louder than he had before in his life. The mere sound and power that came out of him caught everyone off guard and froze Ricky in his tracks. Suddenly, Ricky had forgotten about Becky and now started marching toward the mound, where David was standing.

"What did you say, you little twerp?" he demanded as he continued toward David. When David didn't answer, he said it again.

"You heard what I said," David responded, not backing down even as Ricky was steadily closing in on him. "She can do what she wants."

David paused and saw her smile, but then he continued, "And whoever she wants." In that exact moment, David had gone from a hero in her eyes to a monster. Nothing that Ricky said seemed to hurt her, but David's statement brought a rough look to her eyes that he'd never seen before. Ricky liked the statement and smiled as he stopped in his tracks.

"Well, all right, David," he said, smiling with that mouthful of teeth again. He backpedaled toward the outfield, nodding in agreement. He made sure to look over at Becky and enjoy her moment of pain.

With his smile widening, he said, "Now let's see who is the king of this field."

Gary was just as shocked by what had taken place as anyone else. He was still standing closest to Becky and her house. He knew how much David's words had hurt her. He didn't know what to say, so he just looked at her.

"Hit another rope" was all she had to say. She said it with power and conviction. There was no doubt whom she was pulling for this time, and there was little doubt that was going to bring about an end to the baseball for the afternoon.

Unlike the other day when everyone was on the balls of their feet and ready for this matchup, everyone was anxious for it to just be over. Nobody was really talking, and for once, even Dusty didn't have much to say. He started to walk out toward the mound, but David stopped him after a few steps with his eyes. Knowing that Gary was a good hitter, Dusty knew he'd have to mix things up this time around with his pitch calling. He put down one finger for an outside fastball. David didn't even acknowledge the sign and went into his windup.

"Jesus!" Dusty squealed as he caught the ball for a strike. He'd never caught a pitch that hard before, and it stung him. David was tapping into another level. Dusty knew he'd be foolish to put down anything other than a fastball again. Again, David didn't acknowledge the sign and just rocked and fired.

Gary swung and missed. He looked back at Dusty. "What the hell?" He was just as shocked as Dusty. All throughout high school, he had only seen one of two kids who threw that hard.

David hadn't taken his eyes off Dusty the first two pitches. He was breathing fire and throwing it too. He knew that Gary wasn't catching up to him today. Gary and Dusty knew it too; so did Becky. David noticed that now that everyone had turned their focus to the field and gotten quiet, she allowed a couple of silent tears to roll down her slender cheeks. He wanted to tell her that he was sorry. He wanted to tell her that he wanted Ricky to shut up and that he didn't mean to hurt her. He wanted to tell her that he liked her, but there was only one way to do that.

David knew Dusty was going to put down one finger. Dusty didn't even bother. He just nodded to David and smiled. A new king was going to emerge on this field today, and it was going to be his best friend. Dusty braced himself to receive the fastest pitch he'd ever tried to catch and couldn't wait to give his buddy a high five. Even Ricky, who was the only one chirping the first two pitches, was silent now. He knew what was coming, and he knew Gary wasn't going to catch up to it.

David went into the windup and rocked and fired. Whap! An absolute laser into the left-center field gap. Nobody in the outfield moved to go after the ball. They couldn't believe it. They'd started the afternoon waiting for this result, and now none of them could believe it. Ricky, who should have tracked down the ball, dropped to his knees, laughing. Dusty removed his mask and looked at David in disbelief. Gary simply tossed the bat to the side and shook his head.

Becky, who had been silently crying, quickly wiped the tears from her cheeks and gave Gary a woo-hoo. She came down off her deck to give Gary the victor's spoils. Joey just sat and smiled at Gary and his good fortune. As Becky made her way over to Gary behind the backstop, he tried to avoid her, but she wouldn't let him.

"Nice hit, Gary! You crushed him again. Maybe next time, we'll invite you to the game instead of him." She made sure that David heard every word as she wrapped her arms around him. "Let's celebrate tonight. We can hang at the Dairy Barn later." Gary nodded and said he would be back to her house at around six thirty. With that, she shot David one more look and went inside her house.

With that, the game broke up, and everyone started to go their own way without saying much except that they'd try to get back together and play again on Monday. Ricky and Joey were patting Gary on the back and putting their arms around him as they made their way back toward his house. Dusty was still in disbelief. The older boys knew to leave Dusty and David alone, so they took off without them. Eventually, it was just Dusty and David at the field, waiting for him to finish putting away his gear in his equipment bag.

They stood there in silence before Dusty lifted his bag in David's direction. "I'm assuming you're coming over to my place?" Dusty began. David nodded. "Good, then you can carry this because we've got a lot to talk about." With that, the boys headed back toward Dusty's trailer, making sure to go a different way so that they wouldn't have to walk past Gary's house.

7 CHAPTER

They started off taking the long route back to Dusty's trailer. They walked past the front of Becky's house, and David tried not to look, but he glanced out of the corner of his right eye, straining to see if he could somehow catch a glimpse of her inside her house. He felt horrible about what he had said. He wanted to tell her that, but he'd have to face Dusty first.

"So we gonna talk about what the heck just happened?" Dusty asked directly and angrily.

"Talk about what?" David replied, hoping that Dusty wouldn't press him but knowing better.

"Oh, I don't know. Where would you like to begin?" Dusty fired back. "How about we start with you serving up a meatball to Gary and letting him hit another missile off you?"

"What do you want me to say?" David said, looking down as they slowly shuffled together down the tree-covered street.

"I want to know why you let him get that hit off you." Dusty stopped to let David know that he wasn't going to keep playing along to this song and dance and wanted an answer. David hesitated and looked away, so Dusty continued, "Those first two pitches you threw were the two fastest pitches I've ever seen or caught in my life." David raised an eyebrow but still didn't say anything. "It was like you were possessed out there. There was no way that Gary was going to touch you. You and I both knew it. Heck, even Gary knew it. Look what you did to my hand." He raised his left hand and touched the area under his index finger to show David the slight bruising and swelling he had caused with his first two pitches. "He was dead meat, and we all knew it, and then for some reason, you decide to throw a ball right down the middle about five to six miles per hour slower and let him ride you to left-center. What's up with that?"

"I must have spent all I had on those first two pitches." David shrugged, hoping that Dusty would buy his story.

Now Dusty stopped and grabbed him. "Bullshit! You let him get a hit off you. If you don't tell me why you did that right now, you're going to have to go back to your own house for the rest of the weekend." Dusty knew how to play his cards and get David to talk.

"All right, fine," David admitted with a defeated tone in his voice. "I did let him get a hit off me."

"But why?" Dusty barked back at him. "That moment was everything you had hoped for since we were in sixth grade and started playing back there. We used to talk about the day that we'd be the kings of that field. We had that moment right in our hands, the chance to shut Ricky up and get the respect of Gary. We could be going to the Dairy Barn with Becky tonight instead of him."

The fact that Dusty kept using "we" was hitting home with David. Not only had he let himself down with how he acted toward Becky but he had let Dusty down too, the one guy who would always stand by his side and stick up for him, and David denied him of his moment because he was trying to do right by a girl who didn't care about him and Gary, who already respected him.

"Do you mind if we go to the park and talk?" David said, motioning ahead to Dusty. The city park was at least another quarter mile down the street and well out of their way to Dusty's trailer, but he knew that David didn't ask to talk very often, so he obliged.

The boys really didn't say much as they made their way down to the Riverview City Park. The park was mainly an open field that spanned a couple of acres and was bordered on the back edge by the actual Fox Creek that ran between the main river and the town on top of the bluff. There were a tree line off to their right and a completely unobstructed view of the city skyline off to their left. At the entrance off to the left, there was a good-sized playground that had a large pavilion area adjacent. The boys were surprised but happy to see that there was nobody there as they made their way over to the pavilion area. David set down Dusty's bag and his own glove under the pavilion, walked over to the large metal jungle dome, and climbed to the top, facing the city skyline.

"Well, let's hear it," Dusty said, giving the floor to David whenever he was ready.

David bowed his head and started off apologetically. "Look, man, I'm sorry. I know how much we talked about being the kings of that field, but I just couldn't today." David looked at Dusty, and when he realized Dusty wasn't going to insert himself, he continued, "I messed up and hurt Becky's feelings. I don't know why I said what I did. It's like I . . ."

"Really like her," Dusty said, both finishing David's sentence and wanting to know what this had to do with serving up a meatball to Gary. David was caught off guard that Dusty was so certain that he liked her. He hadn't said anything to him about it before, and he had tried to be careful to hide how much he looked at her when Dusty and the other guys were around. "Look, it's obvious you like her, and she likes you. She——"

"Wait a second," David interrupted. He couldn't believe what Dusty had just said. How could he be so certain that Becky liked him. It was almost as if she had said that to David herself the way his heart and spirits lifted, but being fifteen and trying to play things cool and not show his hand, he had to redirect.

"So why would you say that I like Becky?" David sniped back.

Dusty stopped to think about how he was going to come back at his friend, who he knew was trying to play dumb. He knew David's emotions swung on his response, so he did what David wouldn't. He knew he'd have to explain why David let Gary get that hit. "Look, it's nothing to be embarrassed about. It's not like you're the only one," he said, trying to get David to smile. However, he saw David's face tense up and realized he was taking the wrong tactic, so he changed his course. "I can't blame you, man. I know you didn't mean to hurt her. I'm proud of you for sticking up for her and telling Ricky to shut up. Sometimes that guy . . ." Dusty caught himself before he got off track, so he reverted to the task at hand. "I know you were sticking up for her. She knows that too. I just don't think you realize why she does some of the things she does."

"What do you mean?" David asked, trying to figure out what Dusty was getting at.

"That's not really for me to get into, but the important thing is that you care for her. For the first time today, I saw you actually care about somebody other than yourself. After you blew those first two pitches by Gary, I looked over at her too. I saw her crying. I know you saw her too. I know that's why you served that pitch up to Gary. You felt horrible about what you said, and you would have rather seen yourself fail than to say what you did and then succeed, even if it meant she'd go out with him tonight. That shows how much you care for her. She knows it too."

"Really? How?" David asked, still a step behind Dusty.

"Dude, we all saw the same thing out there today. Everybody knows what really happened, well, except for maybe Ricky." They both smiled. "Why do you think nobody was celebrating, well, except for Ricky? Heck, even Joey knew what was going on."

"They all know that I like Becky?" David asked like he was speaking to a parent.

"Ha ha ha! No, dufus. They know you let up and let Gary get that hit. Why do you think Gary just walked off and didn't say much? He was embarrassed. He probably won't even take her out tonight." That made David happy and lighten up a bit.

"So why does she act the way that she does? Always hanging out with different guys and treating us like crap?" David wondered out loud. Dusty just patted his innocent friend on the back and left him to sit and try to figure it out as he readjusted himself atop the jungle dome. David sat there staring at the skyline. The park, like most of Riverview, sat on the base of the bluff that gave them a perfect view of the city off to the west. The Dairy Barn was just a couple of blocks east from where they were, and the summer traffic flow of treat seekers was increasing, but David didn't care or notice. He only looked at the skyline for answers about Becky and life. While he was starting to find peace, the longer they sat there and stared off into the distance, the more agitated Dusty started to become.

"So you going to just sit here all night thinking about yourself and your own problems?" Dusty unexpectedly sniped toward David. "You know, the city isn't all that great, David. I see you always thinking and acting like you're better than us, but you're not."

Off guard and uncertain why his friend who had just tried to build him up was now on his case, David responded unevenly, "What do you mean?"

"I mean you can't even say that you're sorry. You couldn't say you're sorry to Becky. You couldn't say you're sorry for bringing the game to an end today. Do you even care that you backed out of the moment we'd been talking about for five years? Striking out the best player on that field with everyone there and watching? Nope. All you can do is sit and stare at buildings off in the distance, counting down the days until you can leave this town and trying to figure out how you can speed that up."

David didn't know what to say. Everything Dusty had just said was correct. It was like he had a lens into his mind. As usual, he froze. Dusty hopped down off the jungle dome and grabbed his stuff. "Where you going?" David asked as he didn't understand what had come over his friend.

"I've got to be back before five o'clock. Thanks to you, we're farther away from my house than we were at the field. Of course, you probably don't care!" Dusty barked out to his friend.

"Yeah, and I'm twice as far from my house as yours," David said, trying to combat the barrage he was facing from Dusty. He hopped down off the jungle dome, grabbed his glove, and started after his friend.

"So what's gotten into you, Dusty?" he said as he caught up to Dusty at the edge of the park.

"Me? I'm not the one who is sitting there thinking about life beyond Riverview. So what's your plan, David? You going to go off to college as far away from here as you possibly can? You going to promise that you'll be back for the holidays and that you'll write and call whenever you get a chance?" Dusty was on fire, and David couldn't figure things out. They were walking briskly, and David could hear Dusty slightly straining, trying to keep the pace he had set with his equipment bag slung over his shoulder.

"What's wrong with wanting to get out of here? What's so great about this place?" David was trying to defend himself and get an honest answer from Dusty at the same time.

"I guess I just don't see what you hate about this town so much. Plenty of other people seem to like it." Dusty motioned his head toward the mass of cars and people a couple of blocks down at the Dairy Barn.

"Oooh, we have good ice cream," David griped back sarcastically. "I don't see those people flocking here like sheep in the winter. Unless they're hiding in one of the two dozen bars we have here in Riverview." They strolled past one of the endless neighborhood bars that made up the fabric of their town. He briefly thought about his mom, who was probably just beginning her shift. He pictured her dressed up in her Saturday best to impress a bunch of other men. David looked quickly to make sure his dad's car wasn't parked outside the bar they were walking past as it was one of his desired breakfast and beer places. He was relieved to see his car wasn't there, but now he was getting worked up like Dusty.

Dusty seemed to sense David's rising anger, so he backed off a bit. "Look, I'm just saying that it doesn't mean you're a failure if you stay in Riverview your whole life."

"I didn't say it did," David implored back to his friend. He was still confused why he was coming at him like this, so he decided to go on the offensive. "It's just that the only good thing I enjoy about this town is you and playing baseball at the field. And let's be honest, even that isn't much fun anymore. Remember when we used to play there all day every day?" Dusty nodded as David continued, "Now we've barely gotten enough guys to play, and we've all gotta work. Plus, it just seems like now we're always at each other's throats over something."

"Well, that's your own doing," Dusty sniped back.

"Yeah, I guess," David admitted. "It's just that, what comes after this?" He paused and looked at Dusty, who didn't give any sort of response. "I mean, in a couple of years, what are we going to be doing? I don't want to be working at Jay's and dealing with Ricky. Don't you want to get out of here?"

Dusty just kept plowing ahead, but he knew David's silence meant he'd have to answer, so he started back at him, "You know, people that leave here don't come back because when they do, they get laughed at for being one of the ones who thought they could leave and go on to something better. So I guess that means you'll just leave here and be one of the ones that never comes back too, huh?" Dusty was in near tears as they turned the corner to his street. David didn't know what was bothering him so much.

They walked the last few hundred yards in silence, but as they approached Dusty's trailer, he turned to David and climbed on him one more time. "Why couldn't you have just struck Gary out today? I know you're going to leave here one day, but you're never going to make it if you're always afraid of hurting someone's feelings. It's the ones that don't care about hurting people's feelings that get out and don't come back." With that, Dusty moved ahead of David the rest of the way to his trailer. He chucked his equipment bag in the garage, and they walked up the steps to the trailer together.

As soon as the boys entered the trailer, they were simultaneously greeted by the smell of fried chicken and Dusty's stepmom, Bonnie. She'd gotten her hair all done up and was bathed in perfume. She was wearing a pair of stonewashed jeans under her apron with a NASCAR shirt tucked in. Dusty's father was just finishing up at the table and patted Dusty on the back as he walked past him to head to the refrigerator. He can see that Dusty was upset but didn't want to make a scene in front of Bonnie and David.

"I was hoping you boys were going to be home soon," Bonnie began, oblivious to anyone's mood. "Your father and I are going to the drag strip tonight, so I made a bunch of food for you boys to enjoy while we're gone. How did things go with baseball today?"

Dusty and David just kind of looked at each other, but neither said a word. They were both still processing their emotions from the field, park, and subsequent walk, and they weren't about to spill everything to Bonnie. She was oblivious to them as she had her head over the counter, breading chicken.

Dusty's father knew that something was up, and he had a strong notion about what it was, but he didn't want to get caught up in it before he and Bonnie headed out. He kissed Bonnie on the back of her neck and said he'd be out in the garage. Half-heartedly, he said, "You boys are welcome to come along with us." He looked at Dusty in the eyes for a good long second.

David was really hoping that Dusty would say no. He and his friend needed to finish their talk, so he was relieved when Dusty said he didn't feel like going. He didn't even look at David to see if he wanted to go because he knew the answer.

"All right, suit yourselves. I'll be out in the garage. Bonnie, we've to get going if we're going to walk the pits beforehand." With that, he was out of the trailer, leaving the boys alone with Bonnie and her fried chicken.

"Will you boys be okay with this, or should I make you another side? I've got mashed potatoes and green beans, but I forgot to make any rolls," Bonnie said with a tone of disappointment toward herself.

Dusty didn't respond. He just wanted her out of the house to leave them to eat in peace. He hated how she would cook a meal and then watch him eat it while constantly asking if it was good or if he was enjoying it. Sensing that Dusty wasn't going to say anything and that he wanted her gone, David answered for them, "It's perfect, Bonnie. We'll be just fine. Better not keep Mr. Scott waiting too long, or he might leave without you."

Bonnie smiled at David and wiped her hands off on her apron as she removed it. "You're so sweet, David. Would you boys mind cleaning up the mess? Leave that chicken in the frier for another ten minutes and then remove it. You can empty the grease behind the garage. I love you, boys." She wanted to give Dusty a hug, but as she was speaking, he moved away from the door and into the living room area to avoid her. Instead, she would have to settle for rubbing David's shoulder on the way out.

David walked over to the chicken frying on the stove and began cleaning up the flour and breading crumbs that remained on the counter. Dusty sat on the couch until he heard his dad's car leave. Once they were gone, Dusty walked to the window at the kitchen table and looked out the curtains just to be sure.

With a little bit of a chip on his shoulder, David started in on Dusty. "Why are you like that to her? She's so nice and would do anything for you, and quite honestly, whenever I'm around, you treat her like crap." Dusty didn't say anything as he sat at the table and picked up a drumstick and then put it back down. "Seriously, you need to—"

"Need to what?" Dusty fired back. "Since when are you one to start giving advice about how to treat someone or act around your family?"

Dusty didn't care if he hurt David's feelings now. He wasn't going to listen to David discuss family life with him, but David wasn't backing down either.

"All I'm saying is that she's really nice and is trying to be a good mom to you," David implored as he continued to clean the kitchen.

"Well, she isn't my mom, and she won't ever be my mom, David!" Dusty pounded the table and looked down before looking over at David to gauge his reaction.

"I know, man, but—" David started.

"No, you don't know," Dusty cut him off. "You don't know what it's like to have your mom walk out on you. You don't know what it's like to never see or hear from your mom. You don't know what it's like to have your dad bring a stranger into your house and pretend to be someone she's not. Your biggest issue is that your mom buys you nice things to keep you happy and out of her business. Real tough life you've got there, David. No wonder why you've got everything figured out and can give advice to everyone. Heck, we should all be so lucky to have your family life!" Dusty began fighting back tears again.

As Dusty was in the middle of trying to tear David down, David remembered what today was. He looked at the calendar hanging on the refrigerator to confirm his memory and suspicion and then slid into a chair next to his friend, who was gripping the edges of the table. Everything suddenly made sense to him, and he was mortified as he quickly replayed the entire day and conversations over in his head. "Hey, Dusty, I'm sorry. I honestly forgot what day it was. I wouldn't have said anything had I remembered," David said as he reached out to put his hand on Dusty's shoulder.

David hadn't realized that it was the third anniversary of Dusty's mom walking out on him and his dad. It was a weeknight, and they had celebrated his sister's high school graduation with a big party the weekend before and gotten her situated in an apartment with some friends the next day. David remembered Dusty talking about how weird it was not having his sister around that first night and how empty everything felt around their trailer. He remembered how when he swung by Dusty's house that following Monday morning to walk to the school and play baseball together, Mr. Scott was at the door with tears in his eyes and told him that Dusty couldn't play today. Apparently, Dusty's mom had been seeing a guy for a while and was waiting for the right time to move out. She didn't want to do that before his sister's graduation, so she waited until she was gone and then made her own move. In a matter of a couple of days, Dusty's family had literally fallen apart. His mom tried to stay in touch initially and explain things to Dusty, but eventually, all Dusty knew was that she had moved somewhere that she wouldn't share and that she stopped calling altogether. Mr. Scott quickly took up with Bonnie, and not long afterward, she was living with them, trying to be something she never could be for Dusty.

"It's okay," Dusty squeezed out. "It's not your fault. It's none of our fault. You don't deserve the shit that goes on in your house, and I know you're right, but it's just that I can't let her be my mom. She's not my mom. My mom doesn't care about me." He was growing stronger and steady with his words. "It's been three years since she walked out and over two years since I've heard from her, and I'm okay with it. Looking back, it wasn't hard to see that she and my dad weren't happy together, but she didn't care about hurting people's feelings. That's why she got out and hasn't come back."

David knew he wasn't okay with it, but he wasn't going to interrupt Dusty or correct him. He also knew that last comment was directed at him as much as his mom. He knew Dusty needed to get this out, and he was going to give his friend the time and the space to do so. He sat and listened as Dusty continued on.

"She must have felt trapped here. I know it wasn't because of me. You know my dad. As the fire chief, he works long and weird hours, and he's not the most social person in the world outside of going to the racetrack or drag strip. As many times as he would ask her to stop dancing, I think it was the only thing that made her feel good about herself. I don't blame her for wanting something better for herself, but I just can't let Bonnie be my mom. I know she tries and she means well, but every time I see her in that kitchen, I think about my mom. I wonder what she's doing and why she can't call me anymore. Every time Bonnie sets a plate on the table, I think about how much my mom hated cooking. I guess it makes me hate Bonnie because she loves doing that stuff."

David remembered that the last of the fried chicken was in the frier, so he rubbed his friend's arm as he got up to walk over and remove the last of Bonnie's chicken. As he grabbed the last drumstick out of the frier, Dusty looked up at him. David smiled at him and flipped the drumstick over his shoulder with the tongs and into the trash can by his side. Dusty smiled and grabbed the drumstick he had been playing with and shot it across the kitchen and right into the trash can for two points. They both smiled at each other and began laughing as they made a game out of disposing Bonnie's meal that she cooked for them but they knew they couldn't eat.

The rest of the night they spent eating frozen pizza, watching movies, and talking about their lives and their futures. They both knew and realized that they could empty their feelings toward each other and still be friends, best friends. That's what best friends do for each other. David confessed his feelings for Becky, and Dusty tried to give him advice on how to gain her affection. Dusty opened up about his mom, and David told him that he understood what it was like to have a mom who didn't care. Dusty tried to convince him that she did. Like usual, Dusty could always read David's mind better than he could, and he could push him to places he didn't think he could go or get through.

They watched TV and talked long after Dusty's parents returned. David argued that if he weren't from Riverview, Dusty would hate him. While Dusty initially put up a fight, he eventually conceded that he would probably hate David if they weren't placed in the same reading group in kindergarten. David fought with Dusty and persuaded him to be nicer to Bonnie. It was a monumental night in their friendship spent in the living room of a double-wide trailer, the kind of night that ensured a lifetime friendship.

"Man, I sure wish you'd struck Gary out," Dusty said as he was falling asleep.

"Me too," David said out of obligation. He laid there for a few moments, listening to Dusty's heavy breathing. As much as he enjoyed talking with Dusty and being there for his friend, he wanted another chance to make things right with Becky.

8 CHAPTER

The following day, the boys slept in late. There was very little going on in Riverview except trying to avoid having to do household chores. Dusty's dad was out in the garage, working on some project, while the boys sat and had cereal while listening to Bonnie recap her night out and inquire about theirs. When she asked about why all the chicken was in the trash, the boys just looked at each other and laughed. Bonnie looked a little hurt, but she was more pleased her boys were sitting at the table, having a good time.

"So what are you boys up to today?" Bonnie said as she finished a sip of her coffee.

The boys just looked at each other without saying anything. Dusty realized if he didn't say something quickly, he'd be asked to clean up his room. "Uh, probably just walking to the Dairy Barn and then just hanging out." He floated that out there, hoping that Bonnie would accept his answer and not notice or care about the mess they had left in the living room.

"That sounds nice," she started. "Just make sure to pick up the living room first." Dusty rolled his eyes and then looked at David, who was waiting for his response. Remembering their conversation last night, Dusty agreed to pick up the mess before leaving.

"Why don't you get started with that, David, while I go take a shower?" Dusty said while snickering and patting his friend on the shoulder as he headed off toward the bathroom.

Bonnie tilted her head and looked at David as if she felt bad for asking them to clean up. She set her coffee cup down and started heading toward the living room. David managed to grab her leg as she was walking by. "Mrs. Scott, you asked us to clean it up, and we're going to clean it up," David asserted. Bonnie looked at him in a way that told David she didn't believe him, so David tried to reassure her. "Things will be different from now on. I promise." With that, David got up and began to pick things up in the living room.

Bonnie sat at the kitchen table with her cup of coffee and watched quietly, a little unsure of what to do. When it was David's turn to get in the shower, he gave Dusty a pat on the butt and told him what he had already done. He locked eyes with Dusty as if to say, *Don't screw this up.* While David was showering, all he could think about was if Dusty was actually cleaning up or if he was back to his usual way of taking out his anger toward his real mom on Bonnie. To his delight, when he came back out into the living room, everything was spotless, and he and Bonnie were sitting on the couch, watching TV together.

"You ready to go?" Dusty said as he sprung up from the couch. Smiling and for once feeling like the big brother, David nodded. As the boys made their way out the front door, David looked back at Bonnie, who was still sitting on the couch. Dusty went down the steps first, and Bonnie looked at David with tears forming in her eyes and silently mouthed the words *thank you.*

Once they were clear of the trailer and a little down the street, David thanked his friend for taking the first step toward treating Bonnie like she deserved. "Hey, thanks, Dusty. That really meant a lot to Bonnie and me."

"Thanks for what?" Dusty replied, trying to play dumb. They walked slowly through the neighborhoods of Riverview toward the Dairy Barn. Though the houses were small, the trees that shaded a number of the streets were enormous. The shade was welcome on what was turning into a hot mid-June day.

"So when are you going to step up and try to make things right with your parents?" Dusty started in after a lull in the conversation. David kept walking, hoping to avoid the question, but Dusty pressed on.

"I mean, you can't spend every weekend at my place forever. At some point, you need to try to talk to them."

David sulked for a few paces before admitting that Dusty was right and saying that he would go home later today. He wasn't sure what he was going to talk to them about, but that would not change anything. He wasn't even sure his father was capable of talking outside of fighting with his mom, but he tried to push all that aside while he was still hanging out with his best friend.

As the boys made their way to the main road through town, they could see that there were already a significant number of people in the parking lot of the Dairy Barn. It was a typical Sunday postchurch stop for families who actually enjoyed spending time together. The boys really didn't have an agenda, so waiting in line and killing time wasn't that big of a deal. Just as the boys were about to reach the Dairy Barn parking lot, they heard a car roll up on them. Without turning around or looking, they knew it was Joey's car from the volume of the stereo and a familiar voice yelling at them from the passenger seat.

"What's up, losers?" Ricky said loud enough for people in line to hear as they cut in front of the boys in the entrance to the parking lot. Ricky was hanging out the window with his toothy smile in full beam. "You guys come here to lick your wounds?" Ricky and Joey both laughed at his attempt to properly use a pun, but David and Dusty weren't finding the humor in things.

"Where's Gary?" Dusty asked.

"Don't know. Haven't seen or heard from him since he met up with Becky last night," Joey said, chuckling and poking Ricky. They both laughed as if his triumph was somehow benefiting them as well. David tried not to show it, but he wanted to punch both of them. He knew this was their nature and that they weren't attacking him, so he decided to just let it be.

"Hey, you guys want to have a little fun today?" Ricky said as he contorted his body to dig in his pocket and reveal a huge wad of cash. David and Dusty both looked at each other and simultaneously declined. They noticed that even Joey had stopped laughing. "Well, suit yourselves. We're going to get a couple of milkshakes and then go hang out by the creek and try out this guy." As he finished his sentence, he opened the glove compartment to reveal a shiny new handgun. Before either of the boys could say anything, another vehicle had rolled up behind Joey and began honking as they were blocking the entrance and backing up traffic on the main drag. Ricky smiled out of the corner of his mouth as he put the gun back into the compartment, and they screeched into the parking lot of the Dairy Barn.

David looked at Dusty as if to say there was no way they were going to hang out with those two alone again, and Dusty confirmed his thoughts by simply responding, "I know." The boys decided the best way to avoid Ricky was to just keep walking past the Dairy Barn. They could hang right on the next street past the Dairy Barn. That was the road that led into Fox Creek. It was a really steep and winding road up the bluff, but a little less than a mile up the road was a bridge that spanned the actual creek, and underneath was a nice shaded area that the boys had hung out a number of times when they wanted to disappear for a while.

Just as the boys were getting a sense of relief that Joey and Ricky hadn't followed them up the street, another familiar vehicle came toward them. The boys could see Ryan's dark hair blowing in the breeze as he was behind the wheel of his red Mustang convertible. He was just with one other guy, and neither boy really thought much of it until they noticed that he was slowing down as he approached them. There was nothing that David or Dusty could do except stop and wait to see what they wanted.

Ryan didn't hesitate as he came to a stop across the street from them. "Hey, David, what are you up to?"

David looked at Dusty, seeking approval to speak for them. Dusty gave a quick nod to David. "Just killing time," David said quietly but firmly.

Dusty wasn't going to wait for them to get to business. "So what do you want? Why are you stopping in the middle of the road?"

"Well, actually, we were coming down here to look for you, guys," Ryan said with a hint of uneasiness. He looked at both David and Dusty. "We were hoping to talk to David." This time, he was honest and direct. "We figured we'd grab a milkshake before we came to the field and hoped to find you. You guys want to hop in?"

David looked at Dusty for an answer. They had just avoided the Dairy Barn because they didn't want to have to deal with Ricky and Joey, and now they were being offered a ride back. "It's your call," Dusty said to David, leaving it all on him.

David stood there, unsure of what to do. He figured they wanted to talk to him about baseball and playing for their Legion team, but he didn't want to betray his friends. Then he thought about his friends who were at the Dairy Barn with a wad of cash that they certainly hadn't come about honestly and a gun in the compartment. He also remembered what Dusty had said yesterday about being willing to hurt people's feelings if you wanted to get out.

Ryan looked over his left shoulder and noticed a car coming up behind them. Dusty's face showed that he really didn't care what David decided. David also noticed the car coming up behind Ryan and another car coming from the direction of the Dairy Barn up the road. He had to make a decision quickly. "Sure," he heard himself blurt out, almost as if he was out of body.

Ryan smiled and tapped the side of his car, motioning for them to hurry up and hop in the back seat. Once they were in the car, Ryan punched the gas, and they made the quick trip back to the Dairy Barn. Thankfully, there was a back entrance to the parking lot, so people up front in line were obscured by the building itself. Ryan settled his car into a spot in the half-full parking lot as David and Dusty spotted Joey's car about six or seven spots down.

The boys hopped out of the car and began to walk toward the front of the Dairy Barn, but Ryan and his friend stopped at the trunk of his car, suggesting that they wanted to talk more than they wanted a milkshake. David and Dusty both knew that either way, if Ricky and Joey saw them with the Fox Creek guys, it would likely cause a scene. They figured it would be easier to play off if they were in line around other people, but the Fox Creek boys weren't moving from the car until they said what was on their mind.

Ryan started in first by looking right at David. "Look, first off, I want to apologize for the scene at your work the other day. That was truly embarrassing and not what we're all about." He tapped his friend on the arm, who also nodded. His friend wasn't there but obviously had heard about what took place. "We wanted to talk to you and see if you would be interested in playing with us this summer for our Legion ball team. We're in a lot of big events, and we could really use you. I've seen you throw, and quite honestly, you're just as good or better than anyone we've got. There are lots of college coaches at these events, so it's a good opportunity to be seen. Plus, we're not half bad. If you come on board, we've got a chance to advance to the regional and possibly the national tournament."

Before Ryan could fully finish his sales pitch, all four boys are greeted with "What the hell?" from Ricky as they had come from around the front of the building with ice cream on the way back to Joey's car. All four boys simultaneously looked in the direction of the voice to see Ricky and Joey storming up to the convertible, but nobody responded. "What the hell is going on here?" Ricky angrily asked again, ready to fight at a moment's notice.

Dusty decided to play the cooler and put his hands on Ricky's chest as he said, "We're good. They just wanted to talk to David about baseball."

When Ricky heard that, he burst out laughing. "You want to talk to him?" He couldn't stop laughing, and Joey joined in as Ricky continued, "Gary's lit him up the last two times he's faced him. What do you want with him anyways?" He stopped laughing and turned to Ryan, waiting for an answer.

"Well, I was telling him that we wanted him to join our Legion team this summer, how we're playing in some big events with a lot of college coaches. It's a big opportunity, and we could really use his arm," Ryan said, sounding more like a friend than a salesman.

Ricky resumed his laughter again as he grabbed David's right arm. "You want this arm?" he said, trying to squeeze him. David pulled his arm away, and Ricky seemed somewhat surprised. "Little more muscle there than I thought, David. Anyways, why don't you boys run along? Nobody from Riverview has ever played for Fox Creek. Anybody that plays Legion ball from Riverview plays for the East Side Legion team anyways, and David knows better than to cross enemy lines. Right, David?"

David sat there angered by Ricky but taking in his words. Thankfully, Dusty was there to articulate what was running through David's mind. "You aren't his agent, and you don't answer for him. If he wants to play with them, he can." Dusty turned to David, but he was still processing everything in his mind. "Plus, the East Side Legion couldn't get a team together this summer, so David or anybody else from Riverview is free to play for the Fox Creek team this summer."

Ricky didn't need time to process things in his mind. "Give it up, boys. Nobody from Riverview has played for Fox Creek, and it won't start with him." Ricky slapped David hard enough across the back to cause him to lunge forward.

This bothered Ryan's friend, who now stepped forward and sniped back at Ricky, "Well, the reason no one has ever played for us from this town is that nobody has ever been good enough." After he said this, he postured for what he assumed was going to be an aggressive act from Ricky.

Instead, Ricky just laughed and started to walk back to his car. As he did, he called the Fox Creek boys a couple of choice words. Just as Dusty and David thought they were about to leave, they heard Ricky call out, "Let's go, boys! Leave those pricks here to play with themselves!" Neither one of the boys wanted to go with Ricky, but they knew that if they wanted to avoid escalating things, they should give in and go with Ricky. Ryan nodded as if he seemed to understand, but he saw the disappointment on David's face.

"Hey, I've got an idea," he said in a raised and excited voice to Ricky, who was just about to duck down into Joey's passenger seat. "Why don't we bring some guys down here and we'll play you in a game? Then we'll see who can play and who can't." He stood there with his chin raised for a moment, proud of himself for coming up with such a good idea on the spot.

Ricky stood up straight and then looked at Joey, who had no opinion. He then looked at Dusty and David, who were literally caught halfway between both vehicles. "So you want to play us in a game to show us how good you are and how much we suck? Ha, what's the point?"

Ryan stepped forward, giving David a glance before declaring, "We want to play you to show you how good David is."

Sensing that he needed to play up the rivalry to pique Ricky's interest even more, he said, "He might just be good enough to keep you guys from being completely embarrassed, and if he is, maybe it will persuade him to join us despite what his 'friends' tell him he should do."

This more than piqued Ricky's interest as he closed the door and began to come back around the car to get closer to where Ryan was standing. "If he's good enough to beat you guys, I'll pack his bags for him. Plus, we don't need him anyways. We can kick your ass without him."

Knowing that he won and Ricky was playing right into his hands, Ryan widened his smile and raised his chin again as he asked, "So when do you guys want to do this?"

Dusty didn't wait for Ricky to answer. "Wednesday." He looked right at David. "You're off on Wednesday's, aren't you?" David nodded. "Then Wednesday it is. Be at our field at eleven. We'll be sure to have nine guys."

"Wednesday should work," Ryan said as he turned to his friend to confirm. Then he looked right at David. "Bring it. We want your best."

With that, the Fox Creek boys began the walk across the parking lot to the front of the Dairy Barn. David and Dusty looked at each other and made the half-hearted walk over to Joey's car. "Don't let us down, wimp," Ricky sniped to David as he slid into the back seat.

"Oh, now you're on his side?" Dusty fired back. Ricky looked at Dusty with a puzzled look on his face. "Yeah, asshole. Ryan came down here to talk to David about an opportunity that could really help him, and you open your big mouth before he can get a word out. How do you know he doesn't want to play with them? How do you know he's not good enough? If they want him on their team, what do you care?"

Dusty wasn't kidding around, and Ricky knew it. "Well, I was just—"

"You were just being an asshole," Dusty interrupted.

Turning over his left shoulder and to the back seat where David was sliding across to the driver's side because the other door didn't work, Ricky squinted as he said, "So what do you think, loser? Do you really want to go play on a team with those pricks?"

"He doesn't have to answer to you," Dusty fired back at him. "Come on, David, get out of the damn car. We're done with this clown."

As David was scooting his way back out of the car toward the passenger side, a souped-up black BMW came ripping into the parking lot and screeched to a stop right behind Joey's car, blocking him in. David couldn't see into the car because the windows were tinted, but he could see a massive man dressed all in black with gold chains around his neck, black Raiders hat, black sunglasses, and rings on every finger of his right hand spring out of the front passenger seat. Ricky inched closer to the car and dropped the glove compartment to give him quicker access to the gun he was bragging about a little while earlier. He was searching for the gun with his right hand while not dropping his eyes off the man who was screaming at him. All the other boys were frozen in place, in complete terror of moving.

"I thought I might find you here, you horse-mouthed piece of shit!" the large man boomed loud enough to draw the attention of everyone in the parking lot and get them to cease their activities and conversations. Sensing that he didn't want the entire parking lot to hear what he said next, he gritted his teeth and seethed. "If you ever mess with my money or try to lie to me again, it will be the last thing you do. You understand me, Ricky?" Ricky was still fishing for the gun blindly with his right hand. David looked out the window at Dusty and had never seen him look so scared.

"You understand me, you little bitch?" the man repeated. "I'll end you." With that, the man ducked back into the car, and it tore off through the parking lot, nearly hitting two little kids who were playing hopscotch while eating an ice cream cone.

All four of the boys sat there in stunned silence for a few seconds. David could see Ryan and his friend peering from around the front of the building at Joey's car. It was Dusty who broke the silence as Ricky stood there, trying not to look like he wasn't scared to pieces. "What the hell was that, man? Huh? What the hell was that?" Ricky just stood there.

"Get out of the car, David," he ordered. "We're freaking out of here." David slid out quickly, trying not to look at the compartment drawer or Ricky on his way out.

Sensing that he needed to try to gain some sort of respect back, Ricky tried to seem in control as he grabbed the gun from the compartment while saying, "We're good. We're good. He knows better than to mess with me." But the boys weren't buying it.

"Put the thing away, man," Dusty said as he swiped down at the gun. "There are freaking kids and families around here everywhere. What the hell is wrong with you?"

Even Joey was freaked out. "Who the hell was that, man? What the hell was that all about? Get in the freaking car. This is the last damn ride you're getting." Joey fired up the engine, but as the engine rose, he turned the music off.

Ricky looked at David and Dusty and knew that his best friend was about to lay into him, so he decided to get one last shot in on them. "I'll see you boys at the field tomorrow. Wouldn't want the golden boy to not get his practice in before Wednesday." With that, he put the gun away, slammed the glove compartment door closed, and shut his door, and Joey ripped back out of the parking spot and then the parking lot. Whatever conversation they were about to have wasn't going to be a pretty one.

David and Dusty turned to each other in disbelief. They were where they set out to be when they left Dusty's trailer, but now they wanted to get the heck out of there. They were worried the BMW might come roaring back into the parking lot and see two of the guys Ricky was associated with standing there. They were also mortified and embarrassed about what had just taken place in front of Ryan and his friend. They didn't want to head back toward Fox Creek, so instead, they headed back down the main road.

"That's why you've got to play for them," Dusty began. David looked at his friend, confused. This was the same guy who, less than twenty-four hours ago, was coming down on him for wanting to get out of town. Despite their long talk last night, David still hadn't gotten Dusty to concede that life outside Riverview was any better or that he was right for wanting to get out. Now he was telling him to play for the enemy? "You've got to get out of here if you can, David."

David wasn't sure what to say. He was trying to process everything that had just happened and his best friend's sudden change in tone. "I'm not good enough to play with them," David mumbled as he looked to the sky.

"The hell you're not," Dusty snapped back. "You've got something special, and it's only going to be pissed away if you keep hanging around guys like Ricky and me."

"What do you mean and guys like you?" David said, suddenly sure of himself and looking at Dusty.

"Look, I'm not Ricky, but you know I'm not you. I'm going to look for fights and enjoy them when they come my way. I'm always going to be around trouble. I may not be in it, but I'll be around it. I don't have the grades to do anything else but work behind a bar or in a kitchen in this town. You, you've got something special. Yesterday nobody in the metro area was going to touch you with those first two pitches. You owe it to yourself and to your true friends to go as far as you can with baseball." That was as heartfelt as anything Dusty had said to David in his entire life, so much so that he had tears in his eyes.

"But I'm scared," David said as he felt his throat tightening up.

"What are you scared of?" Dusty implored.

"I'm scared that I'm going to fail. I'm going to screw up. I'm going to be the athlete who tried to get out of here and ended up at the end of the bar or, like my dad, worked a job I hate. I don't want to let anyone down. Worst of all, if I leave or if I play for them, I can't come back and hang out with you guys anymore if I fail. I'll be a laughingstock. Plus, either way, there is no way Ricky would allow me back," David confessed.

"Oh, so you're going to let Ricky Rogers determine your future? You'd rather try to stay friends with a guy like that than do something special with your life? My god, it's just a game. You said it yourself. Our games at the field aren't fun anymore. We're not little kids. This is a chance for you to latch on to something good, and you're too afraid to even take a chance?" Dusty replied.

"Yeah, I guess I am," David said, defeatedly. "I've always been afraid. You're the only person who has ever believed in me." Dusty stopped and smiled at David. "What are you smiling at?"

Dusty continued to smile as he said, "Ryan Harding believes in you." David couldn't deny that, so he just smiled back at Dusty.

"God, I hate you sometimes," David declared. Dusty only smiled even wider.

"You're going to hate me even more when I tell you this," he started, waiting for David to say what.

"What?" David predictably replied.

"I'm going home, and you're not coming with me. You're going to go home and talk to your parents like we discussed last night. You're going to tell them about the opportunity that you have. You're going to have a real conversation with them," Dusty said while smiling continuously.

"And if I don't?" David replied, trying to sound like Dusty.

"If you don't, I won't catch you on Wednesday. I'll tell Ricky that you told me you were too scared, so I didn't think you were going to show," Dusty declared triumphantly.

"How will you even know if I talked to them or not?" David asked, thinking that he would catch Dusty in a loophole.

"Like I wouldn't be able to tell if you talked to them or not. You can't keep anything from me. I can read you like a book. Like right now, you're racking your brain, trying to think of a story you could tell me that would convince me that you talked to them when you really didn't," Dusty declared victoriously. He was absolutely correct.

David couldn't do anything but smile and shake his head. "All right, you win. I'll go home and try to talk to my parents."

"Attaboy," Dusty said as he gave his friend a little fist bump, the same one he gave every time after David struck somebody out. "So I'll see you tomorrow for breakfast?"

"I'll be there, but if you're not nice to Bonnie, I'm walking out," David said, smiling.

Dusty took a quick look at traffic and then dashed across the main road as he yelled over his shoulder, "Deal!" With that, Dusty took off down a side street toward his trailer park.

David began the trek home by himself, alone with his thoughts and how he was going to try to explain things to his parents. He figured he'd try his dad since he knew he at least enjoyed baseball.

9 CHAPTER

When David's house came into view, he noticed that his dad had already cut the grass, so he knew that he would be inside when he got there. Sundays around his house were pretty predictable. His parents would both sleep in late. When they got up, his mom would usually go shopping and return with groceries. She would have an array of frozen meals for the men to choose from, along with fruits and vegetables galore for herself and anyone else who wanted to eat healthy and simple. She would usually drop them off on the counter and then ask the boys to put them away because she had to get ready for work.

David's father would get up late in the morning and head outside to do yard work. David had asked many times if he could help or take over for him, but the yard and landscaping was his dad's outlet, and they had a decent-sized yard with plenty of shrubs and bushes to also maintain. Once he finished up in the yard, he would then come inside and turn the baseball game on the TV and lounge around until the game was over or he had to help put away groceries. When that was done, he'd go and grab a nap before going in to start his first shift of the week. Normally, David didn't mind Sundays because he knew his parents' schedule and when to avoid them, but today he knew he had to talk to them.

As he made his way up the driveway to enter through the garage, David wasn't sure what exactly he was going to say or how he was going to begin, but he knew he wanted to tell his dad about the opportunity to play Legion ball with Fox Creek. Walking up the stairs toward the kitchen, he could hear the baseball game on in the living room. He figured this would be the perfect time and way to talk about his own baseball life with his father. As he grabbed the knob to open the door, he could feel his throat tightening a bit, but there was no looking back. He had to do this for Dusty and for himself.

It was a little before two in the afternoon, and David poured himself a tall glass of water before sitting on the couch across from his father's chair. The game was in the middle innings, so it wasn't getting too intense. His father didn't even seem to notice or acknowledge that he had even walked in, so David would have to press the issue. David waited for the score to flash across the screen to try to break the ice.

"I see the offense is still sputtering a bit," David began. His father somewhat jolted in his chair. After all the games they had watched together, it was pretty rare that there was any conversation during the games. Sensing that his dad was a bit shocked and slightly irritated, he tried to press on. "Doesn't seem to matter who they face these days. They can't generate any offense."

He looked over at his dad for any sort of response, hoping that he would at least want to talk about the game with him. He never understood how he could just watch those games in silence, unlike his grandpa, who talked about every little thing the entire game. Finally, after a few seconds, he responded, "Eh, just a little rough patch. They'll get it together." With that statement, he was clearly trying to end the conversation.

David sensed it too, but for once, he decided he needed to press forward. "I guess, but they're digging themselves a pretty decent hole in the standings." He hoped that would get his father to engage, but at the same time, he was a bit worried because he knew how prickly he could be on Sunday afternoons as the reality of another workweek began to set in. Unfortunately for David, it was the second option that came out.

"Boy, you're just full of brilliant observations, aren't you?" he began to tear into him. "You're gone all day and night, no responsibility, and then you show up to watch the game in my house and point out the obvious. I tell you what, son, forget broadcasting school. I think you should go into the business right now. Some of these idiots spend years in school or playing the game to spout out the same observation you just made in the first minute you were home. Aren't you special?"

Normally, David would have taken this as his cue to go to his room or grab the transistor radio and get lost for a bit, but today was different. After what he went through at the Dairy Barn and his conversation last night with Dusty, he was going to make his dad hear him, no matter how scared he was. "Listen, I was just trying to make conversation—you know, like most people do when they watch a game together."

David's dad snarled but didn't move. He took a deep breath and flipped his hair back, but he kept looking ahead at the TV. Finally, he said in a somewhat defeated tone, "So what do you want?"

David was a bit surprised and unsure of exactly how to answer. "What do you mean, what do I want? I just told you I—"

His father cut him off before he could finish, "I mean, just tell me what's on your mind. For nearly sixteen years, you've sat in silence watching these damn games with me. And suddenly today, when I've got to go back to work tonight, you choose to get all chatty? Just come out with it."

David was taken aback by how perceptive his father actually was, but it was out there now, so he had to respond. He wanted to tell his father that he hadn't talked in almost sixteen years because he was afraid of him. He didn't know what to say to the man because his father had never talked to him about anything. He wanted to tell his dad about how he hated feeling so alone in his own house, but he didn't want to go down that road today. Today wasn't about their past; it was about his future. If his father wanted to be a part of it, that was up to him.

David tried to keep his tone even as he began, "Well, I wanted to tell you about an opportunity that I have and see what you think."

His dad squeezed his eyebrows together a bit to suggest that he was a bit confused and surprised with David's opening sentence. David saw this, so he continued, "Some guy from Fox Creek asked if I wanted to play with their Legion team this summer. They said that they needed my arm and that it would be a chance to play in front of some college coaches. I wanted to know what you thought. Do you think I should play with them?"

When David's dad heard this, he leaned back in his chair, slapped the armrest, and laughed out loud. "You want to know what I think? I think you're not good enough to play for them," he started in on David while still smiling to himself.

"I think their baseball program has gone way downhill since I played if they're looking for you to join them," he concluded, still laughing.

David wanted to get up and walk out on his father initially, but after that first instinct, he felt another one. This was the opportunity to get his initial thoughts out when his father was bothered by his son's odd request to try to speak with him. He leaned forward on the couch to get a little closer to his dad so he'd be sure to hear every word he had to say. "How would you know if I'm any good? How many games have you been to in the past few years? Huh?" He said it angrily and with the force of a peer, not of a son who had been afraid to speak to his dad his entire life.

His father was caught off guard by David's response. He sat there for a second, thinking of what he could say that would cut his son down the most, searching for that perfect statement to put him in his place. "Why would I come watch you guys play? You couldn't even finish with a winning record this past year. You think you're a big shot because you played varsity the last two years? I played varsity for three years, and every year we had a winning record. If we weren't in the same sectional as Fox Creek, we could have gone on a run. Of course, you're going to think you're good when you play with those bums down at the school field every day. Those are the same guys that can't hit, which is why you guys had a losing record the last two years." His dad looked over to see if his words had their desired effect on David, and they had. David sat there, leaning forward but with his head now slumped a bit toward the floor.

His father looked at the clock and knew that his wife was going to be home really soon, so he had to finish him off while he had the chance. "The only reason those boys want you on their team is so they can make fun of you. You're not half as good as I was, and I never got asked to play for them. I thought you had brains, David, but you sure can't see straight through this mess. If you think you're going anywhere with baseball, you're dreaming. If you were any good at baseball or any sport, you'd have a girl all over you by now. Every girl in this town sees a boy with any athletic ability, and they cling to him, hoping that he's their ticket out of town. Next thing you know, you end up getting her pregnant, and you're stuck here for good in the middle of this shitty life that you didn't want."

As his father finished, they could both hear the car door of David's mother close in the garage. His father gave him a victorious smile as he squirmed his way up from his chair to go hide in the bedroom. "And she's right on cue," he said to David with a smile while making a gesture as if he was cheering him with a drink.

David sat there on the couch, looking at the TV in disbelief. He had tried to talk to his father and seek out advice, forge a relationship, yet his father decided to use this platform to try to destroy him. Worse off, it was as if he had waited his entire life to give David this speech. When David's mom emerged from the stairs, she was delighted to see him sitting there.

"Hey, sweetheart, can you help me with these groceries?"

David didn't move, even though he knew that he was the sweetheart she was referencing. He could hear her put down the groceries in her hand and knew she was walking around the front entrance of the living room through the kitchen.

"Did you hear me, David?" she asked as she emerged from around the corner in front of him.

As he came into sight, she noticed that he had tears in his eyes. "Honey, what's wrong?" she said as she placed her hand on his shoulder. All David could do was gesture his eyes down the hallway. That was all his mother needed to hear.

She sighed and said, "I'll take care of this and him. Why don't you go and cool off a bit somewhere?"

David wanted to tell his mom what his father had said, but he knew she didn't have the time to listen. He was also afraid that she might say the same thing. He grabbed the transistor radio and headed out into the woods behind the house. He could listen to the rest of the game there to help keep his mind off things. He didn't want to be in the house for the fight that was sure to ensue, and soon enough, his mom would be off to work and his dad sleeping before he had to go to work. He just had to kill a few hours.

He managed to avoid his dad the rest of the night as best as he could. David went and sat in his room after his mom had left for work. He made himself some eggs and ate in there while waiting for his dad to leave. He could hear his dad pacing up and down the hallway and in and out of the bathroom before he had to leave for work. When it was time to actually leave, he cracked open David's door and looked at him for a few seconds. The look was supposed to say "I'm sorry" because he wouldn't actually allow those words to come out of his mouth. Instead, it said, "Thanks for causing another fight with your mom." Before he closed the door, he just shook his head and walked away. David laid there thinking that this was a stellar reward for trying to build a relationship with his dad. He was thankful that at least he'd be able to play baseball with the boys tomorrow.

Monday morning came, and he had inadvertently slept in. He wouldn't have time to stop by Dusty's house before getting to the field, so he decided to walk straight there. He didn't want to call because Dusty's dad often worked odd hours at the station, so you never quite knew when he might be at home, trying to catch up on some sleep. He knew Dusty would be concerned when he didn't show for breakfast, but there wasn't anything he could do except apologize once he got there. Moreover, Dusty's feelings were the last thing on his mind as he made his journey toward the field. He knew Dusty would understand.

His bigger concern was that he hadn't seen Becky since Saturday, and he didn't know how she might react to him today. On top of that, there was the whole scene at the Dairy Barn with Ricky. Plus, he couldn't help but dwell on what his dad had said to him yesterday. No matter how much you dislike a person or convince yourself that you don't care, the opinion of one's parents always matters and carries weight. The entire way there, David began to convince himself that he was no good and neither were his friends. By the time he reached the field, he was in a bit of a rage within himself. Fittingly, everyone was already there, except Dusty. Knowing him, he was probably still waiting at his place to see if David was going to show.

Everyone seemed to be standing around, just waiting for David to show up. He could see them talking quietly to one another and gesturing at him as he approached. There was no doubt in his mind that they were talking about the game on Wednesday and whether or not they should back him up or purposefully tank to make him look bad. His suspicions were confirmed by Ricky once he got into earshot. "Well, here comes the man of the hour, the prized prospect of Riverview. Where's your escort?"

"I was running late and didn't want to risk calling and waking up his dad. He knew we're supposed to be here, but he's probably just waiting for me," David said, dropping to a knee to retie one of his shoes. He was relieved to see Dusty coming around the corner out of the corner of his eye as he rose to his feet.

"Uh-huh," Ricky groaned. "We figured you guys had spent the night spooning together, trying to decide if you had the stones to show up today or Wednesday." He nudged Joey as he finished up, but Joey wasn't responding. It was clear that he was still disturbed by what had taken place yesterday and hadn't quite forgiven or worked things out completely with Ricky.

Being the true leader of the group, Gary didn't want things to go down a negative path right off the bat, so he stepped up. "David, we've been talking, and we decided that we've got your back on Wednesday. I . . . I mean, we . . . we know that you've got something a little special. If we can help you and beat those guys from Fox Creek, we're all in."

Ricky rolled his eyes and sneered at David. It took about everything inside David not to fight through the group and punch him. Instead, he looked at everyone else and quietly said, "Thanks, guys. I'll try not to let everyone down."

Just then, Dusty walked up and dropped his bag. Speaking to the group but mainly David, he asked, "Everything okay? Everyone all right?"

Gary slapped David on the shoulder to turn him around as he told Dusty that everyone had agreed to go all in on Wednesday and that they were going to kick Fox Creek's ass. Dusty smiled but looked with concern as Gary guided David away from the group. Once they were a few feet away from everyone, Gary spun David around to face him. "I just wanted you to know that I'm happy for you. I'm okay with trying to play at the junior college. You're a couple of years younger than me, and the way you were throwing the other day . . ." He stopped to shake his head. "Nobody was touching you."

He glanced over his shoulder to make sure nobody was looking before he continued on again. "And just so you know, I met up with Becky on Saturday night, but things didn't go anywhere. She didn't even want to get ice cream." David looked at Gary, trying to hold back any sort of smile from his face. "Just thought you'd like to know," Gary said as he gently slapped his glove onto David's chest before jogging out to the field to stretch.

That was the first good news of any kind that David had seen or heard in the last twenty-four hours. For the first time since talking to his dad yesterday afternoon, David felt a little bit better. He started to do his own stretching when Dusty approached.

"Hey, man, where were you this morning? Everything okay?" David stood there thinking about what Gary had said and how good it felt hearing all those things from him, but then there was Dusty, who was now literally slapping him on the cheek to get his attention. "How did it go yesterday? A million things ran through my mind when you didn't show up this morning or answer when I called to see if you were still at home."

David didn't know what to say, so he didn't say anything. He bit down on his lower lip and looked off in the distance while tightly shaking his head.

"Really?" Dusty begged. "He really didn't want to talk to you about things?"

David carefully gathered himself. "Oh, he had plenty to say." He started to say more but could feel the lump in his throat returning, so he stopped.

Dusty took a step back as if to do a full-body analysis of David to see if he was being truthful. Being best friends for over a decade, he quickly knew that David wasn't lying. "What an asshole!"

"Yeah," David breathed out, trying not to cry.

"What about your mom? Was she there? Did you try talking to her?" Dusty now had both hands on David's shoulders.

David broke Dusty's grip as he said loud enough for others to hear, "She had to work. She said she would handle it. You know what that means—hours in the woods until they stop fighting or have to go to work." Dusty tried to grab him, but he wiggled free and walked out to the row of elms to try to compose himself.

"Girlfriend on the rag?" Ricky giggled in the direction of Dusty.

Dusty turned with fire in his eyes toward Ricky. "You better lay off him today. I swear to god, you say one word to him, and that guy in the parking lot yesterday will be the last of your problems." Ricky tried to smile things off, but when he looked at Joey for a sense of protection, he could see that he was with Dusty on this one.

As things were getting a little tense, Gary once again became the leader. "Everyone gets a good round of batting practice today. After that, we're taking ground balls and working on cuts. We've got a ball game to win on Wednesday, boys!" The boys all let out some whoops as they began to organize who would hit in what order. Dusty joined in while trying to keep an eye on his friend in right field by himself under the elm trees.

Eventually, things settled down a bit, and the boys got down to work. They were having fun, but they were focused. Even Ricky was serious and keeping to himself. For the most part, they had nine of the best high school baseball players in Riverview on that field. Even though Ricky and Joey decided not to play this past season, they were good enough to make the team and help. Unfortunately, they had other priorities. The younger guys were hungry and talented. Gary had just graduated, and he was all conference the last two years. David was all conference this past season, and everyone on the team was disappointed that he had pitched the first game of the playoffs, which they won, instead of saving him for Fox Creek the next game.

The boys had finished up with everything they had planned, but since it was a cloudy day and not too hot, they decided they all wanted another round of batting practice. Nobody complained despite the fact that they only had three baseballs, so it took a while to retrieve each ball and get it back in so everyone could get sufficient swings. As the boys were cycling through the order again, Becky came out to sit on her deck.

Despite the fact that it was a cloudy day, it was still warm. All the clouds did was prevent it from being a scorcher, yet Becky was out in sunglasses and a sweatshirt. She wasn't her usual chipper self, and a couple of the boys were nudging each other and talking about her quietly. David was standing in left field, retrieving balls. He would get upset every time someone made an error or mistake, and he knew they were going to get killed tomorrow. With each error or someone goofing around, he became more and more agitated. He could hear his dad's voice and could picture him laughing at them.

He tried to block it all out as much as possible by standing in left field. He liked left field because most guys pulled the ball during batting practice, and he enjoyed shagging fly balls. It was a way to eliminate some of the horrible plays he was seeing others make; plus, he was in the perfect spot to keep his eyes on Becky and the batter at all times. It was the only thing that kept him from completely losing his mind after someone booted an easy play.

He was already getting extremely frustrated with what he felt was certain defeat and embarrassment, so he couldn't figure out how she could tolerate being in a sweatshirt in the warm weather. He was glad she was out there, though, as he was trying to figure out what to say or how to say it when Dallas pulled a ball well foul and into the weeds and trees at the back edge of her property. David had a line on it and made off into the area where he last saw the ball.

He knew that once a person hit one into the thicket at the back edge of Becky's property, two things were likely to happen. That person would do anything in their power not to pull another ball into there, and if you spent long enough looking, you could probably find another ball that had been lost in there days prior. As David made his way back into the area that divided Becky's property from the house behind hers, he turned his back to the field, knowing that Dallas wouldn't pull another one in there. It didn't take him long to find the ball that Dallas had hit, so he figured he'd spend another few minutes looking for any lost balls from the past few weeks.

Right as he was about to give up his search and return the ball he had retrieved into the field of play, he heard a voice right behind him. "Need any help?" It was Becky. He hadn't heard her come up behind him because he had his head down and was making a good deal of noise stepping on twigs and branches on his own. Her voice sounded sweet, like she wasn't mad at him for the other day, but he still wasn't quite sure what to say.

He turned to face her. As he did, she lowered her sunglasses to look into his eyes. He struggled to get his breath, but he forced the words out. "Well, I got the ball I came in here looking for, but I was checking to see if I could find any more we might have hit in here."

"Ah, I wondered what was taking you so long. I was starting to get worried about you," she said with her scintillating smile.

"Yeah," David uneasily breathed out, not sure whether to laugh or play it cool. There was an awkward pause between them, and he noticed he was staring at her without saying anything. "Becky, I wanted to apologize for the other day. I was just mad at Ricky and was trying to get him to stop running his mouth, and I got carried away. I didn't want to hurt you. It's been eating me up inside the last couple of days. I wanted you to know that."

She looked down as if she was happy and relieved. "Thanks, David. That means a lot coming from you," she started off, seeming unsure of what she was going to say next.

She nervously crossed her right hand on top of her left as she continued, "You looked pretty good out there the other day."

"Really?" He shrugged. "Gary hit a rocket off me."

"Did he really?" she questioned. "That might be what some people saw."

David wondered if she knew that he gave in to Gary to try to make her happy. Did Gary tell her? Did she just figure it out on her own? He was trying to figure out all these things in his head as he tried to continue their conversation. "Did you hear that the Fox Creek guys are coming here on Wednesday for a game?" he said while trying not to brag a bit.

She smiled and gave him a playful touch. "Yeah, it's a bit exciting and unusual, huh?"

He smiled back. "Yeah, kind of like wearing a sweatshirt on a warm summer day." He tried to touch her back, but she quickly pulled back. Her face crinkled up a bit, and she folded her arms as if she'd had a chill come over her. David could tell that he had upset her, but he didn't know exactly what he said or did. He tried to apologize and ask if she was okay, but she started to retreat toward her house. "Becky. Becky," he pleaded again, trying to figure out why she was so perturbed. "Are you okay? I wasn't making fun of you." But she was now on the move back to her house. He called her name again, this time loud enough that the boys on the field took notice.

Ricky was throwing batting practice and had been on good behavior all day, but now he stopped and couldn't resist making a comment. "Looks like David is the first person to ever make Becky cry while she was alone with him." All the boys on the field started laughing, and even though David couldn't see her face, he knew that, by this point, she was crying. She flipped Ricky off as she stormed up onto her deck and back into her house. He had no idea what he had done, but he had just upset the girl he liked and spent hours trying to think of how he could apologize to, and his friends had just added insult to injury. Ricky refused to let up on David as he stood in her backyard, staring at the house.

David got so upset that he marched toward the field and threw the ball he had so hard at Ricky that it nearly took his glove off, but he was having too much fun to mind or care. The boys were getting on David, following his lead. After the day he had yesterday, David had had enough and decided to start walking. He didn't want to go home, but he knew he needed to be away from those guys, and his dad would still be sleeping. If they had his back on Wednesday, they sure weren't acting like it today.

10 CHAPTER

David didn't walk directly home or at a fast pace, but he wasn't concerned about what time he did or didn't get home either. He at least knew where he stood with his dad, and his mom was off work on Mondays, and she had been going out to dinner with David's grandpa lately in an attempt to restore their relationship. Walking home, he didn't care much about the guys and their harassing him; he was focused on Becky. She had been so warm and accepting of his apology, so he couldn't figure out what was so upsetting to her.

He wasn't sure what time it was when he got home, so he wasn't sure what to expect when he arrived. He figured it was still early enough that his dad was likely sleeping. His mom's car was still parked in the garage, so he decided he was going to grab a snack and try to head to his room as quickly and quietly as possible. As he walked up the steps, he saw that his mom was out in the garden just beyond the basketball court. He felt relieved that he'd be able to sneak in without anyone noticing.

David came in through the front door and headed directly for the kitchen. He quickly put together a sandwich for himself, grabbed an apple, nabbed a drink from the fridge, and headed to his room. When he entered the doorway to his room, he looked at his bed, and his shoulders dropped, causing the apple to roll off the plate and onto the floor. Laying on his bed was a camouflage-covered canteen. He set his plate and drink down on his desk as he walked over to examine his parents' latest attempt at trying to appease him. He thought, *A freaking canteen.* He had never once been in a situation where he had needed or felt like he wanted a canteen. His dad liked to go camping, but he had never once invited or taken David along with him. This was no doubt an attempt by his dad to apologize for what he had said yesterday. His mom probably guilted him into it. At least she gave good presents to try to win back his favor.

He sat on his bed staring at the canteen, and just as he was about to chuck it into his closet, he looked up to see his mom in his doorway. She had a perfect brown tan and was wearing tiny jean shorts and a white tank top. In the moment, David noticed that his mom didn't look entirely different in age or generation than Becky. She leaned against his doorway, tilted her head, and smiled at David the same way she would smile at one of her customers. "Wasn't that sweet of your dad?" she said as she motioned to the canteen in his hands.

David wasn't going to play along anymore. He told his dad what was on his mind yesterday, so he figured he might as well do the same with his mom today. "Not really," he began in a low tone partially because he wasn't sure what he was going to say and partially because he didn't want to erupt and wake up his dad. He held it away from him a bit to give it one final look over. "When the hell have I ever needed or asked for a canteen?" With that, he took it and flung it into his closet.

"Sweetheart," his mom moaned as she stepped toward his closet to try to retrieve the canteen.

David stopped her when he spoke up with a grin on his face. "Go ahead and take it. There's a bunch of stuff in that closet that I'll never need or use. It's a nice walk down memory lane of all the fights that go on in this house." After that statement, David sat back on his bed as if he'd achieved his goal. He had finally gotten a burden off his chest, and he really didn't care what kind of reaction he was going to get from his mom.

David's mom stood there for a moment, looking into David's closet. She had the look of a woman who had just been caught in a web of lies and wasn't sure where to begin. She rubbed her face and made her way over to David's bed. Without asking, she forced him to scoot over and allow her to sit next to him. She had her bottom lip completely tucked under her top lip and was fighting back tears as she now ran her fingers through David's hair.

"Sweetheart, I know we've messed up. I'm so sorry," she began nervously. "I have been thinking about myself and our family for a while now, and I know I've messed up. But I'm not sure how much you really understand. We were just kids when you were born. We didn't know what we were doing."

She paused for a moment and then continued, "We still don't know what we're doing. You don't need to know our entire history, but I know we have been horrible parents for a variety of reasons. We haven't been there for you. You're so quiet, just like your dad, that we just left you alone instead of trying to deal with any problems. We figured if you didn't say anything, then you were happy."

She was full on crying now at this point and went from running her hand through her hair to hugging him. "This isn't the mom I wanted to be when I was your age, but then I became a mom when I was a little bit older than you, and I couldn't be that person I had pictured in my mind. Your grandparents were so disappointed and ashamed of me that when I refused to leave your dad, they left town. I resented you because I thought that you were the one that drove my parents away."

She pulled back to look him in the eyes through her tears. She grabbed his arms, squeezing his biceps and stopping to notice the emerging muscles on her son's arms. "Now I know I couldn't be more wrong. I am the one that drove my parents away. It's why I meet with your grandpa every Monday for dinner. He won't even meet me anywhere near here because he doesn't want your dad showing up." She looked at the clock on the stand next to David's bed to make sure she wasn't going to be late for their date. "When my mom died, we realized how important time was, and no matter our differences, we had to try to get things right between us."

David now tensed up a bit and gave his mother a stern look. "And where and when did I fit into all this? You can make things right with Grandpa but not me?" Again, he felt the knot building in his throat that felt like it had permanently been there for the last few days.

His mom now burst into tears, shaking as she embraced him. "I'm so sorry, David. I'm so sorry. I know I can be that mother that was in my mind when I was young. I just don't know how to find her or where to begin."

David gently pushed her back to look her in the eye. Sounding more like the adult than her and remarkably cool, he told her, "This is a good start, Mom."

She temporarily stopped her sobbing and panting to look at her boy, who was turning into a man right before her. She realized that she had missed so much in his life that she would never be able to get back. She embraced him again and resumed sobbing. David sat there uncomfortably on his bed, trying to calm her. As a kid, it is never easy seeing one of your parents become an emotional wreck. It was even more trying when it felt like it was a stranger.

After a few minutes, she regained control of the sixteen years of guilt that came spilling out of her and peeled herself off her only child. She reached toward his nightstand to grab some tissues and tried to simultaneously wipe off her face and David's shirt of her mess. She continued to confess to David about how embarrassed she was about her life and the way she and her father were acting. She sobbed as she recanted how amazing her mother was when she was growing up and how pitiful of a mother she had been to David.

While she was talking, she looked at the clock and told David that she had to get ready but that she was happy he had called her out. "Maybe we should start trying to make a habit of this," she said, trying her best to smile without starting to cry again.

"Maybe without all the tears next time," she added with a subtle smile.

David laughed quietly and agreed, "Yeah . . . this was . . . nice." He didn't feel good about causing his mom to break down, and he couldn't just forgive her for the past fifteen-plus years, but this was a start.

Her next action was an even bigger bridge. She got up from David's bed and walked over to his closet to retrieve the canteen. "I don't think this belongs in here," she said sarcastically, picking up the canteen.

She then turned and plopped it into the trash can next to his desk and said, "There. I think that's a much better place for that, don't you?" She was smiling as if she'd achieved her first family victory in years. David couldn't help but feel guilty because the item was probably not cheap and had been tossed into the trash, but he knew it was better to smile in approval of his mom. Besides, he wouldn't use it anyways, he reminded himself. Her bright smile as she shoved out of his doorway and into the bathroom told him he had made the right decision.

Once he heard the water from the shower running and was sure she was inside, he grabbed his dark hair and pulled it back off his forehead, falling back on his bed. He thought about Dusty. He wondered if things at home with Bonnie were nearly as intense as what he had gone through the last two days with his parents. He felt completely drained, and his appetite had completely evaporated. He knew things would be better with his mom, but he knew it would likely get worse between her and his dad before it got any better for any of them. He laid there listening to some music on the radio as he pondered what the next few days at home might be like for him.

Lying there, he heard his mom finish up in the shower and make her way back to her bedroom quietly. Neither one wanted to wake up David's dad, so she quickly got dressed and tiptoed back to the bathroom to finish getting ready. It wasn't long before she reemerged in David's doorway, looking radiant and beautiful. It looked like the weight of the world had been lifted off her shoulders as she looked at her son and was about to set off to go see her father.

She was putting her earrings in as she smiled at her son like a normal, loving mother would. She was excited to tell him, "I almost forgot, but just before you got home, a girl named Becky called looking for you. She asked if you could call her back sometime tonight." She was beaming because it wasn't often that girls called their house looking for David. When they did, it seemed to bring back a bit of nostalgia and excitement for her.

"Is that the Becky that lives next to the elementary school?" she said, not really needing an answer. "She's gorgeous." She walked across the room as if she'd suddenly found a gossip partner and son in her home and tapped him on the shoulder.

"Don't screw that one up!" she exclaimed. "Let me know if you need any advice with her." She seemed like a new woman, and her happiness somewhat repulsed David while making him feel happy to a lesser degree for his mother. She had confessed her sins, but David really hadn't said much.

While his mom was practically skipping her way out the door, David lay on his bed laughing to himself, thinking that his mom would die if she actually knew that he actually did need her advice, anyone's advice. He couldn't and wouldn't let on in front of her, but David was excited and confused about why Becky would have called after walking away from him earlier today on the verge of tears. The longer he laid there, the more confused he became. What would he even say to her? In all the years they had known each other, why was she calling now?

As he heard his father's alarm go off, he began to think about what his dad had said. Maybe he was right. Maybe she was suddenly interested because he could be going places and she wanted to use him as her ticket out of town. The longer he laid there with his thoughts, the more upset he became. He was a prisoner to his thoughts and to his room. He didn't want to call Becky, and he didn't want to leave his room and deal with his father. Instead, he decided to listen to some music loud enough to drown out any noises his dad might make before the baseball game came on the radio. Once the game started, he could let the announcers take him to another world.

He fell asleep early, listening to the game. His mom hadn't returned yet, and he was wondering what she and her grandpa could have been talking about for so long. David figured that his mom had told his grandpa about what had happened, which was why she was gone so long. He guessed it was a good thing, and he didn't feel like talking to his mom again if and when she got home anyways.

He wondered if Becky was sitting around, waiting for his call. He couldn't bring himself to call her. He figured that he would just try to keep things the way he had with them, staring from a distance and jealous of others. With all these things running through his head, it was a surprise that he fell asleep so early, but he had worn himself out thinking about everything.

The next day at work, David practically jumped every time he heard the bell above the front door ring. He kept expecting Ricky or one of the guys to show up. Even worse, he was worried that someone from Fox Creek would show up to tell him that the gig was up and that they were just messing with him. At one point, he thought his dad might have somehow noticed the canteen in his trash can and would come in to give him another piece of his mind. Time couldn't move fast enough as he stocked the shelves.

A little before noon, he was in the back room, getting ready to haul out a dozen or more cases of soda when he saw Becky walk in. He was standing in the back room and could see her perfectly through the two-way mirror. She was nervously walking up and down the aisles, holding her own hands. She was wearing short tight pink denim shorts and a gray T-shirt with three-quarter pink sleeves. She looked lost and unsure of herself. David knew she wasn't in there to buy anything but to look for him. He felt so bad that he hadn't called. Obviously, she wanted to talk to him about something, but he couldn't face her. What would he say when she asked why he didn't call?

Eventually, she made her way to the front and bought a pack of gum. Before she left, she walked to the front of the aisle that led back to the stockroom. She stopped and stared at the stockroom doors that had mirrors where the windows would be. She dropped her head as if to tell David that she knew he was hiding behind those doors and that she was disappointed he wouldn't come out. She looked so lonely and defeated. Seeing her like that, David figured he had nothing to lose, so he summoned up the courage to finally go and talk to her.

"Collins, you gonna stock that soda today or wait until next week?" It was his manager. She had been sitting in her office, apparently taking notice of how long David had been standing there with the cart idling by his side as he stared out the stockroom windows. He turned his head around to face her as he snapped back into reality.

"Huh? Uh yeah, sorry. I was just thinking about if I could get more soda onto the cart," David replied as he shriveled his face at this own stupid response. As he turned back around, he rolled his eyes at how idiotic his response was and how annoying his manager was sometimes. He was going to come through those doors and talk to Becky, and the cases of soda might not get stocked until next week. She would just have to deal with it, but as he pushed through the doors, he didn't see her anymore. Frantically, he pushed his cart full of cases of soda to the front of the store, almost picking off a lady who was headed back to the pharmacy with two young kids. Once to the beverage area, he abandoned his cart and began looking down each aisle, but she was gone. Knowing that he had missed his chance, he slowly opened the front door, only to see her already at a good distance walking back toward her house—another time where he had let his own fear cost him an opportunity.

He spent the rest of his shift in anger, taking little regard or care for the things he was dropping on shelves. He enjoyed slashing and breaking down the boxes as it gave him an outlet for his frustration. The rest of his shift, every time the door opened and the bell clanged, David was filled with hope. He would strain to look in the surveillance mirrors in the hopes it was Becky returning, but it never was. Finally, at the very end of his shift, the door opened, and it was definitely who he was hoping it would be.

"You almost out of here?" Dusty said as he was surveying the snacks and junk food.

"Yeah, I'm pretty much done. Let me go tell my boss I'm leaving, and I'll meet you out front," David replied.

David had a mountain of things to unload on Dusty, and he had no idea where to begin. He figured Dusty would guide the conversation, and he did as the boys met up in the parking lot and began walking back toward Dusty's trailer. "So you ready for the game tomorrow?" Dusty said as he nudged David.

"Game?" David asked inquisitively. He had so much running through his mind he had forgotten about the showdown with Fox Creek tomorrow.

"Oh yeah, I guess," he said half-heartedly.

Since he really hadn't had his friend to himself much the last couple of days, Dusty was going to do the talking for a bit, and David was just fine sitting back and listening. "The boys are really pumped, and you should be too. In fact, just about everyone showed up to get extra practice in today. Don't worry about what happened yesterday either. After you walked off, Gary let Ricky have it pretty good. He promised that he wouldn't get on you at all tomorrow. I think Gary is looking forward to this more than anyone. You know, there's always been a part of him that wished he could have played for Fox Creek. Heck, if he had, he probably could have gone to a bigger school. Of course, he would have probably had to work a lot harder than he's used to, but people just don't pay attention to us here. A number of guys from this town could put on a Fox Creek jersey, and suddenly, they're getting looks from colleges and whatnot. Don't you agree?"

David had only been partially listening to Dusty, so he nodded. He kept thinking about what his dad said about Riverview and his friends. "I guess" was all he could mumble, suddenly getting annoyed with Dusty's optimism. Plus, he knew where this conversation was eventually going to swing.

"So what the heck happened with Becky yesterday?" Dusty inquired with the complete sincerity of a loyal friend. "What did you say to her to make her come out of that brush in tears?"

David had been wondering the same thing for nearly twenty-four hours. He stopped walking, looked at his friend, and raised his arms. "I have no clue!"

"You have no clue as in you can't remember, or you don't know what you said that would have made her cry?" Dusty responded, playing couples counselor.

David paused and thought for a moment. He had replayed their conversation over in his head a million times, so he knew exactly what the exchange was. "I mean, she said that it was exciting and unusual that the Fox Creek boys were coming here to play a game tomorrow. So I responded by saying, 'Yeah, kind of like wearing a sweatshirt on a warm day.' Next thing I know, she gets superupset and goes inside and doesn't want to talk anymore." David hesitated because he wanted to make sure he wasn't leaving anything out before he continued. Dusty shook his head while looking at David, but he continued anyway. "And then I get home to find out she called looking for me. It doesn't make any sense. Then she was in here today looking for me."

"Did you talk to her?" Dusty said excitedly as he began walking again.

"I couldn't," David dejectedly admitted. "I didn't know what to say. I mean, what could I say? The last time I talked to her, I made her cry over nothing."

"Well, she's got a lot going on," Dusty said, imploring his friend to ask a follow-up question. "A simple 'I'm sorry' probably would have gone a long way."

"She's got a lot going on? What am I supposed to be sorry for?" David fired back, letting everything that had been going on the last few days come spilling out. "Did her dad tell her that she's a loser and that her friends are losers? Did her mom confess that she's been a horrible person and mother? Did her friends all make fun of her before her big game? I doubt it. I make one flipping comment about what she's wearing, and she loses it on me."

"Hey, she's got a lot going on in her life," Dusty said, trying to get his friend to follow up, but David was focused on his own problems.

"We've all got a lot going on in our lives. Seriously, man, I can't take it," David said, determined not to have that knot in his throat return. "Can we just go back to your place and I'll fill you in on everything?"

"Of course," Dusty said, trying to get his friend to calm down.

"And can we please just not talk about Becky?" David implored.

"But—"

"Please, Dusty. I don't want to talk about her. Okay?" David said, almost pleading.

"Sure, David, but there's some stuff you've gotta know." Dusty said that as his last effort to get his friend to take the bait, but David wasn't biting.

"There's a lot you've got to know too," David said as he was waiting to unload about what had happened with his mom and his dad.

When the boys got to Dusty's trailer, nobody was home. They grabbed a couple of sodas from the fridge and decided to go hang out in the garage. David filled Dusty in about all the things his dad had said. He told Dusty about how his dad had ragged on him and his friends. Dusty said he admired David for not punching him. David shared how he called out his mom after he had received the canteen for what happened between him and his dad. Dusty laughed and said that he would take it if he didn't want it. David shared that his mom threw it in the trash and how his mom seemed so happy, but he couldn't quite forgive her.

Dusty reminded David about the things he has said about Bonnie. He told David how he and his dad had a long talk about his mother and his feelings toward Bonnie. He learned some things about his mother that he didn't know. Dusty said the conversation really helped him understand his dad a lot better and opened his mind to Bonnie. He said the last couple of days had been pretty good around his house. He felt bad for David about his father, but he tried to persuade David to focus on his mom and the chance for a new start with her.

Eventually, the conversation turned toward baseball as Dusty's parents came back home. Bonnie hopped into the kitchen to start making dinner. She was excited that David would be joining them. Mr. Scott went back to working on restoring the classic Studebaker he had in his garage. David and Dusty went and lay down in his room to continue their conversation. As usual, Dusty was the one to start asking the tough questions. "So you nervous about tomorrow?" Dusty began, trying to get the conversation going.

"Psh . . . yeah," David definitively replied. "You saw us out there yesterday. We're going to get killed."

"Why would you say that?" Dusty asked, now sitting up in his bed. "You know, we're not as bad as you think we are." David just shrugged and continued to look up at the ceiling. "You know, your dad doesn't know shit about us. You can't let what he said affect you."

"Right," David said out of obligation without flinching.

"Seriously, man, we can beat those guys. If you throw like you did the other day, they won't have a chance. Everybody is behind you. Don't let us down," Dusty implored.

"Yeah, well, that's what I'm afraid of," David confessed while still staring at the ceiling.

"What are you afraid of, David? Do you know how relieved Fox Creek was when you pitched the opening round game in sectionals? It's all they could talk about. They knew they didn't have a chance against you then. I know Carterville wasn't as good as Fox Creek, but you only gave up five hits and one run in the opening round of sectionals. My dad and I went back for the sectional championship game, and we overheard the Fox Creek parents talking about how glad they were that you threw the opening game and not against them." David perked up a bit and sat up. "Yeah, I'm serious, David."

David took a deep breath and pondered what Dusty had just said before speaking. "It's just that I feel like nobody has anything to lose except for me. I mean, if we get beat, it'll be my fault. If we lose, it's what we were expected to do anyways, but the Fox Creek guys will see that I'm not good enough to pitch with them. What do guys like Ricky and Joey have to lose? We're already at the bottom, and this will just be another reminder, and it will be my fault."

Dusty now got off the bed to look at his friend and walk out a bit of his growing anger. "You see, that's the type of crap I get sick of with you sometimes, David. Is it possible for you to think about anyone but yourself for a few minutes?"

Dusty paused to let that sink in. David looked at Dusty, which signaled that the message was delivered. "Yeah, you know there are other people that are going to play tomorrow besides you. Did you ever think of that? Beating Fox Creek in baseball might be the highlight of their athletic careers. Did you stop to think about Gary? Did you think about how he stepped up for you the last couple of days despite losing every game he's ever played against them in his career and never being asked to play for them? Do you think he would agree to play them and lose again if he didn't think we had a chance? What if me or the younger guys go out and play well tomorrow? We could send a message that they'll have to deal with us for the next couple of years. You ever think of that?"

Again, he paused to let things sink in with David. "Tomorrow isn't just about you. It's okay to be scared. I'm nervous too. I don't want to embarrass myself. Nobody does, but it's about all of us in Riverview, not just you."

Both boys sat motionless after Dusty's speech. David, as usual, was sitting there processing everything that Dusty had said and realizing that he was right. Dusty took his nonreaction differently and called him out even further. "Heck, if you had an ounce of ability to think about anyone but yourself, you'd understand what's going on with Becky too."

Just as David was about to question what Dusty meant by that, Bonnie knocked on the bedroom door and invited the boys to come out for dinner. She looked at them and sensed that something was off. "Everything okay with you, guys?" she asked, trying to offer up an olive branch between the two.

Dusty gave a hard glance to David that Bonnie couldn't see before facing her with a smile. "Yeah, we're fine. We were just talking about our little scrimmage tomorrow."

She perked up right away and looked at David. "Oh yeah, Dusty's told me all about it. Big day tomorrow for you, huh, David?"

Now it was David's turn to give Bonnie an eye roll. All the times he'd seen Dusty do it, he knew it wouldn't crush her spirit or enthusiasm. "Yeah, I guess it is, Bonnie," he said with dry sarcasm and a glare back at Dusty.

As the boys sat down at the table, Mr. Scott was already there, waiting for them to join. Apparently, word about this game had spread pretty quickly because he too was talking about it. "Big opportunity tomorrow, David," he said, half-declaring and half-asking.

David just wanted a break from having serious conversations with people. He tried to keep his head down and eat, but obviously, Dusty had spent some time going over everything with his parents, and they had their own questions. They knew all about David's situation at home well, which was why he spent so much time at their own place.

"So, David, if you decide you want to play with the Fox Creek guys this summer, do you have a way of getting to practices and games?" Mr. Scott asked with care and concern. David hadn't spent a lot of time even thinking about logistics. He appreciated Mr. Scott's concern. He had coached him all throughout Little League, and he knew that when it came to baseball, he had his best interests at heart.

"Well, I guess I thought my grandpa would be able to take me," David answered as he was thinking on the spot. It seemed to make sense. His grandpa loved baseball and didn't have much to do. He'd been the one who got him to practices and home from games the past couple of years anyways.

"Well, that's good," Mr. Scott answered. He paused for a second and looked at Dusty, who was still a bit bothered with David. "If you ever need a ride or help with money to pay for any of this, let us know. Dusty and I don't want you to miss out on this opportunity." He nodded at Dusty, who looked at David and cracked a slight smile as he chuckled to himself.

Opportunity? David thought. *What opportunity?* He hadn't even pitched the game yet, and people were acting like this was a done deal, an opportunity that he couldn't refuse. How were they so sure they'd want him after tomorrow? He bit into a piece of his hamburger to allow him time to think as he chewed and digested his food.

He then said with complete sincerity and gratitude, "Thanks, Mr. Scott. That really means a lot. I'm pretty lucky to have you and Dusty in my life." He looked over at Dusty to see if he would accept his public apology. Dusty's smile confirmed that they were good. It was the beauty of being young; fights and disagreements among boys usually don't last long and bring friends closer.

In a strange way, Dusty's dad now seemed more engaged with the boys. Dusty's sister wasn't much into sports growing up, and Dusty was a hard worker but didn't have much of a future in athletics. That night, Mr. Scott hung out with the boys, watching the baseball game on TV after dinner and telling old stories. He talked about the importance of getting a good night's sleep and reminded the boys how to set up hitters. He was a catcher back in his day too. He talked about how Fox Creek had always been good for as long as he could remember in all sports and how Riverview didn't have much success against them in the past, even when Fox Creek wasn't nearly as big and developed as it was now. He mentioned that the best teams Riverview had were gritty teams that were close together. The guys hung out together and had that fighter's mentality. This made Dusty smile, but it only made David more anxious. He learned throughout the night that this simple game meant a great deal to a number of people. It was going to be anything but another day at the field. David spent the night at Dusty's, but he barely got any sleep as his heart pounded and his mind raced all night.

11 CHAPTER

The next morning, neither boy had trouble waking up. They had set an alarm extra early so they would have plenty of time to get the field prepared for the big day. Bonnie was waiting for them in the kitchen when they strolled out of Dusty's room to see what they would like for breakfast. They quickly scarfed down their food and began making arrangements. David would have to borrow Dusty's bike to go home and change; today was one day where he didn't care about what looked cool and what didn't. He also had to get a pair of baseball pants. All the boys had agreed that they didn't care what the Fox Creek kids were going to wear; they were wearing pants and cleats today.

They agreed to meet back at Dusty's trailer in an hour, so David would have to move relatively quickly. David wasn't thinking about much on the bike ride back to his house. He was enjoying the silence and the relative coolness of the early morning sunlight. When he got home, he was surprised to see that his dad's car was already in the garage. He must have either come straight home from work or skipped the beers after breakfast. He tried to block him out as he made his way through the basement and up the stairs into the kitchen. *Maybe he is already sleeping,* David thought.

As he opened the kitchen door, he was surprised to see both his mom and dad sitting at the kitchen table. Everyone froze for a second when David emerged from the stairs. His mom asked if he wanted anything to eat, but David just put his head down and said he had to rush back out. He went to his room and changed as quickly as he could. He could hear them having a serious conversation, no doubt some of it centered on him, but he didn't have time to think about that now. He put on a pair of gray baseball pants, his lucky white Nike shirt, and his school baseball cap and grabbed his glove and cleats, and he was ready to head back out the door.

From the kitchen table, one could see the short hallway that led out to the front door. David tried to be invisible as he passed through that doorway, but his mom saw him and called out to him, "Sweetheart, what's with the uniform today?" She was smiling while holding her coffee cup with both hands.

"Uh, nothing. We're just playing a game against some kids from out of town," David said, hoping that would appease her.

"Fox Creek?" David's dad said as he started to chuckle.

He continued to laugh even more as he sarcastically said, "Good luck. I'm sure you guys will need plenty of it."

David wanted to storm across the kitchen and punch him right then and there, right in front of his mom, but instead, he just turned and walked out the door. When he got out onto the front porch at the top of the stairs, he looked into the window and saw his mom slap his dad across the arm as he continued to laugh.

Riding his bike back to Dusty's house, David's head was again filled with doubt and anger. Dusty sensed it as David rode up and put his bike away in the garage. "Hey, man, everything all right?" Dusty asked, looking David up and down.

David hesitated for a moment, trying to decide if he wanted to share with Dusty, but figured he'd get it out of him anyway, "My dad—"

"Screw him," Dusty inserted before David could continue. "He's the last person you should be thinking about right now. We're going to show him what an idiot he is anyways." Dusty clapped his hands together to punctuate his point. It did put David a little at ease that Dusty was so excited and optimistic, but he couldn't put everything to rest with his dad. Fortunately for him, the boys had a lot to get done.

They walked as quickly as they could while pushing a mower and carrying a rake to the field in relative silence. Everyone wanted the field to look really good today, so they agreed that anyone with a mower and within walking distance should bring it to the field. They were going to cut and groom things as best as they could. In addition to stealing the required newspapers, the boys brought tape measures and tent spikes to make sure that their bases were the correct distance and wouldn't be going anywhere.

When all the boys arrived, they had three mowers and decided that the younger guys were responsible for cutting everything. Gary and Joey had some mixture of dirt and clay that they were busy stamping down on the mound. Ricky had gone down to the Little League fields in town and stolen a pitching rubber last night, so he was hammering that into place. David and Dusty were busy taking care of the area around home plate as best as they could by pulling weeds and raking things as evenly as possible. Brooks was busy spray-painting the foul lines orange as straight as he could with paint he had stolen from his dad's work truck. Whatever problems the boys might have had with one another in recent days, nobody would have been able to tell as they looked like a real grounds crew getting the field ready.

David kept looking over to see if Becky had made her way out. There was no doubt that she would be there, trying to look her best for everyone. The field prep had calmed David's nerves, but as the boys started to finish up, he could feel the butterflies start to bounce in his stomach and throat. The boys had a nervous energy about them as they quietly stretched to work out some of their nerves. Nobody was saying much, even Ricky.

They were standing on the first base side of the backstop when Joey was the first to notice the Fox Creek boys starting to arrive in their cars on the street beyond left field. "Well, here we go, boys!" he bellowed in his deep voice.

Gary stepped forward and motioned out to them with a thumbs-up to say that they should leave their cars along the road there. "If anybody hits a ball out there today, it's going to be me." He smiled as he turned to face the group. "All right, boys, bring it in. Everyone, try to relax and have some fun today. No matter what happens, we don't turn on one another today. David's going to keep us in this game . . . and we're going to find a way to win it for him today."

He gave David a nod, the kind of nod as if to say, *I've got you, and I know you've got us.* David nodded back, but his heart was pounding.

The Fox Creek boys all got out of their cars together and were dressed in their practice uniforms. They moved together in harmony as they made their way in from left field. David was glad that they all decided to wear baseball pants today. Even though the Riverview boys were all dressed in different shirts and hats, they looked like they were there to play a baseball game. It was clear that the Fox Creek boys meant business.

By default, they assumed the area on the third base side, closest to Becky's house. As if she'd been waiting for them to arrive, she came out barefoot with light blue bikini bottoms on and a long-sleeved light pastel-colored top that was appropriate for a fall or spring day. David couldn't figure out why she was wearing that top, especially after she had gotten upset with him the other day when he commented that it was unusual for her to be wearing a sweatshirt on a summer afternoon.

The Fox Creek boys were busy lining up their equipment, and Becky was busy making sure to greet them. She and Ryan had a short exchange that sent a hot rush up David's spine, and he wasn't the only one whom she was chatting up. It was apparent that she was more interested in them than she was in the boys who played there routinely. Dusty noticed his friend staring over at her and gave him a tap on the butt with the one hand that wasn't holding his catcher's gear and mask. "Don't worry about her right now," he said. "You've got other things to focus on."

The boys went down the right field line so David could start warming up. David felt good. His arm was loose, and his legs felt strong. He and Dusty had warmed up like this countless times growing up, and David knew that Dusty liked what he was seeing because he didn't say much. David kept looking over and getting upset with Becky, who was constantly flirting with the Fox Creek boys and parading back and forth from her deck back inside her house to give them a show. Both teams continued to loosen up as Gary looked out David's way and gave him a thumbs-up. David stated back with a thumbs-up that he was ready, fired one more warm-up pitch, and then started walking in.

As both pitchers made their way in, both teams started moving toward the home plate area to go over the unofficial ground rules of the field. Ryan and Gary stepped forward as the de facto captains, and Gary started going over things. He explained how they ruled on balls that went up into the elm trees or balls that rolled out into the street where their cars were parked. They agreed to play seven innings and that Riverview would be the home team. The longer Gary spoke, the more upset David's nerves grew. He couldn't tell if he needed to throw up or go to the bathroom. Either way, he needed to go to the thicket at the back of Becky's property, yet he didn't want to exit the meeting at the plate.

Just as the boys had gone over just about everything, they heard a car door close from out in left field and saw a well-built man in a baseball cap and shorts get out of a car and start walking toward home plate. "Who is that?" Joey blasted out in his deep, raspy voice while motioning out to the man who was walking across the field like he belonged there.

"That's Coach Bell," Ryan replied. "We didn't think you guys would have an umpire, so we asked if he'd come and call balls and strikes."

Coach Bell looked like he had been born to coach baseball. He had thick forearms that were covered in muscle and hair. He was thickly built and had a large belly that somehow appeared to be muscle too. He was in his midfifties but looked like he wasn't afraid to mix it up with men much younger than him. He had an intimidating voice that matched his physical stature.

"Wait a second," Ricky objected. "There's no way we're letting your coach call balls and strikes." He said it loud enough for Coach Bell to hear. He was just about to the infield when he heard Ricky's objection.

"You got a better idea, son?" he replied. His voice was so rugged that a couple of the younger guys started to back away from the meeting area at home plate.

"I thought we were going to call our own balls and strikes," he mouthed back. "Besides, we don't need a coach out here to help us."

"How about I call balls and strikes?" It was a voice coming from down the right field side that sounded just as confident as Coach Bell's. Everyone turned and saw Officer Smith getting out of his squad car that he had parked in the shade. They all had this look of surprise and confusion on their face, so he figured he needed to clarify a bit more. "We heard about this game and didn't want any trouble, so if it's okay, we'll hang out and make sure there aren't any problems." He motioned to the other squad car that was rolling up to the field. "If you can't trust a cop to be fair, who can you trust?" He was smiling and walking to the area behind the mound.

"Well, I guess we don't have any Rodney Kings out here," Coach Bell sarcastically mumbled to himself as he threw his hands up and started walking toward the third base side where his boys' gear was.

"Well, I guess it's settled," Officer Smith proudly declared.

Gary and Ryan walked out to him to review the ground rules and go over things again. This gave David the opportunity to go relieve himself. He jogged past the Fox Creek boys and Coach Bell on his way out to the thicket. He could hear them saying something and laughing as he walked by. He thought he was blowing his chance before the game even started.

When he reached the area of trees and bushes, he went a few feet in and decided that he didn't need to throw up, just relieve himself. He could feel his heart pounding as he was standing there. He was trying to control his breathing as he zipped up. After a few seconds of short breaths, he figured it was useless and turned to head back out on the field and meet his fate.

"Good luck, David," Becky said as she was standing not far behind him, with her hands nervously wiggling by her sides.

David jumped as he hadn't heard her walk up on him—again. Any hopes he had of getting his heartbeat under control were now gone. He found himself going over a million things in his head that he wanted to say to her, that he had wanted to tell her since they had last spoken, but all he got out was "Thanks, Becky."

She lifted on her toes a bit as if her spirits had been physically lifted. He took another look at her and then started his walk out to the field. The entire way, he could hear the Fox Creek boys laughing and making fun of him and Becky. "She can't help you out there, Collins!" one boy yelled.

"Looking for Mama in those woods, David?" the kid who had been looking to fight at Jay's last week chuckled. Even Coach Bell seemed to be laughing and encouraging it. Ricky, who was playing shortstop and taking warm-up ground balls from Gary at first, looked at him to see if he could respond, but Gary just shook his head and motioned downward with his hands to tell Ricky to keep his emotions under control.

When David got to the mound, Officer Smith flipped him a nice white baseball and asked him if he was ready. David nodded as he still couldn't quite control his breathing. He took a few warm-up pitches, and the game was ready to begin.

The first batter up was the kid who was with Ryan at the Dairy Barn the other day. He stepped into the left-handed batter's box. Before David began his windup, he looked over at Becky, who was settling into her sun chair and putting on her sunglasses. With his heart pounding, David threw the first pitch for a ball outside, followed by a second, a third, and then a curveball that stayed way above the zone. A four-pitch walk did nothing to settle his nerves or quiet the Fox Creek kids.

Ryan was the next kid up, and again, David couldn't find the strike zone. With each pitch going outside the zone, the chatter kept rising. After the second ball to Ryan and sixth in a row, Dusty called time and came out to the mound. On his way out there, David noticed Becky smiling and enjoying the razzing that the Fox Creek boys were giving him. He also noticed that a few more cars were now pulling up along the streets, with various people from Riverview stopping by to see what all the commotion was about on a Wednesday afternoon in June.

"Hey, settle down," Dusty said as he put his arm around David's back. "Where's the guy from the other day that was throwing smoke against Gary?"

David just looked everywhere but Dusty's eyes. He couldn't focus. His mind was drifting back to what his dad had said. He looked back at Ricky and Joey, who were conversing by third base. He imagined that they were talking about the choke job that had just begun and how foolish the Fox Creek boys were to think that David could help their team. Dusty said a few more things to David before returning to the plate, but David wasn't focused on any of them.

131

Ryan stepped back into the batter's box, and two pitches later, he was standing on someone's newspaper at first base after another four-pitch walk. The next kid up was a big strong kid whom David had seen before but didn't know. Dusty put down the sign for a curveball. He knew that David was struggling to locate his fastball and that this kid would be expecting a first pitch he could jump on and drive. David focused and got his breathing a little more under control as he delivered a great curveball that dropped on the outside corner at the last second. Expecting a fastball and seeing a pitch that looked center cut out of David's hand, the kid swung and was out in front. He hit a routine two-hopper to Ricky at shortstop that was a tailor-made double-play ball, only Ricky booted it.

This incited more hooting and hollering from the Fox Creek side. Ricky knew he made a mistake, so it didn't help when Joey started barking at him from third, and they began to go back and forth. Gary tried to calm everyone down, but the Riverview boys were just as busy chirping at one another as the Fox Creek boys were chirping at them. To make matters worse, Becky was now joining in with the laughing and taunting. "Let's go, boys. He's scared of you," she said while leaning forward and clapping in her chair.

The next kid up was the instigator from Jay's last week. He was a well-built tall kid who had already committed to play division 1 baseball before his senior year. He came to the plate with all the confidence in the world and blew a kiss out to David. The first pitch David threw, he roped into left-center field for a two-run double. Before the growing spectators even got comfortable on the hoods of their vehicles, it was 2–0 with men on second and third and nobody out. This entire game was based on David being able to shut them down. If there was any concern that they were going to go easy on him to make him look good for their coach, those thoughts were quickly gone.

All David could think about now was that his dad, who had taken the previous night off to be with his mother, would be eagerly awaiting him when he got home to ask how things went. In nearly sixteen years, his dad had hardly asked him a question, but David knew that he would be waiting for him to come home today to find out just how horribly things had gone. He couldn't wait to be right and put David back in his place. In those moments when he stood there thinking about his father, a rage built up inside him, similar to what he felt the other day. When he looked over and saw Becky clapping for the Fox Creek kids, it grew even more. He saw her talking to Ryan as he just scored and flipping her hair. It was all he could take. His breathing finally slowed as his entire body seemed to reach a slow internal boil.

"Keep it going, boys! Keep it going!" Becky cheerfully cried out, now standing on her deck.

David now turned toward home plate with his entire insides ablaze. He saw Dusty put down two fingers. It made sense since the last kid had just roped a first-pitch fastball for a double, but David wasn't going to throw a curveball here. He shook him off. Dusty again put down two fingers, this time with more emphasis, but David shook him off again and came set. Dusty knew what was coming; he just hoped it would reach his glove if it was a strike.

The first pitch was a strike, and it did reach Dusty's glove—in a hurry. After that first pitch, everyone got quiet for a second but then started back in. Again, Dusty called for a curveball, but David shook him off. Again, David blew a fastball by the Fox Creek kid, same thing with the third pitch. Dusty shook his hand a bit as he lobbed the ball back to David. Gary smiled and let out a "Let's go, boys!"

David only needed four more pitches to get out of the inning, limiting Fox Creek to those two runs. The Riverview boys came walking off the field, and the first person to greet them was David. He huddled them up and suddenly, like a commander to his squad, announced, "They're done, boys. They aren't getting any more runs off me. That's all on me."

Ricky was standing toward the back of the group with his head down. "Ricky!" David barked at him. "It's all on me. We got this. They're done scoring." With that, he gave Dusty a nudge with his fist. Everyone looked at Dusty, who was just as stunned as everyone else with David's speech. David waited for Ricky to cross past him and grabbed his arm. "Hey, fuck those guys. Plenty more ground balls coming your way, just the way I want it."

Ricky, who didn't respond to David's first speech, now looked at him with fire in his eyes that worked its way into his familiar smile. "Yeah, fuck these guys." He patted David on the back and went and grabbed a helmet.

Now it was the Riverview boys' time to chirp at the Fox Creek pitcher, who looked a little nervous himself to start off the game. His anxiety only increased as Ricky slashed a base hit to right field, and David ripped a ball right back up the middle for base hits. Joey popped out, but Gary then drove in Ricky with another base hit to left. Just like that, they had cut the lead in half, and Coach Bell asked for time to go out and talk to his pitcher.

This prompted the Riverview boys to get all over them as the entire infield met on the mound with Coach Bell. Whatever he said seemed to work, however, as the pitcher was able to retire Dusty and Brooks promptly to limit the damage. Nonetheless, the Riverview boys had responded and let the Fox Creek kids know that they weren't going to be a pushover today.

When the inning was over, David rushed back out to the mound. He couldn't wait to get back out there and prove his dad wrong. He also couldn't wait to shut up Becky, who was encouraging the Fox Creek kids as they came off the field. "Don't worry, guys, you can get that run back. You saw what David's made of that first inning."

It was only fuel to his fire as he went out and set down the side in order, striking out two kids. Dusty gave David the familiar nod as they trotted off, the nod that told David these guys didn't have a chance. Whether they had a chance or not, Becky wasn't deterred with her cheering throughout. Each time David got one of the Fox Creek guys out, she made sure to try to build him back up, but it didn't matter. David was in a zone now, and he was setting them down in order inning after inning. The only problem was that they weren't scoring themselves. After the first inning, they only managed a couple of base runners, and it was clear that the younger guys were overmatched. If they were going to get anything done, it was going to have to happen with the top of the order, and they were due up to start the fifth inning.

Ricky led things off again, but after fouling off a few pitches, he struck out swinging. Next came David. As he was walking to the plate, he heard Becky yell out to the pitcher to throw him fastballs inside, saying that he struggled with that pitch. Everyone turned to look at her, including Coach Bell, so she sat back down in her chair while still nodding out to the pitcher. David seethed and swore if he got an inside fastball, he was taking this kid yard. Naturally, the first pitch was a blistering inside fastball that David fouled off, rattling his hands. The next one was a curveball off the plate for a ball. Stepping back into the box and noticing the pitcher looking back over at Becky again, David knew what was coming; and this time, he was ready for it. He took the inside fastball and roped it for a double down the left field line, yelling back to his teammates to bring him around. He then looked over at Becky, who just turned her head to the side.

Joey came up next and hit a sharp ground ball to second, but it was an out. It moved David to third, but there were now two outs, and Gary was coming up with nobody at first base. Coach Bell motioned over to his catcher to put him on base. The now twenty to thirty spectators started to boo from down the right field line. One even yelled, "It's good to see you guys are scared of one of our kids!" But it didn't influence Coach Bell, who steadfastly held up four fingers and motioned to first base. Gary looked over his shoulder while shaking his head. Even Officer Smith was muttering something under his breath behind the mound.

Dusty came up to the plate with runners on first and third and two out. He looked visibly nervous. The Riverview boys were doing their best to chant and rattle the kid on the mound, but he blew the first pitch right by Dusty. The second pitch was in the dirt, but the third pitch was blown right by him again. Everyone on the Riverview side dropped their head a bit. Dusty couldn't catch up to this kid all day, and nobody seemed to have much faith that he would now either, except David. "Come on, Dusty!" he shouted from third base. "One time, kid, I believe you!"

The rest of the team followed suit. Dusty's dad, who had come down with part of his crew and one of the fire trucks, even joined in, supporting him. Everybody knew what was coming; it was only a matter of if Dusty could time it up one time. As the tall pitcher for Fox Creek came set, David said a quick prayer for his friend as he began to deliver the ball.

Whack! David's prayer was miraculously answered. Dusty had timed it up perfectly and sent a ball screaming over the center fielder's head on a line. The game was definitely tied as David jumped up and down, making his way down the third baseline and turning to watch the play. The ball rolled up one of the giant elm trees in center field and right back down to the instigator who was playing center field. He was able to scoop it up and fire a strike to Ryan, who had come out from shortstop to receive the cutoff throw. The ball hit him perfectly chest high on his glove side as Gary was rounding third base. The Riverview boys were all screaming for him to get moving. Ryan hesitated for a second before turning and releasing a ball that was seemingly shot out of a cannon from short center field. Gary was moving down the line as best as he could while David was standing there, watching the play develop.

As the ball came in, David could see it was slightly high and up the first baseline, so he frantically motioned for Gary to slide to the third base side of the plate. The ball beat Gary to the plate, but by the time the catcher reached up to make the catch and swipe back in an attempt to tag him, Gary had slid in just safe by an eyelash. The Riverview boys and spectators all erupted as the Fox Creek boys and Coach Bell protested the call. Then there was Dusty, who stood on third base, smiling from ear to ear as his pudgy stomach violently fluctuated in and out. The Riverview boys had their lead, and now it was up to David to get the final six outs and shut them down like he had promised.

In the top of the sixth, it was David's turn to go through the heart of Fox Creek's order for the third time. It started with Ryan. Before he could make his way to the plate, Becky came down from her deck, made her way across the gravel driveway in her bare feet, and began whispering in his and the instigator's ears as they were putting on their batting gloves. David didn't need any extra motivation or adrenaline at this point, but if there was ever a doubt about whose day it was going to be, he erased that as he faced those three kids, striking each of them out with a fastball. After the last pitch to the instigator, David let out a roar as he ran back to the first base side. Even Becky sat back in her chair and didn't say much.

The Riverview boys went in order in the bottom of the sixth, setting the stage for the seventh and final inning. As he was warming up, David knew he'd emptied the tank last inning and was most likely going to have to rely on his defense for the final three outs. He got ahead of the first batter but hung a one-ball, two-strike pitch more than he wanted. The Fox Creek kid blooped the ball into shallow center field for what seemed like a certain hit, but out of nowhere, Brooks came diving in to make the catch. One out.

David fell behind the next batter, who had also been at Jay's last week. He hadn't reached base yet today, but David knew he had good swings on his first two at bats. Behind two balls and no strikes, David reached back for the best fastball he had left. The kid smashed the ball to third, but Joey slid to his left, dropping to a knee to knock the ball down. Then he got up as best as he was able and threw the ball to first, where Gary handled the short hop like a pro. Two out.

Now everyone was into it from Riverview, even the officers and firefighters, who were definitely taking a long lunch on the taxpayer dollar. By this time, there were nearly forty to fifty people who had gathered to watch David try to slay Goliath, including a good number of Riverview parents who wanted to watch their boys try to take down Fox Creek. As they anxiously cheered, he fired a first pitch fastball for a strike. The next pitch was a fastball that was fouled right back. The kid was on David, and he was running out of gas. He looked over and noticed that Becky was back in her chair, leaning forward with her hands cupping her face. She was clearly nervous, but David didn't care about her. He didn't care about anything except this next pitch.

Dusty sensed that David's fastball was dropping off, so he called for a changeup. David agreed, thinking, *Get this kid to put the ball weakly in play and get this thing over with.* David threw a nice changeup, but it got too much of the plate. The kid hit the ball hard right back up the middle. David kicked at the ball, trying to knock it down with his leg, but he missed. It hit off the mound and was targeted for center field, but Ricky came sliding across on his right leg just behind second base to snag the ball. He then popped up and fired a strike to Gary at first, who lifted his hands in the air. Three outs. Victory for Riverview.

The kids on the field all went crazy as if they had won a sectional championship. The people watching along the streets were equally excited as if all their failed attempts had somehow been redeemed in this game. Gary ran toward David with his hands raised to start the mob scene, but Officer Smith had already beat him to David with a congratulatory handshake and pat on the back. David then turned and gave Ricky a big hug as he was sprinting in to join the celebration. The two friends, who seemingly could not stand each other, both smiled at each other with respect and joy. Then Dusty came flying in and tackled both of them to the ground. At one point, David thought he was going to be crushed, but he managed to wiggle free and get back to his feet.

The Fox Creek kids were all just quietly standing on the third base side, gathering their gear and exchanging quiet fist bumps with one another. Ryan and Coach Bell were standing side by side, watching the melee on the mound, both with a half smile on their faces. Becky was standing up on her deck with her hands still on her cheeks as if she was in disbelief herself; after all, she had seen these boys play more than anyone.

Slowly, the Riverview boys began to break up and start walking back to their side of the field; but as they did, they started to get greeted by the spectators. David knew most of them in some capacity, but he really enjoyed getting a handshake and a hug from Mr. Scott the most. Even Randy Black, the Riverview legend who made it to Double-A, had watched the last few innings before returning to his construction site. He came over and shook David's hand and told him what a great game he had pitched. As the adults filtered out and back to their daily lives, the boys' next item of business was to figure out when and where they were going to party. Gary suggested they meet at the Dairy Barn at around six and go from there.

Exhausted and emotionally spent, David dropped to a knee to start removing his cleats. As he did so, he noticed that Ryan and Coach Bell were making their way across the diamond and were coming his way. He knew what the conversation was going to be, but he was still nervous. He stood up and walked toward them as he didn't want to have the entire conversation overheard by his teammates and friends.

Coach Bell extended his right hand while Ryan stood there with the same half smile he had when the Riverview boys were celebrating. "Heck of a job, young man," Coach Bell said while shaking his hand firmly. "After that start, I wasn't sure I believed Ryan here when he said that we had to find a way to add you this summer, but now I clearly see he was right. I don't think I've ever seen anyone in all my years in Fox Creek or Legion ball set down twenty-one straight hitters in our lineup."

David didn't know what to say. He had no idea that he had been perfect after the first four batters reached base. He thanked Coach Bell but wasn't sure what he was supposed to do or say next, so he let him continue. "You've got a really lively arm, but I was most impressed by what is between your ears and in here." He tapped David on the chest and gave him a quick smile before resuming in his gruff coaching voice. "Not too many kids your age would have been able to get through that first inning like you did with all the boys chirping at you like that. Plus, striking out my two through four hitters in the sixth inning was something. You knew that was the spot, and you took your game to the next level. Not many guys your age have that in you."

Coach Bell again extended his hand to David and then turned to Ryan. It was his turn now to give the sales pitch to David. "Like I said the other day, we'd love to have you join us this summer. With you on the mound, we can be pretty special." He laughed as he said, "Believe it or not, we can actually hit. We've got a chance to go to do well in the state and invite events. It's where a lot of us get offered by college coaches."

He paused to try to get a read on David, but like usual, he wasn't giving much to go off, so Ryan continued, "And despite what you may have heard today and dealt with the last couple of weeks, the guys on the team aren't that bad. They just wanted to see if you could handle the pressure."

David snickered to himself at the "last couple of weeks" comment but tried not to let it show. Guys from Riverview had to deal with Fox Creek guys their whole life, and what did they know about pressure? Regardless, Ryan was being sincere and had always been honest and forthright with him. David believed he was a good guy, so he didn't have to force a smile and a nod when Ryan was done.

"So what do you think, David? Do you want to play with us this summer?" Coach Bell was looking to close the deal and move on with his day.

"I'd like to, but can I talk it over with my parents? I don't have a license or a car, so I'd need to rely on them—" David began before being cut off by Coach Bell.

"Absolutely, young man. We want all families to be a part of this and enjoy these experiences. We know it's a commitment, so everybody has to be on board." He pulled out a business card and gave it to David. "Give me a call by this weekend and let me know. We've got our first big event next weekend, and we'd love to have you there."

With that, he and Ryan headed back to their cars. David stared at the business card for a moment, and he heard someone come walking up behind him. He turned to see Dusty, who was still a sweaty mess, approaching with concern on his face. "Everything okay?" he asked.

"Yep, everything is good," David replied with a smile and a tap to Dusty's shoulder. "Let's get everything back to your place and start thinking about tonight."

Dusty smiled and nodded. David dropped to one knee to again try to remove his cleats. As he did, he caught a glimpse of light blue moving through his sight line. He looked up to see Becky getting ready to head back inside her house. They locked eyes for a second, and she flashed him a huge smile.

David and Dusty made their way back to his trailer side by side, with David pushing the mower and Dusty carrying the rake. The adrenaline was starting to wear off, but the boys were still smiling and enjoying the moment. They weren't walking alone for too long as they had walked with Gary back to his house and firmed up the plan to meet at six before seeing him inside. Finally alone, they began to dissect things as best friends.

"Man that was a huge hit," David said to Dusty with a huge smile.

"Ha, yeah. Close your eyes and swing hard in case you hit it, right?" Dusty chuckled. Both boys laughed and replayed the moment over in their heads before Dusty continued, "You know, it was pretty cool what you did out there today."

"Yeah, I guess I had it working," David replied.

"Yeah, but I wasn't talking about your pitching. I mean, that was awesome, but what you did for Ricky and the boys today, that was special." Dusty sounded more serious than he ever had. David looked at him with a slightly confused look as always, so Dusty knew he would have to further explain. "I'm talking about how you picked up Ricky after his error. You were thinking about somebody besides yourself for once. That entire game, you put everyone on that team in front of you, and look what we did. It's a game I'll never forget."

David smiled. He hadn't really thought about that as he had got lost in the moment. "Yeah, I forgot about that, I guess. I just didn't want to lose. I wanted to prove everybody wrong." He paused for a moment to reflect on what had happened. "I can't wait to get home and tell my dad about everything. I can't wait to tell him he was wrong."

"He deserves to eat a big turd sandwich," Dusty replied.

"I can't believe they didn't even come down to watch," he said, referring to David's parents. "Didn't you say they were off today?"

David didn't really want to address them or think about that, so he changed topics. He could feel the adrenaline surging in him a bit. "So what was up with Becky cheering for the Fox Creek guys?" he began, starting to sound angry. "Seriously, can that girl make up her mind about anything? How can she root for them right in front of us?"

"Well, what do you expect when you don't call her back?" Dusty replied matter-of-factly. "Besides, you should be thanking her."

"Thanking her?" David ripped back at Dusty.

"Yeah, it wasn't until she started cheering that you started dealing. The louder she cheered, the harder you threw. That girl knows how to push your buttons. You've got something in you, David, and when it comes out, we're all just along for the ride."

With that, they reached his short driveway. Dusty dropped the rake he was holding and took the mower from David. "Don't hurt yourself too much thinking about that one." Dusty laughed while pushing the mower to the garage. "I'll see you at the Dairy Barn at six." David just shook his head and turned to make the long walk back to his house.

As David headed down Dusty's street, he had a hard time not thinking about what he had just said. He had been so angry at Becky, but he had her smile frozen in his mind. Maybe Dusty was right; maybe she had been the difference, but as he continued to head home, he couldn't focus on her. He had no idea what to expect when he got home. As the game got going, he had completely pushed his dad out of his mind; but with each step closer to his home, she was all he could think about. Seeing both of his parents' cars in the garage when his house came in sight only raised his anxiety level. He slowed down as he approached the house and decided to enter through the garage below the house. This would allow him to hear any fighting if there was any going on.

Before opening the door to his basement, he froze and listened intently, but he didn't hear any yelling. He almost hoped that they were fighting because he was nervous about what he was going to say, but since it was good news, he pushed the door open and made his way upstairs with a level of confidence. When he opened the door, he heard his mom and dad laughing together in the living room. It was almost as shocking to David as what had taken place on the field earlier in the day. It was a rare moment where it seemed like they were a normal family. He turned left into the kitchen to grab a drink from the fridge when he heard his mom call out to him. "Hey, sweetheart, how did it go today?"

David grabbed a drink and made the slow journey to the living room to deliver the good news. He started off slowly, but as he started to tell the story, he became more excited. "Well . . . we won." His mom jumped up and came over to give him a hug, but David's eyes went to his dad. His dad slumped back in his chair, and he didn't say anything. "It started off kind of ugly. I walked the first two guys, there was an error, and then I gave up a hit. It was 2–0 before I even got settled." He looked over at his dad, and he saw a slight grin on his face, so David became angry and started talking faster. "After that, I got mad, and I shut them down. In fact, I didn't let another kid from Fox Creek reach base the rest of the game. Afterward, their coach came up to me and said that he'd never seen anything like it against one of his teams before."

"Their coach was there?" David's dad interrupted.

Bothered that this was the only thing his dad could say, David continued on, gently moving his mother aside to address his father specifically. "Yeah, and they offered me a spot on their Legion team. He said I had a lot of heart and potential." His dad just sunk back in his chair speechless, so David turned back to his mother, who was still standing by his side. "I figured I'd ask Grandpa if he could take me to the practices and games. The coach said I had until this weekend to get back to him."

His mom rubbed the side of his face and just smiled adoringly. "I'm sure he'd love to take you, David," she replied, referring to his grandpa.

David smiled and felt relieved. Then he confessed to his mom, "I think I really impressed Becky today too, Mom. She started off rooting against us, but when I left, she gave me a smile."

"What did I tell you about girls and baseball, David?" his dad said, now pushing himself up to his feet.

He shot a hard glare at his mother and continued, "Nobody from this town goes anywhere with baseball. This is all just a waste of time."

David took a step toward his father as if he was going to hit him, but then he just looked at his mom, went to his room, and slammed his door closed. He laid there on his bed, wondering why his dad, who loved watching baseball, couldn't congratulate him. Why did he take the previous night off but not show up like some of the other dads? His fingers intertwined through his thick dark hair as he could now hear his parents start arguing out in the living room. He heard his dad blame his mom for getting pregnant and keeping him in town and from pursuing his dreams. She fired back saying that she had a million better options than to stay with him.

The arguing continued outside as his mom got in her car and attempted to drive away. Eventually, she cleared the driveway and went tearing down the road toward the interstate. David heard his dad come storming back in the house and right to his door. He flung the door open and opened his mouth as if he was about to start in on him, but he stopped before anything came out. He looked at David, who was laying there with tears in his eyes, and just closed the door gently shut and walked away.

David laid there for a while, trying not to cry like a baby, and eventually dozed off. When he woke up, he realized it was getting close to six, and he hadn't yet showered. He didn't think about or care if his dad was home; he hopped into the shower and was going to get out of the house as quickly as possible. He returned to his room and put on a pair of light pink and blue Jams shorts and a white plain top before grabbing a pair of flip-flops and heading out the door. He noticed that his dad's car was gone too, so he briefly wondered where he might be before dismissing him entirely. He was ready to be with his friends and celebrate.

Making his way down the main street in town, David would get the occasional honk from a car passing by. Word had traveled fast to the people who cared. By the time he reached the Dairy Barn, all the other boys were there and started hooting and hollering at him from a distance. He couldn't help but smile and feel like he was on top of the world. Eric and Dallas had even gotten him a banana milkshake for him to enjoy upon his arrival. The boys sat in the parking lot on the hood of Joey's car, laughing and recapping the highlights from the game earlier in the day.

It was the perfect start to a grand celebration when Ricky rolled up in a new silver GT Supreme Subaru Alcyone. He was smiling from ear to ear, oblivious to everyone staring at him and wondering how and where he had gotten that car. He was proud to announce that he had two cases of beer in the trunk on ice. He told everyone that he was going to drop off the cooler at the creek at the back of the city park, and they could all make their way down there when the sun started to go down. Gary gave him a look and said that he would ride down there with him to help set things up down by the creek. When Gary got in, he rolled his eyes to the group as they tore out of the parking lot and headed toward the park.

The boys sat there for a while, talking and retelling stories to other people from town who came up to them, asking about it. Eventually, Brooks, Eric, Dallas, and Jason all agreed that they didn't want to risk getting caught drinking in the park, so they were out. Joey, Dusty, and David looked at one another and smiled, thinking that they really didn't want the younger guys there anyways. As the sun began to start dropping, the younger guys said their goodbyes and headed their own way.

Joey told Dusty and David to hop in his car. They drove down to the park and saw the last few families that were playing on the playground packing up and getting ready to head home. Joey told the boys he was going to look for Gary and Ricky and that they would be back as soon as he found them. Everyone thought it was odd that neither Gary or Ricky had come back after they left the Dairy Barn.

David and Dusty made their way to the back edge of the park. They stood at the top of the bank to the creek and looked down. Just as they had expected, Ricky and Gary had placed the large green cooler on the other side of the creek that had a large dirt area and stones large enough for the boys to sit on. The two boys made their way down the bank and settled on separate rocks with a cold beer in their hands. From their little nesting spot, they could see the sky and the top of the nearly ten-foot embankment where their friends would be approaching.

Neither boy had much experience drinking beer, but they'd seen others do it plenty of times, so they knew how they were supposed to look and act. They sat there quietly, both tired from the day's events but still reflecting on things. As David sat there looking up at the fading blue sky, he started to think of his dad. A few sips later, he started talking to Dusty as if he'd asked him a question.

"You know what I hate about my old man?" David began. "I hate that not only did he try to ruin my day but I also know he ruined my mom's day. I swear, Dusty, I don't know why she stays with him. I know as soon as I get a chance, I'm out of that house."

Dusty sat there just kind of listening. He surmised David's mood and didn't want to say anything that would provoke any more anger, but his silence only seemed to bother David even more. David crumpled the can in his hand and went and grabbed another beer. As he was closing the cooler, he could hear people approaching.

It wasn't long before Joey, Gary, and Ricky all poked their heads over the embankment. Now it was the older boys turn to rehash the day and celebrate the victory. Each boy retold their favorite story from the day as the sun went down and the sky fell black. It was the first time in a long time that there hadn't been any friction between the boys. They told old stories from when they were younger and laughed. As they were working their way through their fourth round of beers, they saw headlight beams flash across the top of the embankment.

Ricky nervously asked, "Who is it?" With his eyes wide open, he was suddenly standing and trying to peer over the embankment.

Gary climbed to the top to check things out, and when he got there, he groaned, "Oh, you've got to be kidding me."

"Cops?" Joey asked.

"I wish," Gary replied. "It's Becky and a few of the Fox Creek kids from earlier today."

"Losers." Joey chuckled as he took a large gulp from his can. Gary began to make his descent back down the embankment, shaking his head. He and Ricky had a few choice words about Becky as they sat back down. David just sat there filled with anger. He had had enough beers to lower his inhibitions, so it wasn't long before he couldn't hold his feelings back.

"What the heck is wrong with her?" David cried. "Seriously, are we not good enough for her?" The boys liked seeing this side of David, so they encouraged him and egged him on. "It's like, even after today, she can't admit that we're better than them. I've never seen somebody as messed up as her before." The boys all agreed and cheered one another as they clinked beer cans and smiled.

"Why don't you go and tell that to her face in front of her new friends?" Ricky laughed. "I'd pay to watch that."

"Looks like you're too late," Gary observed as they saw the lights flash, turn, and then disappear. "Who knows where they're taking her now?" He chuckled as he raised his can.

David was in anger and disbelief as he climbed to the top of the embankment to see if they were really gone. When he reached the top, he was surprised to see a shadowy figure sitting on the swing set. He could only see a silhouette from the streetlight beyond the park boundaries, but there was no mistaking who it was.

Becky was swinging alone with her head down. The car full of Fox Creek kids had left her behind, alone in the dark at the city park, a good walk from her house. David stood and stared for a while until Ricky finally asked if somebody was still there.

"It's Becky," David whispered. "She's all alone on the swing set." The boys laughed, but David didn't take his eyes off her.

Dusty, who was unusually quiet that night, finally spoke up. "Now's your chance, David. Go talk to her." Dusty motioned with his hand as the other boys laughed and gave David a hard time. He stood there at the top of the embankment, looking back at his friends.

Ricky reached into the cooler and tossed David a beer, saying, "I hear there's a lot of courage in these cans." He nodded at David and smiled. Even Gary was giving his blessing for David to make that walk across the field to the playground. There was no opting out now for David, especially after his little speech. The butterflies that he felt this morning were now back in his stomach.

Walking across the open field to the playground, David sensed a bit of coolness in the air. It was a perfectly clear night, so as he looked to his right, the city skyline was pristine and colorful, but the true beauty was in front of him. Becky heard David approaching and turned her head slowly. Her hands were positioned above her head as her shoulders and body slumped forward in the swing. She was wearing a pair of short jean shorts and a baggy light green sweatshirt that she had cut the banding at the bottom off. Her hair was up in a ponytail that was angled and fell behind her left ear. David nearly stopped and turned around when the streetlight caught her face as he was intimidated by her beauty, but he didn't want to have to face his friends, who were undoubtedly watching from the embankment a little over one hundred yards away.

She was the first to speak. She had tears in her eyes but was steady and clear with her voice. "Hey, I'm sure glad to see you."

David was a little taken aback by what she had said. After all, she had just been hanging with three kids from Fox Creek. If she wanted to see him so badly, he wondered why she hadn't come to the Dairy Barn early. He couldn't help but be sarcastic. "Really? It didn't look like it a few minutes ago."

Hurt and put off by his tone, Becky swung her head away from him and lowered her hands on the chains. David didn't want to be mean, but he was buzzing from the beer, and his emotions had gotten the better of him. Sensing this, Becky turned back toward David and then looked at the beer he was holding in his hand. "I thought you were different. I didn't peg you for another townie who got drunk in secret spots across town with their friends until they're old enough to do it in the bars together."

David was suddenly aware and embarrassed of the beer he was holding in his hand. He didn't want to be another townie. He had been struggling so much lately to not be like his dad, and now in one sentence, the girl whom he liked had thrown him in that same category. He set the beer down and eased into the empty swing next to her. She was looking at him with tears still in her eyes but could sense that she too had hurt him. "I'm not like them. I don't want to be like that," he said in a quiet and imploring voice. He could hear his friends rumbling from across the way, but he didn't care about them.

Becky shook her head as she now looked down. As she began to speak, she slowly raised her eye level to meet David's. "Well, I haven't seen much lately to prove otherwise, David Collins. It seems as if the only pleasure you get these days is in hurting me." With that, she got up, wrapped her arms around herself, and began walking toward the entrance to the park.

David sat there for a moment, contemplating his options. He thought about just going back to the creek with his friends and having a good time, but his heart urged him to try to make things right with Becky. "Becky, wait," he said excitedly as he rose off the swing. "I'm not going to mess up this time. I've been thinking about you nonstop lately." He caught himself after he made that declaration. The beer was still causing him to speak a bit more freely than he normally would, but when he saw Becky stop and turn toward him, he was glad that it was. "I know I have said some horrible things to you, and I didn't call you back, but I'm not who you think I am."

She looked at him for a few seconds before hinting at a smile. She wiped her eyes and extended her hand as an invite for him to join her. "Oh really? Maybe we can take a walk, and you can explain to me who you are then." Her smile widened, and David's stomach flipped. He walked over to her, smiling nervously as they set out walking back through town.

"So who are you, David Collins?" she said as if she was in control of the conversation, and she had him right where she wanted him. "From my perspective lately, you seem like a guy who's afraid of his own shadow, someone who avoids talking to people that make him feel uncomfortable, a guy who is loyal to his friends even if he doesn't necessarily agree with what they're doing, a guy who is really smart but doesn't know what he wants to do, a guy who wants to get out of this town and is terrified he never will, a guy who—"

"Whoa, whoa, whoa," David interrupted. He was stunned and caught off guard with how well she had him pegged. He didn't even know where to begin, but he knew he wanted to stop her before she completely picked him apart. He wanted to dispute her, but he couldn't, so he responded with the only other thing he could think of. "How do you know so much about me?"

She smiled and relished her position. Now changing to her flirtatious and controlling self, she told him, "Well, we have lived in the same town our entire lives. Just because we aren't in the same class doesn't mean I don't pay attention to people. I've noticed you staring at me for some time." She snickered.

David dropped his head in guilt.

"It's okay," she assured him. "I've been staring too."

David quickly raised his head to look into her eyes, and she wasn't joking.

"You've got a lot going for you, and we're not that different."

David couldn't help himself from snickering and uttering in a sarcastic and hurtful way, "Yeah, right." He looked off in the opposite direction.

Becky grabbed his arm and forced him to look back at her. "So tell me what you know about me, David," she implored, letting him have the floor.

David hesitated but knew that she wasn't going to let him off the hook. "Well, I know that you are the prettiest girl I've ever seen, and your hair—"

She grabbed his arm again and cut him off. "Those are things that anyone can see, David." She was smiling and was flattered by the compliment but not satisfied. "I want to hear what you know about me," she implored, giving his arm a slight tug. "What do you know about me that others don't care to see?"

David took a breath and tried not to let the beer do the talking for him. He thought about what he really knew about Becky and weighed that with what he thought she would want to hear. He started slowly, trying to gauge her reactions. "Well, I know that you aren't shy like me."

She smiled and confirmed that this was what she was hoping he would say, so he continued, "I know that you can make friends with just about anyone. I know that when you smile, I wish I was one of your friends." He stopped and looked at her, and she stopped too.

She was smiling and took her hand and laced it inside David's. "Okay, that's a nice start and about the nicest thing anybody has ever said to me. We can get back to me in a little bit, but tell me a little about you. What don't I know about you?" She squeezed his hand a bit to get him to make eye contact. He looked at her with his heart pounding so quickly that he felt like his neck was pulsating. She sensed his nervousness a bit so she tried to calm him. "I know you're not a liar. You are honest and sincere." This made him smile and relax a bit.

David thought about what to say. Nobody had ever asked him to describe himself before. What was there to tell that she hadn't already named? As he walked, he started to think about his father and his home. He felt a surge of anger come over him, and the beer made him want to blurt out a tangent about how much he couldn't stand him, but instead, he composed himself before speaking. "Well, my homelife isn't the greatest. People think that because I don't live in a trailer or a run-down ranch, I've got it good. They see me wearing nice things and get jealous because my parents spoil me."

He looked to see if this was appealing to her and what she wanted to hear. Her sad eyes and tightening grip on his hand suggested that he should keep going. "Truth is, my parents pretty much ignore me. They only give me nice things after they've had a big fight. Instead of talking to me about things, they just buy me a gift and think that everything is better. My dad tells me that I and my friends are losers and that I shouldn't bother with baseball. My mom means well, but she doesn't know what to do. Plus, they both work odd hours, so I never see them, and they never really ask about me and how I'm doing. Lots of people think it's great that I can come and go as I please, but it's lonely. Sometimes I feel like a prisoner when I'm at home."

He was starting to get angry, and his voice was rising. Becky sensed this was a sensitive area, so she tried to ease him a bit. "Yeah, I know what you're saying," she said soothingly as she pulled her hand away gently. "I had no idea things were so bad for you at home. I guess I was like everyone else when it came to that. I also know what it's like to feel like a prisoner." David looked at her with an intriguing look on his face, but she changed the subject quickly. "But at least you have good friends," she said encouragingly.

David squinted his eyebrows a bit before admitting, "Well, Dusty is my only real friend. You've seen how the other guys treat me. If we didn't play baseball together at the field, I doubt we'd even hang out."

"So then why were you having beers with them in the creek bed?" she quickly replied.

David looked at her with a look of contempt. "What's wrong with having a few beers with them?" He was getting perturbed by her tone.

"Well, I just thought you were different," she said matter-of-factly. "And you even said that they weren't really your friends, besides Dusty. Do you just go along with whatever they do? And you mean to tell me that you really enjoy hanging around with a jerk like Ricky?"

Growing agitated with her accusations and tone, David decided he wanted to turn things around a bit, so he started in on her. "So speaking of friends, why is it that you only seem to hang out with guys from Fox Creek these days? How's that working out for you?" His posture changed from relaxed to stern. He was tired of seeing her with different guys and wanted an answer, but her answer surprised him.

"David, be glad that you have friends," she calmly replied. "Be glad that you can leave your house whenever you want." Her tone was changing, and so was David's stern posture.

"Do you ever see me hanging with friends?" she was asking him but more so telling him because he knew the answer. "I don't have any friends, David. I don't have anyone that I can talk to. I just want to get out of here. I need to get out of here." She was starting to cry now. They had reached the elementary school and the field where earlier that day David had been a godlike figure, but now he felt helpless as the girl he liked was crumbling before him, the girl who seemed to always be in control and have all the answers. The girl whose self-confidence never seemed to waiver was suddenly crying in his arms.

David escorted her to the merry-go-round on the playground, where they sat next to each other in silence. She started to get herself together a bit and pulled back from his arms to look at him. "Why didn't you call me back or talk to me at work? I knew you were there. I knew you were behind those doors," she said in a voice so pathetic that it nearly broke David's heart.

He thought about what to say to her, but nothing seemed like the right thing, so he just admitted, "I was scared. I didn't know what to say to you. You always seem so in control, so when you suddenly got mad at me, I didn't know what to think. I just hated myself for making you so upset, and I didn't want to do it again. I hate seeing you upset." It felt good to finally get the truth out. After he said it, he wondered why he couldn't have said it earlier.

She looked at him and his shameful slumping demeanor and asked, "I can trust you, right?" She looked at him as if he were her only lifeline. His honesty and sincerity comforted her despite making him feel horrible. It seemed to be the exact words she needed and confirmed what she had long believed and knew about the boy who had spent so many hours playing in the field next to her house and in the classroom across the hall from hers.

"Sure," he said, unsure of what was about to come next.

"Even though we didn't always have classes together, I always knew I could trust you," she began. She recounted the various times she had seen him cleaning up someone's mess in the cafeteria without being asked or not joining in when others might be picking on someone on the playground. She told him how she admired that he had always gotten good grades despite the pressure from a lot of people they knew to not stand out in school. She talked about how she had gotten straight As her entire life and wanted to go to school far away. She sensed that David felt the same way. She talked about what it was like to be one of the youngest people in her class, and David agreed. She confessed that her girlfriends had made fun of her because she was the last to go through puberty and develop. David agreed and said he knew exactly what that was like. She squeezed his arm and told him that he was definitely catching up.

They lay back on the merry-go-round, staring at the sky and sharing childhood stories and memories for well over a couple of hours. They talked about how they had long admired each other and how they wished they'd talked like this long before tonight. They playfully laughed and joked about the things they had in common. David opened up more about his family while Becky listened intently. She confessed that she hung out with the boys from Fox Creek in the desperate hopes that one guy might be kind enough to see her as more than a boy toy, but they all only cared about the same thing. She hoped that maybe one might help her find a way to a better life, but when she wouldn't give them what they wanted, she was sent back to Riverview as the butt of their jokes.

He talked about how excited he was to play for them and maybe go away to college to play baseball and prove his father wrong, but hearing her stories made him question if it was worth it. She told him how proud she was of him and that she knew he would achieve his goal. She told him it was worth it and that he shouldn't let her issues affect his thoughts about them, even though she secretly loved him for having those thoughts. They laughed as they talked about various times they had gone to school dances and wanted to dance with the other but were too scared. David was shocked and comforted to find out that Becky Reeves was afraid of something.

However, it was when she started to talk about how she hated her looks that David gave her a confused look and sat up. "How could you possibly hate the way that you look?" he said with a sincere confusion. "I was serious when I said that you are the most beautiful girl I've ever seen." But she didn't smile or react. "Even though that didn't show what I knew about you," he said jokingly, trying to bring back her smile and the comfort with which she had been speaking.

Slowly, she sat up to meet David's eyes. "I can trust you, right?" she said more seriously than anything else she had said all night.

"Of course," David replied, somewhat offended that she would ask that after all the time they had spent sharing things together on the merry-go-round.

She gave him a hard look for a few seconds to size up how honest he was being and just how much she could trust him. When he didn't flinch, she grabbed his hand and gave it a good squeeze as if to tell him that she did trust him and that he needed to brace himself. With that, she took her light green baggy sweatshirt and lifted it completely over her head and off her body. David sat there frozen, with his heart pounding. The reflection from the moon and a light outside the entrance of the school provided more than enough light to see her beauty and curves clearly. He looked at her face, scared and intimidated to look anywhere else. Seeing that his eyes had not dropped from hers, she grabbed his hand and gently moved it over her left breast. David had never experienced this with a girl before, and his heart was pounding as he could feel the warm, soft skin and the smooth satin of her bra cup. His entire body was tingling as she held his hand there for a second before motioning with her eyes for him to drop his. When he lowered his eyes to take in what his hand had been enjoying, he quickly pulled it back and locked eyes with her again. She tightened her lips and motioned with her eyes that it was okay to look again, that David hadn't been fooled by what he had seen.

As David pulled back and slowly lowered his eyes again, he took in the scratches and hickeys that lined and marked good portions of her chest and breasts. He was speechless as his body surged with rage. Those Fox Creek boys had had their way with her and then dropped her off at the park for her to find her own way home. She had put up a fight, but that was the price she had to pay for trying to find her ticket out of town. His body tightened back up as he felt the adrenaline come back to his body from earlier in the day. "Those assholes. I can't stand those pricks from Fox Creek. There's no way I'm playing on that team," he declared as his voice started to rise, and he started to his feet. She cut him off before he could go any farther, grabbed him, and pulled him back down.

"David," she said calmly, "those marks aren't from any boys from Fox Creek."

He felt somewhat reassured but still just as confused. He looked into her eyes begging for the truth.

"They're from my stepfather." As she said that, she dropped her head in embarrassment and relief.

David had no clue what to say. He sat there trying to study her face to see if this was some kind of joke or test, but it clearly was not. He felt ashamed for even touching her breast, removed his hand, and pulled her close as she sobbed in his arms. Suddenly, everything Dusty had been saying made sense, and David felt a surge of guilt for everything he had said and felt toward Becky. He now understood why she wore the sweatshirts in the summer heat and why his comment had been so painful to her. He felt sick for even complaining about his homelife to her.

"Becky," David began slowly, unsure of exactly what to say, "I'm so sorry . . . for everything. I had no idea. If I did, I would have never—"

She cut him off while putting her top back on. "It's okay, David."

"No, it's not okay, Becky," he retorted with a growing menace in his voice, but she grabbed his arm with both hands. He was now looking at her house with disgust in his eyes. She turned his face toward her so they could meet eyes. She stared at him, and this helped calm David.

"It's okay because I've never been able to tell anyone before," she said as she stared into his light brown eyes while hers again filled with tears. "You don't know what it's like being a girl in this town. For years, I wanted to grow up and be like the older girls who would make fun of me and my annoying, outgoing personality. Even the girls in my class treated me like I was a little girl. All I wanted was to be pretty and to physically mature so I, too, could get the attention of the boys instead of having to hop around, trying to be everyone's friend. Then as soon as I got my wish, my stepfather started giving me these looks. Sometimes I'd be lying in my bed, and I'd look up and see him staring at me. I didn't know what to do. My mom works second shift, so thankfully, most nights, she would come home not long after he'd stare at me.

"Then one night last year, he came home drunk, and he finally came at me. I was so embarrassed and ashamed that when my mom came home and I was crying, I told her it was because I was upset about a boy. I couldn't tell her it was because of my stepdad thirty minutes before she got home. In gym class the next week when I had to change in the locker room, the girls started giving me a hard time and asking who had marked me up. To save face, I lied and told them it was a boy from Fox Creek. They all laughed and said I was lying, so then that became my cover. I had to start hanging with kids from there to make my story believable, and I had to start dressing the way I do to make it seem like I was always trying to impress some boy."

She paused and twisted her mouth as she looked up to the sky. "I guess it's better to be labeled as a slut than a rape victim. At least the girls backed off a bit, but it's why I don't have any friends," she said as she started to get angry. "They all think I'm a slut, along with most of the boys in this town and Fox Creek too." She shot David a look that made him feel horrible and guilty because he was one of those boys. "Nobody wants to be my friend. The girls at school hate me, and they wouldn't believe me if I told the truth now. The adults in this town know what goes on, but nobody will stop him. Do you know what it's like when everyone thinks you've slept with just about everyone and the only person you've ever actually been with is your stepfather because he rapes you?"

She started to cry openly now, but a surge of strength came back over her. It was one of the traits that David had long admired about her. "It's okay though," she said, gaining her composure.

"I'm going to get out of this town, and I'm not as weak or as much of a pushover as I used to be. I've just got to be strong for one more year," she said with rising strength and grit. "I don't care if my mom doesn't care or believe me. I don't care who believes me. I will make it out of this town, and I won't let this happen to other girls."

She seemed to catch herself in that moment and looked at David. "I'm so sorry. I shouldn't have dumped all this on you. It's just that I always knew you were different. I could see it ever since we were kids. I saw it a few days ago when you told me and Ricky off." She squeezed his arm a bit to try to lighten his mood, but he sat there still trying to process everything. "It hurt when you said those things about me, but you didn't know. I could tell that you liked me, and I knew that I liked you. I saw you were different when you blew those pitches by Gary and then let him get a hit so he could still seem like a hero and to ease things over with Ricky and me. It's also why earlier today, when you were struggling, I cheered so hard against you. I knew that was the only way to get your best out of you. I didn't want to see you fail. One of us deserves to get out of here, right?" She now shook his arm a bit to try to loosen him up.

"Right," David breathed out uneasily.

Becky sensed that he was overwhelmed by everything as she wiped the remaining tears from her face. She had admired David and his honesty and desire to always try to do the right thing for a long time. She sensed that was eating at him at this moment too, so she repeated herself to him. "It's okay, David. I'm going to be okay. We're going to be okay. No more games. We're going to get out of here."

"We?" David questioned instinctively.

"Well . . . maybe not together," she hesitated, unsure of where his emotions were. "But I know you, David. I saw you on that mound today. I've seen you for years. You're different. It's why I like you. It's why I trust you. Do you think I could share any of these things with anyone else from here?" She now had her right hand on his thigh and was trying to inspire him. "I know I'm going to be okay."

David couldn't help but look at her house and think about the horrible things that she must have endured in there. He wanted to be able to protect her and keep her from that place. He felt guilty for complaining about his own homelife. He felt horrible for not understanding and appreciating why she had seemingly been so mean to him earlier in the day. He felt dumb because it seemed as if she and Dusty both understood so many things better than he did. He put his head down and grabbed at his hair.

She tried to ease his pain by saying, "I called you that day I stormed off on you because I wanted to tell you. Then I came looking for you at work, but when you didn't come out, I knew it was because you liked me and were confused."

She gently touched his shoulder as she said, "David, it doesn't happen that often, and next time it does, he'll be the one with the marks and the bruises. I can take care of myself, just like you can. That's what will make us so good together."

David looked at her, shocked but thrilled that she kept saying words like *we* and *together.* He was still uncertain of how to comfort her and handle the situation, and Becky sensed this, so she gently put her hand under his chin and raised his eyes level to hers. "David, I want you to kiss me. I don't think I've ever been kissed by someone that I trust, by someone that truly liked me for who I am, not just what I looked like."

He looked at her, unsure if what she was saying was true. "No more games," she said, still holding his chin as she moved in to kiss him.

As their lips met, it was as if they had discovered what they had been missing their entire young lives. They started slowly, but quickly, neither could resist pressing closer and deeper up against each other. David put his arms around her and pulled her closer. He never imagined he could feel this way about anyone else, so connected and concerned about anyone but himself. As her breathing grew deeper and slower, he began to run his hand along the back of her neck and down her arm.

Just as their passion was reaching a tipping point, a bright beam suddenly shone on their faces as they heard a car door slam and a familiar voice come from nearby. It was Gary, and he was frantic. "Ricky is being rushed to the hospital. We've got to go."

David and Becky were still embracing each other as the other doors to the car opened, and they heard Dusty and Joey urging David to get in the car. Neither one had any idea what had taken place, and they didn't want to leave each other. Gary was pleading for David to get in the car as he walked up to them. He told Becky that she had to go home, but when David looked in her eyes after Gary said that, he told him that she was coming with them. Gary relented but was still just as frantic about getting them in the car. Quickly, David and Becky rose hand and hand and ran to hop in the back seat while Gary was behind the wheel of Joey's car.

"What the heck happened?" Becky urged to know.

Joey, who was sitting in the passenger seat, turned to fill them in. He looked white as a ghost while he was trying to remain calm. "After you guys left the park, we went and sat at the pavilion for a while. We started to get on him about some of the things he's been into lately. We asked him about where he got the beer and the car he was driving in earlier."

He glanced at Gary to make sure he wasn't leaving anything out before continuing, "Well, you know Ricky. He got all pissed and started to stomp off. As soon as he got to the street that feeds into the park, that same BMW that rolled up at the Dairy Barn the other day came flying up. Two guys jumped out of the back seat, threw him in the car, and tore away headed south toward the interstate past your place. We hopped in my car as fast as we could, but we couldn't keep up." He was fighting back the tears as he gritted his teeth.

Gary picked up for him. "So we just came back to the park. We didn't know if they were going to bring him back there or what. After a while, we decided to just walk to the Dairy Barn before they closed to cool off and get some ice cream." He couldn't finish either as he was getting emotional. Despite some of their differences, Gary and Ricky had been really close ever since they were little. Gary tried to talk to Ricky numerous times about his choices, but Ricky being forever cocky insisted he would always be fine.

Dusty, who was sitting behind Joey, was the best suited to finish the story. He looked at David, who had Becky pulled close to him in the back seat, and continued, "When we got to the Dairy Barn, Officer Smith was there with his family. He still had his radio on him, so while we were in line, we overheard the dispatcher notify police of a body found in the street between Riverview and Washington Grove. They asked for assistance from any nearby units."

Dusty paused to make sure that Gary wasn't about to run a red light. When he felt the car slowing down, he continued, "Officer Smith saw our reaction and noticed who was missing. He knew it wasn't you, so he asked if we thought it might be Ricky. When Gary told him about what happened, he got on his radio and told his wife and kids that he was responding and rushed to his car. As he was leaving, we asked what hospital they would take him to. He told us Memorial downtown, so after that, we ran back to the park to get the car and came looking for you."

"Oh my god, I'm so sorry," Becky said as she put her arm on Gary's shoulder to try to comfort him. David couldn't believe she felt sorry for Ricky, who had seemed to love nothing more than insulting her the other day.

"I tried telling him. I tried telling him, I don't know how many times, to stop messing around with those guys." Gary gritted through his teeth as he pounded on the steering wheel. Becky jumped back into David's arms as Joey tried to console him.

The ride to Memorial Hospital was about fifteen minutes, but Gary made it in about ten. It was coming up on midnight on a weeknight, so the city streets were mostly vacant at that time. Nobody was saying much. They were all focused on the road to make sure Gary wasn't getting too erratic, each thinking about Ricky in their own way. As they flew past the baseball stadium, David turned his head to take an extra look. Becky looked right into his eyes and snuggled even closer. Gary found a spot on the street just down from the hospital, and the group ran into the emergency room area. Gary and Joey began demanding to know if Ricky had been admitted, but neither was successful in getting any information.

It didn't take long for them to get the information that they needed but didn't want. As the older boys were pacing through the lobby and questioning where else he could have been taken, David saw Officer Smith come walking through the doors. He tapped Dusty, and they went over to him as Becky trailed behind.

Before he began, Officer Smith made sure that Gary and Joey were out of sight and hadn't detected him yet. When he was assured that they weren't going to interrupt him, he confided what he knew to David and Dusty, treating them like men. "It's bad, guys. He was beaten really good, and he hasn't regained consciousness at all. His vitals are solid, but if he recovers, it's going to be a long road for him."

He continued to fill them in on other important details like, since Ricky was scooped up in Riverview but found in Washington Grove, it was going to be a joint investigation. He also wanted to speak to Gary and Joey before he left to see what they might know about who Ricky was involved with. He advised that the boys go home as they weren't going to be able to see Ricky tonight or anytime soon most likely.

Both boys took in all the information but just looked at each other in shock. They both seemed to be fixated on the same detail, "if" he recovered. Becky just collapsed her head into David's shoulder. Neither boy knew what to say or how they would tell Gary and Joey. Fortunately, they wouldn't have to because both boys had circled back and saw Officer Smith as he was trying to make his way to the front desk. He corralled them and led them back outside, leaving David, Dusty, and Becky in the emergency room waiting room while Officer Smith relayed to the older boys the same thing he had just told them.

Suddenly, they all became aware of where they were, and nobody wanted to be there. They observed Officer Smith through the lobby windows talking to Gary and Joey while taking notes outside. After a few minutes, Officer Smith returned inside with his notepad. He wanted to confirm some aspects of Joey's story from the Dairy Barn the other day. David and Dusty just nodded as Officer Smith repeated the description of the car and occupant who threatened Ricky and how Ricky had a gun that he was fishing for but couldn't grasp. Becky's mouth fell slightly agape as she heard each detail and realized that David had been there. Once confirmed, Officer Smith thanked the boys and told them again to go home and not to worry. "Ricky made his own choices that led to this, so none of you should be in any danger."

As David, Dusty, and Becky shuffled outside, they saw Gary and Joey looking just as vacant and jarred as they were. They got back in the car and rode back to Riverview in complete silence. David couldn't help but notice how dark the town seemed as they got off the exit and how bright the lights were that reflected in the sky from Fox Creek at the top of the bluff, just a couple of more miles down the interstate, just a couple of miles where everything seemed to always be a little bit better, where kids were sleeping in their homes without any worries or concerns about one of their friends hooked up to machines in a hospital, where Becky had hoped she would find someone who would take her in and keep her away from the evils of her home.

David's house was the closest to the interstate, and he nodded when Gary looked in the rearview mirror to see if he wanted to be dropped off there. No matter how bad things were at home or how uncomfortable he might feel there, he wanted to sleep at home tonight. The beers had worn off, so he was left with a dull headache and was feeling drained. Plus, he had to be at work in the morning.

Gary eased off the main road and stopped at the edge of David's driveway. He just pursed his lips as he looked at the boys in the car. Everybody was thinking the same thing, so they all just nodded. He opened the door and scooted his way out of the rear driver's side door, but when he went to shut it, he was met with resistance. Becky had put her foot out to stop the door from closing as she was also getting out of the car.

"What are you doing?" David asked, trying not to cause a scene but completely caught off guard by her actions.

"I'm not leaving you alone tonight," she said as she closed the door shut.

David just stood there, unsure of what to do. He looked at Gary, who managed to give a slight grin and nod of approval, and with that, he eased back out onto the road. David stood there for a few moments, trying to process everything. He had woken up this morning at Dusty's house, pitched the game of his life and beaten Fox Creek, caused a big fight in his family, gone out to celebrate with his friends, had an amazing night with the girl he had been fawning over, and found out one of his friends was seriously injured and may never recover, and now the girl of his dreams was standing outside his house in the early hours of the morning, claiming she wasn't leaving him alone for the night. He wanted to tell her that he didn't think it was a good idea for her to come inside, but he looked at her standing there with her hair now down. She had wittingly pushed him to greatness earlier in the day as a sign of love, and now she was backing up her earlier actions with her presence in a time of distress.

Even in the moonlight, the light green shirt made her features pop and contrasted her dark skin sharply. He thought of Ricky when he pictured what was under that sweatshirt that Becky was wearing to hide her secrets from the world. He couldn't tell her no, so he grabbed her hand and guided her up the driveway. She didn't want to go home as much as he didn't want to explain to his parents why she was there, and she had a much better reason than he did.

Making their way up the driveway, David was relieved that Mom wasn't working. He figured they would both be in bed, and he'd be able to get out of the house for work in the morning before they woke up. He quietly opened the front door and was relieved to hear no noise in the house when he entered. He poured a large cup of water and escorted Becky to his room, where she nervously sat at his desk by the window. He handed her the plastic cup, sat on his bed, and put his head in his hands.

Becky walked over, placing the cup on the stand next to his bed, and sat next to him. "I'm sorry about Ricky," she whispered in his ear.

David just shook his head, still looking down, as he quietly replied, "You know, I could barely stand the guy, but it's just messed up." He paused and allowed Becky to rub his back. Gaining some strength, he sat up a bit taller. "I've got to get away from this stuff, but if I join the Fox Creek summer team, all they're going to talk about is Ricky. They're going to assume I'm like him. They assume we're all the same."

Becky just continued rubbing his back as she leaned in closer to his ear to whisper, "We're not all the same. You'll show them." She gently kissed his cheek.

David turned to face her. He was physically and mentally drained, but he hadn't noticed how much she was too. He gave her a hug and put his arms on her shoulders as he looked at her. "Thank you for everything, Becky." She tried to talk, but he wouldn't let her. "I don't care what happened. This is still one of the best nights of my life. I definitely won't forget it, that's for sure." He kissed her forehead and pulled her close.

After a few seconds, she pulled back, and she placed one hand on his cheek as she looked at him somewhat embarrassed. "Would you mind holding me for a while?" She almost sounded unsure if she wanted to ask and guilty for saying it out loud. "I really just need to be held by someone I trust."

"I'll do anything for you, Becky Reeves," he said as he pulled back the sheets. They both tossed their shoes and clothes to the floor and slid under the covers together. "No more games."

"No more games," Becky lightly replied as she lay on her side with her back to him. They were both asleep within minutes, too exhausted to even think about the day gone by and what tomorrow might bring or the fact they had woken up that morning with an awkwardness between them and that now they were asleep in each other's arms.

The next morning came soon enough as David's alarm blared for him to get out of bed for work. For a brief moment, he thought everything might have been a dream, but he felt a slight movement next to him and then Becky's warm body turning to embrace his. "What time is it?" she whispered with her eyes still closed.

"Time for me to go to work," he replied, rubbing his eyes and rolling out of bed. "If we get out of here now, my parents will never know you were here."

"I thought they didn't care about you," she said with a joking tone as she was waking up a bit.

"I'm sure my mom will kill me, but it was worth it," he groggily replied.

She smiled at David and gave him a kiss on his cheek as she rose out of bed to put her clothes back on. David was mesmerized by her body and beauty, even as she awoke in the morning. He looked at the marks on her chest and stomach as she put her top back on. He somehow hadn't noticed the bruises on her arms the night before, but somehow he didn't feel as upset. He felt like things would be okay.

He smiled back at her as he cracked the door and told her to stay put. "I'm going to brush my teeth really quickly. If the coast is clear, when I'm finished, I can give you a new toothbrush and get you in the bathroom when I'm finished."

She nodded and sat down at his desk, adjusting the blinds to let a little more of the sunrise shine through. She sat at his desk and looked at some of the pictures he framed along the window ledge. She was drawn to one in particular of a young David smiling in a baseball uniform with a man she didn't recognize.

"That's my grandpa," David said, surprising her as he sat back down on his bed with a new toothbrush in his hand.

"He looks so young," Becky replied while still examining the photo.

"I was seven or so when that was taken. My mom was just shy of seventeen when she had me, so he's not your typical grandpa," David continued with a sense of pride.

Becky thought about David's mom having him at that age, the exact age as she was now, after she had just spent the night in a boy's bed for the first time. She suddenly felt cold and a bit anxious, but she looked over at David, who seemed to be feeling the same uneasiness. "Thanks for the toothbrush," she said with a fake smile meant for a photograph. "Everything clear?"

"Yeah, but don't take too long," he said, looking at his clock. While Becky was tidying up in the bathroom, he quickly got dressed for work.

He thought about her and how nice it was having her in his house. He felt even better when she came back flashing that same smile.

"Ready to go?" he said, extending his hand. She gladly accepted, and they began making the fifteen-minute walk to Jay's convenience store.

Along the way, they talked about Ricky and about their time together last night. Becky convinced David that he was stupid to wait so long to talk to her, and he convinced her that he had just been waiting for her to make the first move. They talked about how they knew each other for so many years but how they couldn't wait to keep getting to know each other now. They promised to be there for each other and to help each other move forward from whatever issues or pain their family might cause. David couldn't help but think about Becky's stepfather and the things he did to her and when he might do it again, but Becky decided to end the conversation on a bit of a lighter note. They reached the back of Jay's, and David stood there dangling the key to open the door. Neither wanted to leave, but they both knew they had to.

"So you going to talk to the Fox Creek coach today?" Becky asked with a wink.

David looked a bit puzzled as he blinked his eyes to jar his memory.

"You know, about joining the team."

David hesitated. It was the immediate reality that he wasn't quite sure how to handle. "I'm not sure. With Ricky being in the hospital and—"

"Hey, no more games," Becky interrupted before he could give any more excuses. "Don't let Ricky's situation, my situation, or any situation keep you from following your dreams. You understand that?"

David looked at her, a bit breathless and awed. She was the voice he needed; she was his strength. "Uh . . . yeah. I'll call my grandpa this afternoon and talk to him about it," he said while trying not to seem too subservient.

"Okay, good," she said as she bounced one time on her toes. "After you talk to him, make sure you call the coach. And after you talk to him, make sure you call me." She walked into his space and gave him a quick kiss on the lips.

"Yes, ma'am," he said, giving her a fake salute. She just turned, smiled over her shoulder, and began walking home.

That day at worked felt like an eternity. David's mind was racing, and he wanted to be anywhere but there. The faster he tried to get things done, the more mistakes he made along the way. He was tired, and his nerves were shot. At various times, everyone from the baseball group checked in to give updates on Ricky, which really weren't updates. They were just reporting that he still hadn't talked or opened his eyes but that his mom was really glad people were stopping by. Dusty stopped in to let him know that his dad would take them over when he got off work, but he said they couldn't stay too long because he had to work in the kitchen that night. David didn't mind, though, especially if Ricky wasn't responding. He had a list of people to talk to and things to do after work anyways.

The boys did make it to the hospital, but just like everyone else had said, Ricky wasn't responding, and there wasn't much to report. They couldn't even see him, so they just spent a few moments with his mom, who was very grateful. David got home just as his mom was leaving for work. She gave him a big hug and told him that they had a lot to talk about. He figured it must have been regarding Becky spending the night, but when he walked in, he noticed a number of things were missing, most importantly his father.

David called up his grandpa to tell him about the baseball news, but he had somehow already found out. However, he wanted David to give the entire recap anyways and relished in every detail, often asking him to be more specific about certain situations. When David asked if he could help him out with getting to and from practices and events with the Fox Creek team, his grandpa practically jumped through the phone with excitement. "I was nervous you weren't going to accept that offer, David," he said with excitement and concern. "But I sense that things are changing with you a bit." He hesitated a bit before adding the next part. "And your mom."

David subsequently hesitated a bit and now thought about what must have happened with his mom and his dad. He didn't necessarily care where his dad was, but he wondered where he was. "Yeah, things are changing a bit, Grandpa," David started. "But they're changing for the better."

David's grandpa chuckled on the other end of the line. His grandpa told him about what had happened between his parents, how his mom put her foot down about how he had acted toward David, among many other things. He said that it was the first time David's mother had acted like the girl he raised in sixteen years. He was full of excitement and hope when he talked about David and his mom. He said that David's father was going to be living with a coworker for a few weeks while they would try to salvage their relationship.

He bounced with joy when David told him about Becky, but he told him to stay focused on baseball and his future, no doubt thinking about how his daughter's life had gotten sidetracked by a high school romance. David assured him that he would and told him he had to go and call the Fox Creek coach. David couldn't tell who was more anxious, himself or Coach Bell, when he called. They worked out the details, and he told David when the next practice was.

When David hung up the phone, he felt like he was on top of the world. He wanted to call Becky right away, but he chose to do another quick inventory of the house. Indeed, a lot of his father's essentials and favorite things had been packed up and were absent. David thought about Ricky for a minute, but he knew Ricky was a fighter and that he'd find a way to pull through. Nothing could bring him down, at least nothing until he called Becky, and she was crying.

"Whoa, hey, calm down," David tried everything to get Becky to stop crying and explain to him why she was so upset. His initial reaction was that it was her stepfather and that he had tried to assault her again. The longer she couldn't get herself under control, the more David felt the rage growing inside him.

"Is it your stepfather?" he demanded to know.

"No, it's my mom," she said, trying to control herself long enough to get the words out. "Please come meet me on the merry-go-round, David."

Even though he was tired, there was no hesitation in his agreement. He told her that he was getting on his bike and would be there in a few minutes. Pedaling down to the school, he tried to imagine what her mother had done that could have upset her so badly. David didn't know her all that well, but she seemed generally quiet and nonconfrontational. Her biggest flaw seemed to be her attraction to men who liked to drink. He also thought about Becky, who up until last night seemed like one of the strongest people he'd ever seen, but now she suddenly was an avalanche of emotions that he wasn't sure he was equipped to handle.

When he got to the park, the sun had only a few more minutes left before completely dropping below the skyline. It was the perfect time of day that made her dark skin look perfect and accentuated her blue eyes, but those eyes were still filled with tears as David dropped his bike and trotted over to sit next to her. He didn't say anything as he sat down and put his left arm around her. It was the exact same position they had been in a little less than twenty-four hours ago when they exchanged their first kiss. She looked up at him with tear-filled eyes and nearly squeezed the life out of him as she wrapped her arms around him. David had no idea that someone so petite had so much physical strength in her. David wanted her to start talking, but she just sat there and cried, so he eventually broke the ice.

Looking over at her house that had no life coming from inside, he asked, "So what did your mom do?"

Becky tried to slow down her breathing a bit as she grabbed at David's T-shirt. She had her head buried on his shoulder and didn't raise it as she confessed that her mom had agreed to start working the third shift. It would provide more money for the family and was an opportunity for her to move up at work. In the ideal work, it sounded like a big benefit for a lower-middle-class family, but David knew exactly why this was so upsetting for Becky.

As he was starting to put the pieces together in his head, Becky spoke up and filled in the details. "She's going to leave me alone in that house with him five days a week, David," she began, trying to be strong but sounding more desperate and hopeless with each word. "How am I going to survive? I could deal with him when my mom worked second shift. I'd tell him that she'd be home soon or mentioned that she might be getting off early, and that would usually get him to go away and leave me alone. Or when he did come at me, I could look at my clock and know that it would be over soon. But now she's going to be gone all night." She started crying openly again.

"Can you talk to her about this?" David asked innocently.

Becky pulled back a bit and sniped, "I've been talking to her about him for the past six months, and she just ignores me."

She was growing a bit steadier and angrier. "I'm going to run away, David," she said with conviction. David looked at her and was worried when she didn't flinch. "Nobody in this town believes me or will help me, so I'm getting out of here."

David couldn't help but feel a bit sorry for himself. "But I'm here. I don't want to be here without you, not after last night."

His words jarred Becky a bit and brought her back to him. "Aww, David, I don't want to be here without you either, but how am I going to handle this? He didn't come at me very often because he knew my mom would be around, but now that she's going to be gone, he'll just get plowed every night, and I'm afraid he'll come at me every night."

David didn't have an answer, and the thought of Becky's words turning into reality made him sick, so he blurted out the first thing he could think of that might comfort her. "Well, maybe you could move in with me?"

She jerked her head up and looked at him as if he had three heads.

David thought for a second how ridiculous his solution sounded, so he decided to give it some context. "I didn't mean with me but in my house. Apparently, my mom and dad split. I'm sure she's going to be a bit lonely, and we've got another bedroom. Plus, she'd love having another girl around the house." It was ridiculous, and they both knew it, but it was also genuine and sweet.

Becky appreciated the offer, and while it didn't fix her problem, it confirmed that David did feel deeply for her and cared about her. She seemed comforted by this and suddenly felt bad for focusing all the attention on herself. She asked David how his day was, and she was pleased to hear everything went really well. She was happy that his dad was gone and that his grandpa was going to step in and make his baseball goals come to life. Despite the fact that her world felt like it was crumbling, she believed she had something special in her arms.

Just like the night before, they sat and talked for hours on that merry-go-round. They never seemed to run out of things to talk about. It felt like they were best friends who had suddenly realized the connection and spark between them. She was glad to finally have a friend to talk to, and he was shocked by how much he had to say. They ended the night with a moonlit kiss and a reaffirmed promise to always be there for each other. Becky felt somewhat encouraged she could endure whatever was to happen at her house if she had David on her side.

The next day was a big one for David. When he finished up with work, he had his first workout with the Fox Creek Legion team. They were playing a doubleheader on Saturday, but David wouldn't be able to play due to some weird rostering rules. Coach Bell said it was fine as the bigger games and events didn't start until the following weekend. He just wanted David to get a feel for how they did things and get to know some of the guys. That was what made David the most nervous.

His grandpa dropped him off at practice and told him he'd be back in a couple of hours. The Fox Creek field was nicer than any other field he'd been on before. He had played there before as a visitor, but now this was sort of like his home field. As a visitor, he didn't feel bad about walking on the grass or dropping his bag haphazardly in the dugout, but now that this was *his* field, he didn't want to do anything to screw it up. Everything looked so pristine and manicured; it was vastly different from what he was used to at the elementary school field. Also, despite pitching extremely well against them two days earlier, David was suddenly scared about how much bigger everyone was than him. The requirements were that you were under eighteen years old by the beginning of summer, and some of these guys looked like the last time they were under eighteen was three summers ago. David still hadn't turned sixteen. Despite the fact that he was growing and physically maturing, he was still smaller than most of these guys.

Coach Bell made sure to come over, greet him, and introduce him to the team. He joked that they all knew he could pitch but that he wanted to work David into the outfield a bit as well and give him some reps. He told the outfielders what drills they were going to be doing and said they'd finish up with batting practice. While David was excited to be given an opportunity to play in the outfield, this meant he'd be spending time with the instigator from Jay's. He was just as cocky now as he was that day. It turned out his name was Dawson Kemp, which David thought was the perfect name for a jerk from Fox Creek.

Ryan sensed that David was a little uneasy, so he tapped him on his back. "You all right, David?" He smiled at him, and David nodded back. Ryan looked like the rest of the Fox Creek kids, but he was different, and David appreciated that. "Come on, let's go," he said, motioning to the field. "No walking on this team." David liked that approach and jogged to the outfield as Ryan joined the others on the infield.

The outfield drills and most of practice went well. In fact, David was starting to feel at home. He enjoyed the structure and focus of the practice. He also enjoyed being on the field with his peers in terms of talent. It wasn't a disrespect to his friends in Riverview, but he knew this was how baseball was supposed to be practiced and played. As drill work ended and batting practice began, he was thinking more and more about how impressed some of his friends would be with everything, and then he started overhearing some of the outfield conversations between the Fox Creek guys during batting practice.

"Did you hear about that toothy kid from Riverview getting the shit kicked out of him? Prick probably deserved it." It was Dawson speaking to a couple of other kids.

"I heard he's laid up pretty bad in the hospital," the kid replied, trying to be respectful.

"Well, he's just lucky it wasn't me, or he wouldn't be in the hospital," Dawson replied while laughing. One of the other kids was laughing with him.

"They were probably fighting over that little whore from Riverview," he continued. "What's her name again? Bridget? Bailey?"

"Becky," one guy stepped in to correct him.

"Yeah, Becky." Dawson nodded while smirking. "That girl has probably slept with half the freaking metro area." They all laughed together. "Who hasn't been with her?" They all laughed again. "But damn, she is one fine piece of ass, even if she is from Riverview," he concluded.

David was standing about forty feet away but overheard everything. When they looked over at him, they tried not to laugh when they saw his scowl, but they couldn't hold it in. Dawson was the worst and continued on, "Well, apparently, we've got the one guy from Riverview on our team she hasn't slept with." They all erupted again.

David couldn't take it anymore. He dropped his glove and was going to put Dawson in the hospital bed next to Ricky when Coach Bell called out his name to come in and hit. David froze about halfway between where he had stared and Dawson. He gave him a glare and then retreated to get his glove and go hit. However, when he got to the dugout, he froze. He could feel the tears in his eyes and the rage in his heart. Even though he knew Ricky had done things to get in trouble and he wasn't his best friend, he didn't like the idea of him being the butt of jokes for Fox Creek kids. Moreover, he struggled hearing how they talked about Becky. Were they right? Had she been with most guys in the area? Had she been lying to him? He didn't care. He knew this wasn't a good fit for him, so David grabbed his stuff, left the dugout, and then left the field.

Coach Bell just kind of threw his arms up, but Ryan, who was standing at shortstop, turned and looked out in the outfield. He saw Dawson and his friends laughing toward David, who was making his way to the parking lot. Ryan sprinted over to David to try to keep him from walking away. Coach Bell just called out another name. "Hey, why are you leaving?" Ryan said as he grabbed David's arm to stop him so he could position himself in front of his face.

"Just leave me alone, asshole!" David barked back at him.

"Asshole? What did I say?" Ryan demanded to know. David just pushed past him and continued to try to walk away, but Ryan grabbed him again. "What did they say?"

David stopped and figured Ryan deserved an answer. He had always been a stand-up guy to him, and David trusted him. "They were making fun of Ricky, and they were talking about how Becky had been with everyone in the area, and they were just making fun of Riverview in general," David confessed. After he said it, he felt a little strange confessing how he cared about his hometown so much. He'd been thinking about ways to get out, and now that he was, he found himself defending it.

"Look, I know it's not easy," Ryan started. "But you've got to try to ignore Dawson. His parents are going through a really messy divorce, and he's just taking things out on people lately."

David seemed puzzled that anyone from Fox Creek had problems.

Ryan continued, "His dad ran off with some other woman, so he's been going around, blaming every girl for his problems. It's his way of dealing with things. Doesn't mean he's right, but we've all got problems, right?" Ryan tapped David on his outer thigh with his glove.

David reluctantly nodded. "Yeah, I guess."

Ryan seemed a bit more relaxed as he figured David was starting to come down a bit. "I'm really sorry about your friend Ricky. I don't know what happened, but nobody our age deserves to be in a hospital bed." Again, Ryan sounded sincere, and David was comforted by his words.

Sensing that he could steer David back to the field but not wanting to push him, Ryan suggested, "Why don't you come back and just take some ground balls next to me? I'll talk to Dawson after practice."

David had no reason not to trust Ryan, and he started to think about what his grandpa would say when he would have to explain why he quit the team, so he agreed. David felt at home with Ryan as they talked about different things. He learned that life in Fox Creek wasn't entirely different from Riverview for a lot of kids. They all had problems at home and friends who annoyed them at times. He finished out practice and even took the last round of batting practice from Coach Bell, who said he was glad that he stuck around and would address the issue earlier in private. All in all, David performed really well at practice; but as he made his way back toward his grandpa's car, one thought started to consume his mind. Was what they had said about Becky true?

In the short car ride to Riverview, David's grandpa demanded to know every detail like he always did. David obliged but left out the part about him temporarily walking out of practice. Satisfied and proud, his grandpa asked David if he wanted to stop by the Dairy Barn for ice cream. Since it was Friday night, he knew it would be packed, but David didn't mind. He needed to clear his head a bit.

When they pulled into the parking lot, they saw the enormous amount of people to be expected on a Friday summer night. David's grandpa somehow managed to find a good parking spot, away from where all the younger people from Riverview did their socializing. David did a quick scan but knew he wouldn't find his friends there as they had all planned to go to the hospital to visit Ricky. Apparently, he was improving during the day, and they were hoping he might be talking a bit by tonight.

As they walked around the front of the building, a large group of Fox Creek kids turned the corner, nearly knocking David over. He wouldn't have really cared much until he saw Becky trailing them to the parking lot with a couple of more guys from Fox Creek. She was stunned to see him and could tell by the look on his face that he was upset. She stopped to talk to him despite the urging of the guys she was with to leave.

"David," she began, trying to make eye contact with him, but he wasn't having any of it. She tried again, but he kept turning to avoid her.

Ready for ice cream and confused by David's demeanor, his grandpa managed to get his arm around David as he saw Becky struggling to get his full attention. "Why, this wouldn't be Becky, would it?" he asked, shaking David a bit to show how proud he was of him. David didn't move, so his grandpa knew he had correctly identified her. "She's every bit as good looking as you described to me." He extended his hand toward her. She was flattered but concerned about David. "Henry Alberts."

"Becky Reeves," she nervously replied, trying to be polite and grant him eye contact while staying focused on David.

"Becky, it's a pleasure to meet you," David's grandpa replied. "I can see you've got some ice cream already, but, David, why don't I get in line and get ours and leave you alone to talk with your gal?" Normally, David would have jumped at the opportunity to talk to a girl like Becky and ditch his grandpa, but now it was the last thing he wanted to do. His grandpa didn't give him a chance, though, as he shoved David toward Becky and made his way to the back of the long line.

Becky could see that David was clearly hurt and troubled but wasn't quite sure where to begin. "Hey" was all she could muster. She got the same reply back. "Can we find a bench and talk for a second?"

"Wouldn't you rather hang with your friends?" David snapped back sarcastically as they sat atop the first open picnic bench they could find. He could see the Fox Creek group sitting at their cars, looking at Becky.

"They're not my friends, and I'd rather hang out with you," she said, trying to make him smile.

"Could have fooled me," David replied coldly.

"What do you mean?" she asked sincerely. "You know I'll do anything to get out of the house when my mom is working and my stepdad is home. They called and asked if I wanted to come up here, so I said I'd join them."

Her story seemed truthful, and David knew it, but he couldn't forget what Dawson had said about her at practice. "You just don't know what I've been through tonight, Becky," David implored, wanting her to know what he was thinking without making him say it.

She looked at him intently and with worry. "Did things not go well?" she said with concern as she touched his shoulder.

"Things went fine," he angrily said back. "Well, at least the baseball was fine."

"So what else happened then?" she asked, not suspecting anything.

He turned to look at her, and he could still see and hear Dawson perfectly in his mind. "They were making fun of you. They were making fun of Ricky. They were making fun of this entire town," David let out. It made him mad, but it also made him feel good to get it out. He knew that she would be concerned about everything, but it is human nature to ask about yourself first.

"Oh yeah," she said, dropping her head. "What were they saying about me?"

David thought back to their conversation the other night and how people had spread lies about her. Seeing her next to him and knowing what she had been through and what she was going through, he suddenly knew he couldn't tell her the truth. He cared about her too much. He heard Dusty's voice, reminding him to think about people other than himself as he said, "They were talking about how pretty you are, and it just made me really jealous. Then when I saw you with a group of other people, I didn't think I was good enough for you."

"Oh, David," she said, covering her mouth as her lips tightened. "That is so unbelievably sweet of you, but you are more than enough for me." She leaned in to give him a hug.

David felt relieved and comforted by Becky's embrace. He felt even better when the cars of Fox Creek kids left without her. He was glad he hadn't broken her heart and even happier that she hadn't broken his. They sat atop the picnic table, and just like David's grandpa, she wanted details about the entire practice. He liked that she was similar to her grandpa in that way, so he obliged and filled her in. His grandpa was even happier to join them and get all the details again, this time with a large ice cream cone in his hand. The three of them sat there for a while, talking about things. David enjoyed how well she and her grandpa got along; it was like they had known each other for a long time.

As the night wore on, David's grandpa reminded the kids that he still had a decent drive home. He asked Becky if she wanted a ride home.

She looked at her watch and then nodded. David knew that after nine thirty, she would be safe from her stepdad as her mom would be home soon. They held hands as she sat between him and his grandpa in the front seat of his 1990 Pontiac Bonneville.

While they had only been together as a couple for a few days, David felt like he and Becky were quickly developing a deep and significant relationship, the kind of relationship that moves like lightning when two old acquaintances realize that they are perfect for each other. He gave her hand a squeeze as he thought about how his first practice with Fox Creek seemed to go well, and he believed that Ryan would handle things with Dawson. He was sad and worried when they dropped Becky off, but her amazing smile and carefree stroll down her driveway made him feel really good when his grandpa dropped him off in his own driveway, but that would quickly change when he walked inside his house.

15 CHAPTER

David was in a good mood and spirits as he waved goodbye to his grandfather. They both had been in such a good mood that neither one seemed to notice that the light in his bedroom was on above the garage. Both garage doors were closed, so David thought that maybe he had forgotten to turn it off when he left for practice, but he didn't remember turning it on. He could hear the music coming from the bar where his mom worked and thought that maybe she decided to not go in. She had put in her notice and told them that she planned to focus on her schooling while finding a job more suitable to her schedule, but David thought that maybe she didn't want to endure another Friday night of being hollered at and grabbed on by locals.

When he reached the porch, he tried to look through the blinds for any movement in his room or the house, but all he could see was the outline of his desk and the shadows in the kitchen. He felt more at ease that he must have accidentally left his light on as he opened the door and sensed no movement. Feeling relaxed, he closed the door behind him and turned right to head to his room.

Pushing his door open, he almost simultaneously jumped as he saw a body lying in his bed. It was his father, lying on his back with his hands laced around the back of his head. He was smiling as David entered into his eyesight. When David froze in the doorway, he held out his arm and invited him in. David looked down the hallway to see if his mom was in her room, but the rest of the house was dark.

"What are you doing here?" David demanded before moving into his room.

David's father didn't flinch as he said, "Sit down, and I'll tell you." David studied his dad's face. In sixteen years, he hadn't once asked to talk to David; now here he was, sitting in his room on a Friday night, waiting for him to come home to a house that he technically didn't even live in anymore. His dad had always been hard to read, but David had no idea what to expect as he worked his way to the chair at his desk.

"I just wanted to say I'm sorry," David's dad began with contrite. David was not expecting to hear those words, so he raised his eyebrows and leaned forward in his chair.

David's father continued to lie on the bed, staring at the ceiling as he continued, "I've been a horrible father to you. I know it. You have called me on it, and your mom has called me on it. I don't know what's wrong with me. I shouldn't have said those things the other day about you and your friends. More importantly, I shouldn't have said those things about girls and your mom."

David shook his head with his lips tightening. It sounded like this was a scripted apology that he was trying out to try to win David's mom back, and he wasn't buying it. A rush of spite filled David as he said, "I don't believe you."

His father sat up and looked at David. He was trying to repeat himself and be genuine, but David couldn't just forgive him like that, so he sternly interrupted his father, "If mom hadn't kicked you out, you wouldn't be here apologizing to me. You've had sixteen years to say that you're sorry, and you couldn't do it once. Instead, you just tried to shut me up with stupid gifts." David turned to his closet, trying to find something to use to prove his point, but nothing readily flashed before him.

His father sensed that David wasn't going to accept his apology easily or at all, so he thought he could appeal to his ego a little bit. "You know, I ran into Randy Black yesterday, and he told me about how you dominated the guys from Fox Creek. He said he thought you had a chance to possibly make it as far as he did." His father nodded and sounded excited, but David was disgusted. Instead of complimenting or believing David himself, he trusted a washout drunk like Randy Black.

David didn't hold back when he responded to his father's feeble attempt to give him a compliment. "So you believe Randy Black, but you couldn't come watch me yourself? You even took the night off, but neither you or mom could come down?"

"But it was just a scrimmage. I didn't think it was a real game," David's dad said, trying to defend himself. "If I had known—"

"If you had known, you would have found an excuse not to be there," David stopped him before he could continue. "Other parents showed up. They were there cheering their kids on, but it was just me by myself as usual. Parents shouldn't have to be told when something is important to one of their kids. They should know. Besides, you would have just wanted to see me fail. You want to hold me back, but I'm not going to let you." He was mad but felt like he had gotten the upper hand.

"I guess Mom decided that she wasn't going to let you boss her around anymore either, huh?" David said as a smile ran across his face.

David's dad started to say something but cupped his hands together as a sign of surrender. Like so many other times in David's life, he didn't know what to say; and unfortunately, he had waited until David was old enough to stand his own ground to start trying to mend bridges. Dejected, he got up and walked to the living room. He grabbed a bag that he had packed and headed for the door. When he grabbed the knob, he turned back and looked at David with the hint of tears forming in his eyes. "Maybe you're right, David. I should have known how important that game was to you, and I know I shouldn't have said those things." He looked at his son, who had grown into a young man. He looked him up and down and took a long pause before he smiled and stated, "You come about a lot of things honestly, David. Take those good traits and develop them and do your best to push past the bad ones."

David just looked down at the floor.

"And, David." He paused to wait for him to bring his head back up. "For what it's worth, I really am sorry—for everything." With that, his dad walked out the door and left David home alone, like he had been many times before; but this time, the house seemed emptier than it ever had. David didn't feel like a prisoner anymore, but if this was the price of freedom, he wasn't sure he could handle that either.

He sat in his room the rest of the night, pacing, replaying the conversation with his dad over and over in his head. Despite all that his dad had done to frustrate him over the years, David couldn't help but feel a little sorry for him. He looked at the clock and wondered where he was at the moment. The professional team was out on the West Coast, but David was having trouble focusing on the game that was playing on his radio.

He started to feel himself falling asleep when he heard the front door open. Panicked, he got to his feet and looked at his radio clock. It was too early for his mom to be home, so he thought that his dad had come back. Before he could make his way to his door, it began to open slowly. "Hey, David, you still awake?" his mom whispered as she opened the door wider. He felt immensely relieved, but he was confused why his mom was home before midnight.

Looking at his face, she knew she needed to give David the reason for her surprise appearance. "Slow night, and apparently, when you turn in your resignation papers, you're the first waitress cut." She smiled and sat down next to David. She studied him for a second and could see that he was a bit troubled. "So your dad stopped by?"

David couldn't believe that she knew. He looked her up and down before predictably responding, "How'd you know?"

She rubbed his back and said, "He came in right after you told him off. He told me all about it."

"Oh," David replied, trying to gauge her reaction.

"Yeah . . . oh," she said as she raised her eyebrows at him. She was wearing a tight black top and tight jeans. She smelled like a well-blended combination of cheap perfume and cigarette smoke.

"I guess we both had coming what you told us the past few days," she said, slapping her legs as she got up to pace the room a bit. "But you don't need to fight my battles for me too."

David followed her with his eyes, trying to figure out if she was going to continue or if he needed to defend his actions, but she continued, "You know, he really was sorry. We're both really sorry about how things turned out between the three of us. Maybe one day you'll get there too." he paused and looked at a picture of her parents on David's desk. "But hopefully not. I just want you to know that your dad moving out is our way of trying to make things right again. We needed a fresh start."

She sat down next to him again, and putting her hand on his leg, she told him, "You may not think we deserve another chance, but we'd like it if you would give us one."

"Mom," he began, but she raised her hand off his leg and put it back down, telling him she wasn't quite done.

"David, can I ask you about Becky?" she said very slowly.

David squinted and pulled back a bit. He wasn't sure why her name was coming up now.

She started off slowly again, careful not to trigger an emotional reaction. "I want to talk to you about Becky. I think it's great that you have someone that you're interested in and someone that is interested in you. However, I'm concerned with how you've been acting the last few days ever since you started up with her."

David was a bit relieved that she didn't bring up Becky spending the night, but he felt his pulse rising as she continued, "It seems that since you've started hanging around her a bit more, you've become more assertive and trying to push us away." As she finished saying this, David literally pushed his mom's hand off his leg, but she was determined to finish. "It's just that I know how strong emotions can be at your age. They can make you say and do things that you'll regret, things that can damage relationships. I was the same way when I first started dating your dad. I knew everything, so I tried telling my parents what they didn't know. Next thing I know, I'm on my own, and my parents will barely see or talk to me. I don't want that to happen to you."

David's pulse was now like a kick drum on overdrive. He could feel himself physically getting hotter as she talked. Somehow Becky was being blamed for him finally speaking up for himself. Her guiding hand had somehow unraveled a family in a matter of days? He was pushing them away? When had they ever welcomed him in to begin with? Worst of all, David's mom was accusing him of making the same mistakes that she had. He wanted to burst out and tell her the same things he had told his dad, but he caught himself. He didn't want Becky getting blamed for his outburst, and furthermore, he didn't want to alienate both parents in the same night. He also remembered what Dusty said about putting others' emotions and thoughts first. He tried to picture his grandpa having a similar conversation with his mom. Even though he couldn't imagine going down the road she did, her past had shaped her response. After taking a few deep, heaving breaths, David looked at his mom and said, "Thanks, Mom."

She smiled and rubbed his back. She asked if he wanted anything before bed, but he told her he was fine and just about asleep when she got home. Just before she exited and turned off his bedroom light, David did have one request from his mom. "Mom, I want you to meet Becky. Grandpa met her tonight, and it went really well. I think you'll really like her."

The last thing David saw was her smile as she turned off the light. "Sure thing, sweetheart. I believe you." The way she said it, David believed that she was being honest. He fell asleep almost instantaneously, exhausted from the past few days.

The next morning, his mom was the first thing he saw. She was sitting on his bed, gently trying to wake him. When he opened his eyes, he could see that the sun was already up as his mom had opened his blinds. He tried to put his pillow over his face, but she told him that he needed to get up because he had company. For a split second, he panicked and thought that Becky had come over unexpectedly or that his mom had arranged for her to visit; but when he sat up, he saw Dusty standing behind his mom. He didn't greet him with "good morning" but instead with "Ricky's awake and talking!" David didn't need more than five minutes to get cleaned up and out the door.

Gary and Joey were waiting in his car in the driveway. David rushed out with Dusty but promised he'd be home with his mom to talk more about things this afternoon. The boys jumped in, and they were off to go see Ricky downtown. All the boys were excited in their own way. Gary was talking about the things they were going to do with Ricky when he got out of the hospital. Joey just agreed and seconded everything that Gary said. Dusty vowed that he was going to kick Ricky's ass as soon as his ass was healthy enough to kick again. David just took it all in.

When they got to the hospital, Ricky's mom met them by the elevator on his floor. She was happy to see the boys, but days of stress had worn her already thin, somewhat gaunt body. She was a chain-smoker and looked the part. She was small boned and aged beyond her years. It was easy to see why Ricky was so wiry and cantankerous with people. She told him that all he kept asking for was to see them.

Excitedly but with a lot of anxiety, they made their way down the hallway and into his hospital room. His entire face was discolored and swollen to the point that it was hard to recognize him, but when he heard their voices, he cracked a small smile that was unmistakably his despite the fact that it was wired shut. The boys sat and talked quietly. They were a bit overwhelmed by Ricky's appearance, but the doctors assured them it looked like he was going to make a full recovery over time, but it would still be a while before he would be able to leave the hospital because they wanted to make sure all the internal bleeding had stopped.

They visited for about forty-five minutes, and they mainly just answered his questions about what had been going on the last few days. Ricky seemed to be most tickled and interested in David's life. He was genuinely excited about he and Becky getting together, and he was happy that things went well with his first practice. David thought about Dawson laughing about Ricky for a second and wished he was there now to see if he thought it was funny. David didn't bring any of that up, though, because he didn't want anyone's temperature rising. Ricky spoke mainly in slurred whispers, so the boys had to listen intently and quietly. Nobody brought up revenge, though, as they knew this was something that Ricky had brought onto himself.

Leaving the hospital, none of the boys felt like talking much. They had seen their friend, but that wasn't their friend. They all kind of wanted to process things in their own way after their visit, so they agreed that they would all go home but meet up at seven at the church festival off main street.

David was a bit relieved when he was dropped off at home. Surprisingly, he found himself wanting to talk to his mom. He called out for her as he entered the house but realized she was outside in her garden. He poured her a tall glass of ice tea and brought it out to her. She thanked him and asked what was on his mind.

David hesitated for a few moments. He wasn't sure how or where to begin with Ricky. She knew who he was, but like most of his friends, she really didn't know him. "I'm just a little off, I guess. Seeing Ricky was a little bit tougher than I realized, than we all realized."

She had resumed her work in the garden but stopped to look at him. She was trying to see if he was okay without having to ask.

"I just didn't think it would be that bad."

"I'm sorry, sweetheart," she said as she arched her back to stretch. "Unfortunately, we all have to deal with the consequences of our choices."

David didn't particularly care for her tone, but he figured she was talking as much about herself and their relationship as she was about Ricky. He tried to remain patient while feeding into her comment. "I guess so, but I don't know if he deserved that. We'll probably never know exactly what he did, but I definitely know he's no saint." He paused to gather himself a bit. He had a number of things on his mind, but right now, he was thinking about his mom and his family with his next question. "Do you think people can change, Mom?" She looked at him with a puzzled look, so he clarified for her. "I mean, do you think people can change and be better?"

She weighed his question for a few seconds as she took another gulp of tea. She knew this was a sensitive question, and she wanted to answer respectfully. "Well, I can tell you that change isn't easy. I don't know if I know anybody who just changed on their own before something bad happened, but I do think people can change for good or for bad." Seeing David nodding she went further. "I'm changing to give myself a better future. I'm going to school to try to be a nurse or substance counselor. I'm trying to change to be a better mom and daughter, but like I said, it usually doesn't happen without something bad happening."

David knew she was talking about his father. He knew that, despite the fighting, there was love between them. He had been there on their drunken nights when things were good, so he knew there was still love and passion between them. "Maybe you're right," he started while twisting his mouth a bit. "I mean, I hope you're right. I've always wanted to leave here, but lately, I've been thinking that maybe I can change some things here."

She smiled at him with her hands still on her hips.

"I guess I grew up thinking that people couldn't change and I didn't fit it, so I should just leave here as soon as I got the chance, but recently, I've been thinking that maybe they can change. Maybe even I can help make some of those changes."

She was a bit puzzled with where he was going, but she was pleased that he wasn't acting the way she had heard about when his father came to visit last night. "One thing I know about you and me," she said with conviction, "is that we can do whatever we put our minds to. We get that from your grandpa."

They both smiled at each other and sat there talking to each other a while longer. Slowly but surely, they were getting to know and understand each other. David told her how proud he was that she was going back to school and quitting her bartending and waitressing work in the local bars. She talked about how nervous she was to start school and how she wasn't looking forward to starting work at Jay's either, but she was thankful for her father and the flexible hours in a stable environment. They both talked about how it would be nice to see each other more often, even if things were going to get tight financially for a while.

They talked about Becky and some of David's other friends. It was the first time in a long time his mom had taken a real interest in him and his life. She wasn't rushing out the door or preoccupied with his father. It made David feel good, and the longer they talked, the more he could see his grandpa in her. He told her that he was going to the church picnic tonight with Becky and the boys. She was excited for him and embarrassed him with some dating tips. He was sad when she had to start getting ready for work, but he was also glad this was the last Saturday she was going to be working until the early hours of the morning. David sat inside and watched the baseball game on TV after his mom left and before it was time to go and meet Becky and his friends. He hadn't felt that relaxed in a while.

The church picnic in town was a huge deal every year at the end of June. Riverview didn't have many churches, and most people would not bother to call themselves religious by any stretch of the imagination, but the nondenominational church served as a de facto community center for a lot of things. The church sat back off the main road and had a couple of acres of parking lot and grass fields that were easily converted into a large gathering place for the community. Each year on the last weekend in June, it served as an entertainment center. The church paid for carnival rides and booths and set up a large beer and gambling tent that featured live music after nine. There was every sort of carnival food imaginable, and just about everyone in town attended. Even people from neighboring areas would come for the entertainment and fun. The best part for David was that the church was off main street on his way into the center of town, not more than a couple of minutes' walk from his house. Even though the city skyline was in clear view, no kid wanted to be anywhere else on those summer nights.

David arrived a bit early and began sifting through the crowd, looking for Becky and his friends. He saw her first from a distance. She was standing by the Ferris wheel. Her brown hair was up to show her neck and collarbones in a low-cut light shirt. She sparkled in David's eyes as he stood still and enjoyed watching her seek him out. Eventually, when she spotted him, she flashed her perfect smile that literally melted the legs of any young man falling in love. When she spotted him, they intertwined hands like they had been doing it for years and tried to figure out what to do next. Dusty found them soon after and gave David a rough slap on the shoulder as he told them to enjoy some time alone together. He said he was sure they'd meet up a little bit later.

David and Becky spent what felt like hours going on the various rides and playing games together. He told her about how he had told off his dad and how it helped bring him and his mom together. He talked about how optimistic he was that things were going to change and how he regretted not speaking up sooner. They both laughed and agreed that he had a bad habit of not speaking up sooner when he said that. They both wished he had spoken up sooner about a lot of things. She was genuinely happy for him, like any partner is when their significant other is happy. They were laughing and leaning on each other, sharing cotton candy, when they spotted some guys from the Fox Creek Legion team, including Dawson and Ryan. David wanted to avoid them, but Becky insisted that they talk.

The happy couple greeted the boys by all the carnival games, with music blaring in the background. They were all glad to see David, except Dawson, who looked a bit put out by all the pleasantries. Seeing his facial expression, he started to think about what he had said about Becky and Ricky. He didn't care for how chummy some of the guys were with Becky and how comfortable she seemed talking with them. She seemed to fall right into conversation with them, which placed further doubts about the victim role she had tried to play when talking about how the Fox Creek guys lied about her and her ways. David hated seeing Dawson smiling and talking with her more than anyone.

"So how did it go today?" David nervously asked Ryan, trying to get the attention off Becky.

"Eh, we won both, but we didn't play very well," he confessed while shrugging.

"It will go better next week though," he quickly added while nodding to David.

David noticed Dawson shaking his head when Ryan made that last comment. He also noticed that a couple of guys had moved in a little bit closer than he cared for around Becky. "What's your problem, man?" David said as he raised his hands toward Dawson.

"Hey, hey, easy," Ryan said, trying to calm him down a bit. "I told you we talked things out."

"Yeah, maybe you did," David started with an edge. "But I'm still tired of the looks. I didn't ask to join your team. Remember that." He pointed at Dawson. Dawson just shook his head and bit his tongue.

"Hey, do we have a problem over here?" a voice came calling behind David. It was Gary, and he had Dusty and Joey with him as well. They must have figured that David was in some sort of tussle with the Fox Creek guys involving Becky.

"We're fine," Becky said. "David was just telling them how excited he was to start playing games with them next weekend."

Dawson had bit his lip long enough and couldn't resist now. "Oh really? Well, it's funny because we were just over there playing that game, and people were laughing at us because we couldn't win. Maybe the hotshot here can win you a prize and show us how much better he's going to make our team." He was pointing toward a booth where you had to knock down three sets of six bottles stacked on one another with three consecutive throws. Judging by the size and the number of prizes still hanging, the owners of the booth weren't used to losing.

Before David could object, the boys on both sides were hooting and hollering as they made their way over to the booth. David stood there looking at Becky, figuring this was her cruel trick to expose how she really felt about him and the Fox Creek boys. "Why would you do that?" he asked her while rejecting her hand as she tried to grab his.

She looked at him and just smiled. "I did that because I really like you and want you to win me a prize." He stood there trying to figure her out, tuning out all the shouting from the boys behind him. "Plus, once you do, those Fox Creek boys will leave me alone, and I'll have something to show them that you're mine." She smiled again and nudged him. He wasn't sure if he wanted to kill her or smile back.

When David walked over there, Dawson already had the baseballs in his hand. He was more than happy to pay the fee and explain how each of them had tried three times, and nobody had even knocked down two sets of bottles. David figured the sooner he got this over with, the sooner he could hopefully be left alone. The booth attendant made sure to point out the line spray-painted in the grass and warned that if he stepped across the line before he released the ball, he would be disqualified. Dusty bragged that it wouldn't matter if the line was ten feet farther back.

Reluctantly, David took the first ball from Dawson and worked the seams in his right hand until he found the perfect grip. Without looking at anyone, he kicked and fired. All six bottles were blown off the stand simultaneously as the ball perfectly found its mark. The Riverview boys roared while the Fox Creek guys warned that they each had all knocked over one set of bottles earlier, and you didn't get a prize for getting lucky once.

Dawson had a small grin on his face as he flipped David the second ball. David looked at Becky, who had her lips tucked into her mouth as she was nervous. He sarcastically wondered to himself what she had to be nervous about, but he regained his composure as he saw Dusty jawing with a Fox Creek guy. Trying not to smile, he fired the second ball. It hit the middle bottle on the bottom row, which went flying;

eventually, the other five bottles methodically fell and rolled off the platform.

The Fox Creek guys were now all screaming about how lucky he was, but David's friends matched them with their certainty that he was going to knock over the last set of bottles. Within seconds, they were each placing their own side bets. David tried to block out all the commotion, but the boys were being so loud that a few police officers had come over to make sure it was just good-natured noise and not the kind that preceded a fight. All the other carnival goers in that area stopped what they were doing to see what was going on.

Dawson now had a big smile on his face as he flipped David the last ball. David wasn't sure if the smile was because he wanted him to fail or if he was actually rooting for him to knock down the last set of bottles. When he got the last ball, David blocked everything out and focused solely on the last set of bottles. He could barely hear anything as he found the right grip and reared back to fire the last ball. Bingo! It was a simultaneous explosion, just like the first ball. All six bottles instantly went flying off the platform, and all the boys rushed to David and hugged him, even Dawson, who seemed to enjoy every last second of it.

The whooping and hollering lasted for almost a minute, and David started to walk away with all the boys, but the attendant called out to stop him. "Aren't you forgetting something, young man?" he said, pointing to the prizes.

He had completely forgotten about the prizes, and he had completely forgotten about Becky in those briefs moments. He quickly turned and saw her standing there by herself with her gorgeous smile beaming toward him. She continued to smile and shrugged, saying, "Well, David Collins, what do I want, besides you?"

David hated the fact that she was right, but all the boys had disappeared to head over to more rides and games. They seemed to forget about the guy who had caused all the commotion and the girl who made it all happen. He just shook his head in disbelief toward her and then held out his arm like a butler opening a door to a vault of prizes for her to choose from. She laughed out loud at his goofy gesture as she stepped forward.

"You can choose anything you want, young lady," the man said to her, proud of his collection of stuffed animals and cheap toys.

Becky surveyed over the prizes. David was certain she was going to choose one of the nearly life-size stuffed bears or goldfish. Whatever it was, he knew it would be something he'd have to lug around the rest of the night and feel like a fool doing it, so he was surprised when she chose a small stuffed lion that was nearly hidden in the corner. "That's what you want?" both David and the attendant asked almost simultaneously and with the same amount of surprise.

"Yes," she said assuredly. When she got it, she gave it a tight squeeze and looked right at David. "Now when you're not around, I'll always have something that reminds me of you." She bounced on the balls of her feet.

"A lion?" David said out of the corner of his mouth.

"Yeah, a lion," she boasted. "You know, an animal that lies in waiting but when provoked shows others that he's the unequivocal king. Other animals might think they're better or tougher, but he always proves them wrong—an animal whose confidence may waver but is never broken, an animal that is known for its courage and one that is loyal to its pride, someone who is calm and cool but when provoked can let out a roar to remind others of his passion and strength. I've seen all this in you, my lion." She pushed the stuffed animal into David's chest to show the zest of her excitement and to accentuate the fact that she was describing him. He just looked at her and tried to play it cool, but he had never been prouder of any prize he had earned in his entire life.

They spent the rest of that night parading around as a handsome couple, enjoying a perfect summer night. Officer Smith even commented on what a great couple they seemed to be together. After that night, David was done doubting Becky and her feelings for him or any stories about her.

The next day, David's grandpa was coming down to pick him up to go get some lunch. They were both a little disappointed because the professional team was out on the West Coast, and this was going to be their last free weekend of the summer to possibly go watch a game together. Nonetheless, David's grandpa said he wanted to get together and enjoy their last weekend of freedom before he and David were running around all over to his own various baseball games and events.

The weather was going to be rather warm but otherwise sunny and typical for the first day of July. David's mom wanted to come along, but she was working the afternoon shift at the bar. David's grandpa was going to take him to a place downtown where they had great burgers and twenty-four-hour breakfast. David didn't really care; he was just happy to spend time with him. He wanted to tell his grandpa about last night, but after he thought about it, he didn't think the story would sound as special to his grandpa as it was to him, so he waited for his grandpa to speak first in the car.

"How are things at home, David?" he began, sounding like a concerned grandpa who was asking about David but also about his daughter.

David hesitated. He sensed that he wasn't going to get off easy with a one- or two-word answer, so he wanted to be as honest as he could with him. "They're going pretty good," he started. "Mom and I had a good conversation yesterday. We've probably talked more in the past week than I can ever remember."

His grandpa didn't take his eyes off the road, but David could see the smile growing on his face as he spoke. "That's good. I like hearing that." He paused a bit before his next sentence. He had probably thought about it for a while but knew it was a sensitive topic. "And how about your dad? I heard you spoke with him the other night. Told him off pretty good?"

David wasn't expecting his grandpa to bring up his dad, so he was caught off guard and unsure of how to answer. He still felt a little bad for him but owed his grandpa an honest answer. "Yeah, I let my emotions get the best of me," he started while looking down at his lap. "He was trying to apologize, but I basically told him I didn't accept and that I couldn't stand him. I told him he was a horrible father. He apologized again before he left, but . . ."

"But what, David?" his grandpa urged.

"But I ignored him. Now for some reason, I feel horrible for him," David said, shaking his head. "Is that weird? How can I feel so bad for a person that has ignored me their entire life? I feel bad because we live in a nice house, and he's tried buying me nice things, and I know he works hard, but I just couldn't accept his apology."

"Kind of like a lion kicking someone out of their pride." His grandpa snickered. David jolted his head up, wondering if somehow he had heard about what happened last night, but he continued on, "I've heard the same thing from my daughter, your mom, for the past seventeen years about your dad."

David looked over at his grandpa, and he noticed that he wasn't happy or sad, just ready to get some things off his chest, so he fed him a line for him to continue. "Really?"

His grandpa looked quickly at David and sighed. "Yeah. That man has made so many promises to your mother, and he's just about broken all of them." He continued on for a while, talking about how he had promised to let her go back to school, to move them out of Riverview, and that he wasn't going to drink as much but failed on all of them. He talked about how his mom kept believing him, and every time she did and he didn't follow through, she sunk deeper into a hole she couldn't climb out of. "Eventually, they both started blaming you for all their problems. She stopped listening to me and rejected our help, so that's why I and your grandma moved away. We couldn't see our daughter like that. You were little, and I promised her that I'd take care of you, but I couldn't help her until she started taking care of herself."

David had heard a lot of these things before, but they carried a bit more weight and implication as he had gotten older and suddenly found himself in a relationship and willing to speak his mind to his parents. The hospital where Ricky was came into view. David tried to find his room as he looked out the window. "So, Grandpa, do you think people can change?"

His grandpa groveled a bit as he readjusted himself behind the wheel. "Well, David, it's hard for a person to change who they are. We're all born with a certain nature about us, so I don't know how much we can change." He was really thinking deeply about this. It was something his daughter had probably asked him many times, and he never quite had the right answer until now. "I think people can grow, and we can learn from our experiences. Those experiences can cause us to reflect, and maybe if we want something bad enough, we can go against our nature."

Both men looked out the window, contemplating the words that he had just spoken. His grandpa wanted to make sure his point was clear, so he continued for David. "I think your parents can grow and try to change their nature. I've seen it in your mother recently. Will they be perfect? Probably not, but I do believe they have a chance to grow and get it right."

David was shocked by his grandpa's answer, but he felt strangely uplifted. "So you think Mom and Dad can work things out?" he asked with a bit of hope in his voice.

"They're going to have to do a lot of growing, and they're going to have to learn from this experience. You speaking up to them has brought a lot of this out," his grandpa said triumphantly.

However, it didn't make David feel good that he was the person who had caused his parents to separate. As much as he couldn't stand that house, he felt horrible for breaking up a relationship by running his mouth. He put his elbow up against the window ledge and used his hand to catch his head. He inadvertently muttered "oh" as he sunk down in his seat a bit.

Sensing that David had felt the literal weight of his parents' failures falling on his shoulders, his grandpa quickly tried to restore him. "David, it's not your fault," he said, reaching over to rub his shoulder. "In fact, if they work things out and things do get better, it will be all because of you."

David gave a look of doubt, so his grandpa had to appeal to his young mind. "Can I talk to you about baseball?" his grandpa asked.

David thought he was changing topics, so he was more than willing to go along. They were passing the stadium, and David wished they were going to a game and talking about the matchup that day instead of how he was going to make or break his parents' relationship. He managed to sarcastically mutter, "Sure thing." He stared out the window and the giant structure.

"Your dad wasn't as good at baseball as he says he was," his grandpa happily fired back.

David quickly turned his head to look at him.

"That's right, he wasn't that great, and you're a hundred times better than he was."

David sat there with a confused look on his face. His grandpa laughed, and his whole body was moving up and down as he was saying, "I thought you might like to hear that."

"But I thought—" David started off, trying to process everything.

"But you thought he was this great player," his grandpa interrupted. "Let me tell you about your dad, David. He could have been a really good ballplayer. He had a lot of talent, but you're going to be way better. Let me tell you why." He stopped to let David catch up and take everything in. "He played on the varsity team for a few years, so when your mom started dating him, I went to watch him play a number of times. Like you, he was a pitcher. It's where you get your arm talent from. But when I watched him pitch, there was one thing I noticed that I could never get past."

"What?" David asked on the edge of his seat. He had always heard his dad talk about how good he was, so he was fascinated to hear another side of the story.

"Your dad always blamed others when things started going south. He wasn't strong enough to push through adversity. If he walked someone, it was the umpire or the catcher's fault. If somebody made an error, he would get on them, and then it would cause another error. He couldn't push through adversity. He could rarely pitch deep into games because he would unravel despite having the talent to do it. If he made an out at the plate, it was because of something that the coach had said to him. Any coaches that might have been interested in him as a player beyond high school saw that, and nobody wanted him. He didn't have any offers to play behind high school because of his attitude."

David was in shock, but he didn't want to interrupt or slow down his grandpa, who was now getting emotionally charged.

"Nothing was his fault. As I got to know him better when he was dating your mom, I saw the same thing in their relationship. Everything was her fault. He blamed her for getting pregnant, and he blamed you and her for all his problems in life. That's his nature."

When his grandpa was finished, David leaned back in his seat. He didn't even realize he had been leaning so far forward, but he was hanging on every word his grandpa had said. "I didn't know any of that, Grandpa."

Catching himself a little bit and coming down from his emotions, his grandpa turned to look at him as they were stopped at an intersection. "I know, David. That's why I wanted to tell you. You're just as much his son as you are my daughter's son. Whatever happens in life, don't blame others for your problems. Look at where it got your father."

David reflected on his grandfather's words as the car eased along down the city street. He suddenly felt keenly aware of his nature to blame others. He could see Dusty and Becky smiling at him for his lack of understanding and quickness to cast the blame onto others. He started to feel bad, but his grandpa wasn't done.

"So, David, that's why you're a great ballplayer. When I watch you play baseball, I see you picking your teammates up. I see you pushing through adversity. I see you making those around you better." He smiled at him the way a grandpa smiles that warms their grandkids' hearts. David was smiling again too. "You're making your parents better too. They may not be able to change who they are, but maybe they can grow and change their nature enough to salvage their relationship with you and possibly themselves." He paused to rub David's head. "And that is because of you, young man, and I'm so proud of you. Your mom has to learn to not let others keep her down and that she has tremendous potential in life, just like you, David. And for your dad to come to you and apologize, well, I'd say that's growth and a sign that maybe he's trying to change his nature."

They pulled into the small parking lot for the restaurant, but his grandpa wouldn't let him get out of the car just yet. He turned off the engine but didn't open his door. "There's one more thing I want to talk to you about," he started. "Your friends."

David just sat there, unsure of where his grandpa was going with this.

"You show me a man's friends, and I can tell you what kind of man he is," his grandpa sternly stated. "You're at an important age in your life, David, and the types of people you hang around are very important."

David was starting to feel a bit defensive and wanted to speak up for his friends. "But, Grandpa," he tried to interrupt.

"No buts," his grandpa quickly struck back. "I just want you to know that no matter where you go in life or what you do, your true friends will support you." He stopped to let that sink in. David wasn't sure what to do or how to respond, so he just squirmed a little in his seat. "You have some good friends, David, but if they're true friends, they will support you. I know what it's like to try to leave Riverview. You'll really find out who your good friends are when you do. Remember that, okay?" He put his hand around the back of David's head as he concluded.

"I won't forget, Grandpa," David replied assuredly. "I promise I won't forget any of this."

David's grandpa looked at David and gave him his nod of approval. They got out of the car and went and had lunch. They spent hours talking that afternoon, and David felt like a man. He and his grandpa talked for hours about life, human nature, and growth. That day in the city with his grandpa turned out to be better than any baseball game they ever attended together. They talked about relationships and goals.

David felt like he finally understood his parents, and for the first time, he felt hope that he could have a relationship with both of them.

He returned home filled with confidence and optimism. He felt like things were falling into place. He was nervous when he talked to Becky on the phone because it was her mom's first night on third shift, and she was terrified, but when he saw her on her deck in a bikini the next day to watch the boys on the field, they were both at ease.

It was strange being at the school field in the middle of the summer without Ricky, but all the boys wanted was a sense of normalcy. They all enjoyed the good-natured ribbing and distraction from everyday life that those few hours provided. Plus, they all enjoyed seeing Becky out there sunbathing each day in her swimwear. All the comments and remarks she made now just made him smile even more, knowing that she was his. The week went quickly, and the boys were excited that Ricky was being released from the hospital on Friday. David was disappointed he wouldn't be there to welcome him back home as he was going to be playing in a big baseball event.

He and Becky decided to spend that Thursday evening together. It was the Fourth of July, but since he was going to be playing most of the weekend and they were unsure of when they might see each other next, they just wanted to be alone together. There wasn't much for them to do in town, so they just walked around the quiet side streets, talking with each other and watching fireworks shot off in various spots in the sky.

"So you nervous about the weekend?" Becky asked with her teeth clamped down to contain her excitement.

David just shrugged. "A little, I guess. Coach said that I'll just be playing the outfield until we get to the championship game. He said we shouldn't have too much trouble getting there."

"Oh yeah, and what happens then?" she said, smiling and giving him a nudge. She liked forcing him to talk about himself.

"And then I have to pitch in the championship game," David said, rolling his eyes.

"And then you pitch the team to a championship," she corrected him. They both laughed together. David loved how she made him feel. She loved how she challenged him. She loved how she understood him. Things had happened quickly, but he knew he loved her. As a teenager, love often happens quickly but not unexpectedly. David had known Becky almost his entire life, and he always knew there was something about her that made her different, something well beyond her looks. It was why things were moving forward even quicker for them.

They had walked for a few seconds in silence, but David's mind wasn't silent. He knew he wanted to tell her that he loved her, and he didn't care if she said it back. Becky was busy pointing out fireworks in the sky ahead when David stepped under a streetlight, stopped walking, and forced her to do the same. Before he could even think, he just blurted it out. "Becky, I love you. I've loved you for I don't know how long, but I love you, and I don't see this world without me loving you."

She pulled her hand away from him and just stared at him. She loved how everyone thought he was this quiet kid who never said anything to anyone, but he had this tremendous passion for things inside him. She loved how she was the one who got to see that side of him, and he saved it for her. She loved that she didn't have to dress a certain way or pretend to be someone she wasn't to get his attention. She had long known that he was different from the other boys, and she loved that she could trust him with anything. Without hesitation, she squealed back that she loved him too. They kissed passionately under that streetlamp until a nearby firework made them both jump. They smiled at each other and looked to the sky together. They had experienced a lot in life to that point, but this was their first experience with love.

After a few minutes of passionate romance, they began to slowly continue their walk, both reassured that this was not some summer fling. They joked around about a life and a future together as teenage couples often do. They were both feeling limitless in the company of each other. They had wandered the streets, talking about endless possibilities, until they found their way back to Becky's house. They stood in the driveway for a few moments, holding hands. Neither one wanted to let go, and they both knew the dangers that were possible each night inside that house. Her mom had already left for her shift, and her stepdad was out somewhere, getting drunk.

"Becky," he asked, suddenly a bit more serious than he had been after they professed their love for each other, "do you think people can change?"

She joyfully answered, "Sure, I mean, look at you and me and how we're—"

David stopped her right there with a gentle finger to her lips. This wasn't what he was talking about. He was thinking about the type of change he and his grandpa had talked about. He shook his head and glanced toward her house as he began slowly, "I mean real change—you know, change their nature and how they treat people?"

She looked at him, suddenly aware of what he was talking about, and dropped her head to her chest before taking a deep breath and looking at him again. "No, I don't think certain people can change. As much as I want to help others when I get older, I don't think I'll be able to change how people act. Some people are just the way they are."

David nodded in slight agreement, but he had seen some changes in his own home, and he felt a little more emboldened with his love standing next to him. "Maybe you're right, but I think most people can change. I've been thinking lately about how I could maybe help with some of that."

"My stepdad?" Becky cried out with her eyes suddenly wide and shaken.

"No, no," he reassured her, "with our town." She again gave him a look of confusion and uncertainty, so he explained further. "For as long as I can remember, I've wanted to get out of this town."

Becky nodded almost with her entire body in agreement for both of them.

"But lately, I've been thinking about how maybe I could change this town. Well, maybe I can't change the town, but maybe I can change how people view Riverview and how people think of people from here. Maybe they won't always get into fights or hang out with the wrong crowd."

She laughed at him a bit but stopped when she could see that he was not joking.

"I'm not saying I want to stay here forever, but there's a lot of good right here. Where else could a guy find friends like these or a girl like you? There's a lot of loyalty in this town that I don't think people appreciate. People stick up for one another here, so why can't they learn to act a little better to support one another?"

Becky just shook her head a bit. "David, I don't think I can stay or come back here. I just can't. You don't understand everything. I have to leave here."

She was getting upset, and that bothered David. He didn't want to ruin a perfect night, so he comforted her the best he could and reassured her that he was going away to play baseball for a college one day. He promised her that he would see where life would take them from there. She liked the fact that he used the word *them* and gave him a long embrace.

He pulled back slightly and gazed into her eyes. He felt like his breath was being pulled out of him by her beauty. He shook his head slightly as he told her, "For the longest time, I wanted to run off to the city and just disappear from this town, but now everything I want in the world is right here in my arms." She whimpered and gently put her head back on his shoulder.

Suddenly, they were both startled a bit when a car came down her street and passed her house. David was relieved it wasn't her stepfather. He hadn't had many past interactions with him, and after Becky's revelations, he didn't ever want to see or talk to him. They were both relieved it wasn't him, but Becky could clearly tell that David was more spooked by the passing car than she was.

"It'll be all right," she assured David. "Ever since my mom started working third shift, he's usually out getting plastered. I think he likes knowing she won't be around to get mad at him when he comes home. Usually, by the time he comes home, he's too wasted to do anything. He just passes out and wakes up the next morning and goes to work."

David shook his head, but she caught him with her right arm.

"He doesn't even check on me. He usually just passes out on the couch." She was trying to force a smile to put David at ease, but he just shuffled his feet. "Besides, if he tries anything, I've got my lion to protect me." She gave him a gentle kiss on the cheek to assure him things were okay. David finally smiled back at her. "Why don't you come inside with me?" She wasn't joking, and she wasn't desperate. She just wanted to be with the boy whom she loved.

David stuttered a bit, trying to weigh what he wanted to do versus what he should do. "I can't, Becky. I told my mom I'd be home tonight."

She just looked at him with her beautiful eyes. She wasn't begging him; she was speaking to him silently. These weren't the eyes of a girl who was scared or wanted to spend more time talking. These were the eyes of a girl who wanted to be loved for the first time. David knew it, and he knew he didn't want to go home, so he told Becky that he could call his mom and tell her that he was going to spend the night at Dusty's. She smiled as she led him inside.

That night was a special night for the both of them. They had laid in each other's arms not many nights ago before this one, but this was the night that no young person ever forgets. They were both unsure of things, but they trusted in the love of the other. Afterward, David laid there with Becky asleep in his arms. The moonlight was peeking in through a gap between the window and the blanket thrown over a curtain rod.

David heard Becky's stepdad come in and stumble around the house, but as Becky predicted, he eventually collapsed on the couch with the TV blaring. Becky never changed her breathing pattern, but David had been terrified. She was sound asleep in the arms of the boy she loved. David glanced up at the shelves above her bed and saw the stuffed lion that he had won looking down over them. He closed his eyes and enjoyed the feel of Becky in his arms as he too fell asleep.

CHAPTER 17

It was hard to tell who was more anxious about his first weekend with the Fox Creek Legion ball team—David, his grandpa, or Becky. David was anxious about his performance and showing the kids that he truly belonged on the team. He got off to a good start at the plate, so that calmed his nerves. David's grandpa spent the hour drive there and back on Friday and Saturday, giving him the scouting reports on the teams they were facing or were going to face. None of it was factual; it was just based on what he had seen and heard about those areas and their baseball prowess in the past.

Becky seemed to have David's schedule memorized and the times they played because it seemed that, within ten minutes of him walking in the door, she was calling for him to fill her in. So far, everything had gone to plan, and Fox Creek would be playing in the championship game on Sunday, and David would be on the mound. Not only would he be on the mound but the winner of this game also would advance to the national qualifying tournament in Tennessee.

David's grandpa swung by that Sunday morning to pick him up and make sure he had a good breakfast. Instead of waiting for the car ride, his grandpa spent most of the breakfast at a Riverview restaurant and tavern not far from his house going over the other team. He had watched them play while David's team had been warming up before one of their games. He talked about how it was one of the better-hitting teams he had seen and that he would be proud of David no matter what happened. He made sure to point out that he was still just fifteen and a junior-to-be, while some of these kids were turning nineteen and going off to college in a few weeks. He made sure that David understood that he couldn't just try to throw it by these kids, that he was going to have to pitch. David nodded along and appeased his grandpa, but he was surprisingly at ease. At least he was at ease until they left the restaurant and started heading the wrong way.

"Uh, Grandpa, you know you're heading the wrong way, right?" David asked, trying to think of why his grandpa was taking a different route from what he had the previous two days.

"Nah, I know where I'm going." He smiled and laughed out loud to himself.

"But the last two days, we've gone that way to get to the fields," David said, pointing in the opposite direction.

David's grandpa pretended to act confused for a moment and then winked at David. "Slight detour," he declared as he slowed down, approaching David's house.

"Are we stopping back at the house?" David frantically asked as his grandpa began turning into the driveway.

"Yep," he smugly replied.

"Forgot something—I mean, someone," he corrected himself as he motioned to the porch.

David took his eyes off his grandpa to look up at the porch in time to see his mom and Becky exiting his house. He shot a surprised look back at his grandpa, which only widened his smile even more. "Your mom wasn't going to miss this game for the world, and she told me how Becky has called you each day as soon as you got home. I figured the best we could do was give them a ride." He winked while reaching behind him to open the back door. "Your father killed her love of baseball, but I guess she's just trying to change her nature."

Becky and David's mom slid into the back seat, both with nervous huge smiles on their faces. "Good breakfast?" David's mom asked, leaning forward to put a hand on each shoulder of the boys in the front seat.

"The best," David's grandpa replied with a huge grin and nod to his daughter.

She continued to slide over and make room for Becky while she declared, "I haven't been to a baseball game in years. Do I look okay?" She primped her hair quickly as she caught a glimpse of herself in the rearview mirror.

"You look beautiful, sweetheart," David's grandpa replied to her. "And you too, Becky."

David couldn't agree more. He peered over his shoulder to get a look at Becky sitting in the back seat of his grandpa's car next to his mom. They both were wearing short jean shorts and light-colored summer shirts with flip-flops. Becky had on a baseball cap that shaded her face but couldn't hide her beautiful eyes. David felt on top of the world.

"You look so handsome in that uniform I can barely take it," his mom joyfully cried out like a proud mother as she shook both his shoulders from behind him in the back seat. "Let's go, Dad." And with that, they started down the road toward the field, the same way his grandpa had taken the two previous days. His grandpa and the girls were bantering back and forth, but David was just taking it all in. Every now and then, he'd catch David smiling out of the corner of his eye and give him a nod. This wasn't just what David needed but it was what he needed too.

When they arrived at the field for warm-ups, they all wished David good luck. He couldn't believe how many people were already there, and he noticed a number of coaches wearing their school's baseball caps, talking to one another behind the backstop. Coach Bell was back there with them and made sure to point directly at David as he walked into the dugout to set down his things. During stretches, Coach Bell asked David how he felt; it was more of a nervous habit than anything else. While he was warming up in the bullpen, he went through a scouting report with him of the other team's lineup.

Up until that point, David felt great about everything. It wasn't until he made his way in from the bullpen that the butterflies started creeping up on him. As he sat down and took a drink of water, he looked over into the other team's dugout and thought there must have been a mistake. Most of the kids looked like minor-league ballplayers, not guys from high school. His heart rate was rising, and they were the home team, which meant he would have to take the mound first.

Standing on the mound to take his warm-up pitches, he could feel everything in himself tighten up. He struggled to throw strikes, but more importantly, his velocity on his fastball was affected. Without his fastball, he wouldn't be able to set up his other pitches, and he knew he was going to get lit up. He saw his mom, grandpa, and Becky sitting in the front row next to his dugout, and he thought about how his mom waited all these years to see this impending failure. The stands were packed, and people were standing down the lines. It felt like the world was closing in on him.

As David prepared to throw his first pitch, he saw all the coaches behind the backstop raise their radar guns and point them right at him. To David, it literally felt like he was in front of a firing squad. The first pitch sailed high and outside to the right-handed batter, nowhere near the strike zone. Waiting to get the ball back from his catcher, David noticed that every coach was scribbling something down on a pad or in a book. The next pitch bounced in the dirt, and when David finally threw a strike on his third pitch, it was laced into right-center field for a double.

David quickly fell behind the next batter before he laced a base hit to left field. The third batter wasn't much different as David struggled to find the strike zone, eventually walking the kid on five pitches. Just like that, on the biggest stage of his life, the first three batters were on, and he was in a bases-loaded jam in a game his coach had saved him to pitch in. He figured it was a good thing that he suddenly wanted to stick around Riverview and help change things because he'd be back there as a reject in a few hours. Ryan came in from shortstop to try to talk to him and calm him down, but it didn't help. He fell behind the next batter two balls and no strikes. A couple of coaches had already put down their notepads and radar guns and just shook their head.

David saw his mom, who was a nervous wreck with her hands over her face. He looked over at his grandpa, who was shaking his head. Then there was Becky. She was sitting there with a smile on her face, watching the boy she loved on the mound in a championship game. She reached into the cloth bag that she had brought with her to carry her suntan lotion and seat cushion and pulled out a stuffed lion—the lion that David had won for her and that she believed kept her safe. She gave it a slight squeeze as she set it on her lap. David looked back at his grandpa and thought about what he'd told him about his dad, how he couldn't handle adversity and would always blame others and bring down his teammates. He figured his mom had seen this scene one too many times. He turned to the outfield to kick some dirt off his spikes and saw his teammates all standing there, kicking at the ground with their heads down. This wasn't what his mom and grandpa deserved, and he was better than he was showing. His teammates knew it, but most importantly, Becky knew it.

He turned back toward the plate with a new determination in his eyes. His breathing had calmed, and he could feel his right arm drop and loosen. He took the sign from his catcher and rocked and fired. Strike one, a beautiful fastball on the outside corner. David noticed a couple of the coaches who had put their radar guns down look over at those who hadn't. The next pitch, David threw a blistering fastball on the hands of the batter, who popped it weakly back and out of play. Suddenly, every coach had picked up their radar guns again and were opening their notepads. Everyone wanted to see the fastball again, along with David's catcher, but this wasn't Dusty, and David remembered the last time he thought he could throw three fastballs by a good hitter; Gary took him for a ride. He shook off and wanted the curveball. David focused and then threw a perfect pitch that completely fell out of the strike zone and had the hitter out on his front foot. He weakly waved at it for strike three and the first out.

Suddenly, the Fox Creek dugout and fans were back alive. He could hear the infielders chatting it up again, talking about how all he needed was a ground ball. Two pitches later, David delivered that ground ball on a beautiful changeup. The second baseman scooped it up and flipped to Ryan at short, who came across the bag and fired a bullet to first for a double play. David had escaped the inning with no runs and in the process managed to fire up his team. Ryan practically tackled him as he was sprinting off the field and back to their dugout on the first base side.

From there, the game was nip and tuck. Fox Creek took a lead in the second inning, but the other team tied it up in the third. They went up by a run in the fourth, but Fox Creek tied it back up again in the fifth. As they moved into the last two innings, David locked everything out.

He was focused on making his pitches, and he held them scoreless in the top of the sixth. Fox Creek then erupted for three runs in the bottom of the sixth to take a three-run lead. All they needed were three outs, and they were headed to Tennessee next weekend.

David retired the first batter on a weak pop-up, but the second batter managed to get a base hit on a seeing-eye single. The next batter flew out to right field, and David was now one out away. He knew the kid at the plate was the out he needed. He didn't want to face the kid on deck again. He already had two hits off him and hit one out of the stadium that was just foul back in the fourth inning. David noticed that Coach Bell sent somebody down to the bullpen to warm up, and suddenly, he was losing focus. For the first time since the first inning, he could hear the other team's dugout trying to make noise. He looked over at his mom for the first time since the first inning, and she was practically in the same pose. Before he knew it, David was behind two balls and no strikes in the count. The more David knew he couldn't walk this kid, the more he couldn't throw a strike; and before he knew it, the tying run was coming to the plate.

Coach Bell asked for time as he slowly made his way to the mound. The rest of the team was there to greet him when he arrived. "Hell of a job, Collins. We'll get you out of this one," he said, patting him on the butt. But David didn't move, even when his teammates tapped him on the back as well.

"Let me finish, Coach," David calmly said as he stared back at his coach.

"Son, normally, I would, but this is a trip to the national qualifying tournament we're talking about here. I've got to think about the entire team," he replied, sounding a bit unsure about himself.

"No offense to Waters down there, Coach," David started as he flicked his head in the direction of the bullpen. "But I think I'm the guy you want to get this out."

Coach Bell looked at the other boys, and they all nodded in agreement. The umpire was making his way to the mound to break up the meeting or force a pitching change, so Coach Bell had to make up his mind quickly. "We going to finish this thing today, Bell?" the umpire said as he reached the mound.

"Yeah," he said, slamming the ball back into David's glove, "this kid's going to finish it soon enough." He gave David a quick smile from the side of his mouth, and everyone else said "yeah" as they hopped back to their positions.

David looked at the kid walking to the plate. He was smiling, pleased that Coach Bell had left in the kid he already had two hits off, but David wasn't fazed. He knew he hadn't really gotten a fastball by this kid all day, so he was going to have to get him with the off-speed stuff. The catcher put down the sign for a curveball, and David delivered a knee buckler for strike one. The kids on the infield were holding back their all-out laughter as the kid had nearly bailed out of the batter's box on a pitch called a strike. Now David was thinking this kid wasn't going to bail on the next pitch, even if it was at his ear, perfect time for an inside fastball to back him off the plate. He and his catcher were in agreement, and David came to the stretch. David let the ball rip, and so did the hitter. The ball was lined and landed just foul down the left field line. The entire crowd groaned in unison, and Coach Bell kicked the dugout fence for letting a kid talk him out of his decision.

Now the confident laughter and chatter from the infield grew nervous. A base hit here would likely put the tying run on base, and a home run would tie things up. That last swing was the same type of swing that kid had taken all day off David. David knew that this was his last batter no matter what, and he wasn't about to stand next to Coach Bell in the dugout as they both prayed Waters could come in and get the last out with the game tied or the tying run on base. He thought about going to the curveball again, but he figured that was what the batter was expecting. He didn't want to throw another fastball, though, because he hadn't gotten one past this kid all day. He truly didn't know what to do, so he stepped back off the rubber to regain his composure and clear his head.

In that brief moment, he caught Becky out of the corner of his eye, squeezing the stuffed lion for all it was worth. David took a deep breath as he stepped back on that rubber and told himself that lions have to eat. He shook off the sign for a curveball and waited until the catcher signaled for a fastball away. David vowed that this would be the hardest pitch he would throw in his life. He took a deep breath and delivered.

As the ball left his hand, David didn't hear anything. He was just focused on the catcher's glove. He saw the ball traveling toward home plate, but it seemed frozen in time, like a pitch that would never get to home plate. He could see the kid starting his swing and momentarily held his breath. He kept focused on the catcher's glove, and when the ball hit the pocket and the cloud of dust popped off the back of his glove, everyone erupted. David couldn't hear anything at that moment, but he was buried under a pile of his teammates a few seconds later. Eventually, they would pick him up and carry him over to the dugout on his shoulders, the same dugout where his new family was watching. Ryan had him on one shoulder and Dawson on the other.

After the chaos had ensued and the boys were gathering their things in the dugout, Coach Bell addressed the parents to let them know about travel arrangements and what info he had on the event. He was struggling to put sentences together because he'd never made it that far before. The team sat in the outfield, anxiously awaiting his postgame speech. He kept it short and simple. He spoke about how proud he was of how they competed and had come together as a team and sternly reminded the team to never try to pull what David Collins just did. He looked at David with a pissed-off expression on his face and then erupted into laughter and celebration. The whole team went crazy again. When they settled, he gave them their itinerary for the upcoming week and then told them to go home and celebrate.

As the boys made their way back to the dugout, Coach Bell grabbed David's shirt sleeve and stopped him in his tracks. David figured he was going to get a stern talking-to about disrespect and following orders; instead, Coach Bell told him to leave his stuff in the dugout and follow him. He had a big smile on his face.

Coach Bell escorted David behind the home plate bleachers, where there were seven college coaches all waiting to talk to him. His mom and grandpa were already back there and had exchanged pleasantries. They all bombarded him with questions and compliments. "So you're not even sixteen yet?" one coach asked, looking to confirm his disbelief.

"That was pretty impressive, young man, to regain your composure like that in the first inning," another chimed in.

"Takes a tough kid to perform like that against older kids," one coached calmly said as he shook David's hand.

"I particularly liked how he told Bell here to take that ball and shove it up his ass in the seventh inning." Another one laughed, causing everyone there to bust out laughing.

"I liked seeing you get stronger as the game went on, young man," another coach said as he extended his hand to shake again.

"Do you know how hard you threw that last pitch?" another coach asked.

"No, sir," David politely replied.

"You sat around eighty-five all day, but that last pitch clocked at eighty-eight miles per hour," he boasted, showing him his pitching chart. "Son, at your age and with your developing body, if you get serious about weights and baseball, the sky's the limit for you."

He handed David a card as all the coaches did. Most of them told him that they were going to be in Tennessee next weekend or would be sending a friend they trusted to watch him there as well. Those coaches gave David the name and number of those guys as well and told him that they would all be checking in with him again soon. They looked at David's mom and grandpa to confirm if this was okay, and they nodded. Coach Bell thanked his mom and grandpa and patted David on the back again as he made his way to the parking lot.

David's grandpa could barely wait for the coaches to get out of earshot before exploding with excitement to David and his mom. She was speechless and just hugged her boy and told him they could go out to eat anywhere he wanted. They waved as one of his fellow teammates invited him over to swim and celebrate with a cookout at his house. At first, David thought there was no way because his friends in Riverview would be pissed if they found out he went to a party in Fox Creek, but then he remembered what his grandpa told him. He knew that Dusty would be happy for him, so he gave the kid a thumbs-up.

After all that madness had quieted down and David's grandpa was trying to put all the coaches' cards in his pocket, David looked over and saw Becky standing there quietly, waiting for her turn. She was still holding the stuffed lion, but as she saw David turn her attention to her, she brought it up to her neck and made it do a little dance while she smiled. It made David laugh. "I told you," she said, looking down at her favorite prize. "You're a lion." She gave him a big hug.

"I'm so proud of you, David. Any of those schools would be lucky to have you," she said with a hint of sadness.

He pulled her in a little tighter and said, "Not as lucky as I am to have you." He gave her a little kiss on her forehead and then asked everyone where they wanted to go.

"Your choice, superstar," his mom proclaimed.

"Well," he hesitated, looking at his grandpa and Becky, "I know a few people around here that like ice cream."

They all smiled at one another and drove off to the nearest ice cream place. They spent the afternoon laughing and rehashing the game, with David doing his impressions of each of them as they were sitting in the stands. David didn't think that life could get any better than at that moment.

The month of July seemed to fly by for David. He and his grandpa went down to Tennessee, where the team played well enough to be invited to the American Legion national championship event in South Carolina the following weekend. The team struggled a bit, but it was still an experience that everyone enjoyed. David and his grandpa spent plenty of time together talking, meeting college coaches, and traveling, and David really grew to enjoy his new teammates and friends from Fox Creek.

The time away seemed to be helping his parents a bit as his mom sounded optimistic about some of the changes she had seen in David's father, but she wasn't about to let him move back in anytime soon. She reported that he wasn't going to bars anymore after he got off work, and he was talking to his supervisors about getting off third shift so he could be home during regular hours. His mom not working at the bar had done a lot of good for calming his nerves and distrust, and he even called David a few times to ask how his games had gone. It was awkward, but David appreciated the fact that he was trying.

During the weekdays when David was home, he spent the days he wasn't working with Dusty and the nights with Becky. He was enjoying working at Jay's with his mom and listening to her talk about her summer school classes she was taking at the junior college. Dusty's parents talked about how they felt a little lonely without him having as many meals with them, but Bonnie was really happy that his life at home was getting better. She kept smiling wide as she looked at Dusty, who had really made an effort to give her a chance. Dusty missed his friend but told him he was happy for him and couldn't wait for school to start up so he could see him every day again. That news shocked David and made him a little guilty for his diminished time with his friend, but Dusty said he couldn't argue against what he was accomplishing with baseball and for spending his evenings with a girl as beautiful as Becky.

On the days that David didn't have to work, the boys gathered at the school baseball field and played together. There were no more really competitive games there, just good-natured competitions or contests. The younger guys especially loved asking David about his events and experiences with baseball over the summer. Since David had risen to prowess, more and more younger kids started showing up. David promised to bring the college coaches to the field if and when they visited like they said they were going to. Becky enjoyed seeing David enjoying his moments in the sun with his friends, and the boys still loved seeing her in her outfits or getting some sun while on the deck or in the inflatable pool.

Ricky was home, and Joey and Gary would bring him down every now and then to hang out with the guys. He still didn't have his fiery nature back and his face slightly discolored, but he was happy to report that the guys who had done this to him had been arrested and that he was done selling drugs and stealing. Gary got his car up and running and found a good part-time job with a landscaping company. He was even working out regularly to prepare for fall workouts with the junior college baseball team. Joey naturally got a job at the same place as Gary but enjoyed his cigarettes too much to keep up with a regular exercise routine.

David had one more baseball event near the state college. It wasn't quite as exciting as going down south, but he was anxious because he had always been a fan of the state school and had never been on campus. He promised the guys that they would spend as much time hanging out as possible the first couple of weeks of August before school started back up. He told everyone that he'd be at the school field early in the morning on Monday when he got back.

He apologized to Becky the night before he had to leave because he wouldn't be able to talk to her most of the weekend because he would be in a hotel again with his grandpa. This had become their new routine the last few weeks, but she understood and said she couldn't wait to see him on Monday morning. She liked knowing that he was spending time with his grandpa and doing what he loved. They sat on the merry-go-round and talked under the stars. He kissed her goodbye on that same merry-go-round where he first kissed her and said he already couldn't wait until Monday morning to see her again.

After his games on Saturday, David and his grandpa walked the campus, and David fell in love with the place. On Sunday, they spoke with the college coach again, and David knew that this was where he wanted to go to school. He figured it was perfect because it was a few hours from home but close enough so his grandpa could come to a lot of games and watch him play. He also remembered Becky talking about how she hoped to one day go there as well.

He couldn't believe how quickly things had changed. He went from needing routine confidence boosts from Dusty to somehow committing to play division 1 baseball for his state school in a couple of months. He was so thankful for his family and friends who pushed him to take advantage of the opportunities he was presented with and those who convinced him that he was more than he ever thought he was capable of. He couldn't wait to get home and share the news with Becky, but his grandpa wanted to celebrate with a steak dinner near campus. Because of this, David didn't get home until after ten at night, and then he had to explain everything to his mom again.

After he showered and got to bed, it was almost midnight. He was exhausted and couldn't wait to see the guys in the morning. More importantly, he couldn't wait to see Becky. He thought it was strange that she hadn't called, but David didn't realize that his mom had taken the phone off the hook earlier so she could study for an exam without any distractions.

David woke up the next morning to his mother kissing him goodbye. She was off to work at Jay's, and she remembered him saying he wanted her to wake him up when she left. He wanted to sleep in a little bit, but he wanted to be ready to head over to Dusty's bright and early for breakfast before they got to the field. He left his house at around eight o'clock and couldn't wait to tell Bonnie about his college decision. She wanted Dusty to go away to school, but they both knew he didn't have the grades or desire to do that, so she would be so happy that one boy at her table was going away for college in a couple of years. He wasn't in a big hurry, but he was walking at a good pace when he got to the church where he had won Becky her favorite prize. He looked at the large grassy area where there had been rides and games a month ago and smiled as he thought about Becky and the memories they had made this summer.

It was then that Gary came to a screeching halt on the side of the road. David figured he was on his way to work and wanted a quick update on his weekend, but he saw Dusty in the car as well. He thought it was really odd that they would both be up and riding around together this early. David racked his brain and tried to remember if they had agreed to pick him up on Monday morning, but he was positive they hadn't. He smiled and waved at them as Dusty rolled down the passenger seat window, but his smile slowly faded as he saw Dusty holding back tears.

"Get in, David," he said calmly but sternly.

"What's up?" David asked nervously. He looked over at Gary, but he was looking out the driver's side window and wouldn't make eye contact.

"David, get in the car," Dusty calmly repeated again. He wasn't sure what was going on, but he could tell that it was something serious. He had only seen Dusty like that a few times before in his life, and it was usually right before a fight when he was so angry that he couldn't hold his anger in any longer. Anxiously, David tossed his baseball gear into the back seat and slid in the middle of the back seat.

He was looking in the rearview mirror and the back of their heads, trying to guess what was so troubling this early in the morning. He was wondering if something had happened to Ricky again, or maybe it was Joey since he wasn't in the car. Neither Gary or Dusty was talking, and they both seemed to be looking at each other and silently asking the other one to break the silence. Gary waited for traffic to clear before doing a U-turn to start heading back into town. That was when he gave Dusty the look that told him he had to say something and soon.

Dusty turned around and was visibly shaken. He no longer looked like a boy who was about to fight but a boy who had his heart broken. As he started to talk to David, he had a hard time keeping from breaking down, so he spoke slowly while taking shallow breaths. "I tried calling you five times this morning, but your phone line was busy."

David stopped to think, and he remembered that his mom had taken the phone off the hook, and they both had forgotten about it, so he nervously smiled and tried to explain to Dusty, but he shook his head and told him not to worry about that. He took as deep a breath as he could gather as he knew the next few sentences were going to be the most difficult he would have to say in his young life. "David, my dad called about twenty minutes ago. They got called down to Becky's house." He now could no longer hold back the tears but fought through them to keep on for his friend. "Her dad got into her really bad last night, beat her up and raped her like never before. When I couldn't get a hold of you, I called Gary because we didn't want you finding out some other way."

David's jaw gently dropped as he wanted to start asking questions and was taking in the news, but Dusty wasn't finished. "David, it's really bad," he started again, gaining some composure to get things out as quickly as he could for his friend. "It was Becky's mom that discovered them this morning when she got off work. He must have been so drunk because he was still passed out on the floor in her room when she got home, and Becky was still unconscious this morning. She had been there like that for a few hours. They were rushing her to the hospital, but my dad said she was in really bad shape."

When Dusty finished, he looked at his friend to try to prepare for whatever reaction awaited. Gary looked in the rearview mirror at David but quickly looked away in silence when David looked up at him. David was in shock. He couldn't believe what his friend had just told him, but he knew that he was not joking. He fell backward into the seat and replayed what he envisioned that scene must have been like over in his head. It made him sick to his stomach, but it also made him angry. He couldn't picture his love beaten so badly that she lay unconscious for hours. Suddenly, this swell of anger came over him; the car was rolling up on an intersection. They were heading back to Dusty's place as David figured they were instructed to do so by his dad. When Gary reached the four-way stop, David flung open the back door and began running toward her house. Neither of the boys even bothered to yell at him to stop.

David sprinted the short distance in disbelief, but as the school and field came into view, so did the mob of police cars and emergency personnel. There was crime scene tape all around the perimeter, just like David had seen on TV, but this was because of his girlfriend. He slowed up as he approached the scene, and he could hear Gary's car suddenly trailing him. None of it seemed real until he saw Becky's stepdad covered in blood, being led out of the house in handcuffs. The sight of that man lit the fuse inside him, and David began running at full speed to go and kill him. At the last second, however, Officer Smith saw him coming and tackled him to the ground. They wrestled briefly, but Officer Smith quickly got the upper hand.

"What the hell are you doing?" he shouted at David, keeping him pinned to the ground.

"Becky!" David cried. "He killed Becky! I'm going to kill that son of a bitch! He killed Becky!" David was openly crying now, and whatever strength and fight he had in him evaporated in Officer Smith's arms, who now began holding him like a small child. David couldn't control his crying, but each time he thought about his beautiful Becky, he lost it even more.

After a few minutes, David began to calm down, and Officer Smith welcomed Gary and Dusty to come over and help console their friend. He sat on the ground with the three boys, putting his arm around David. "David, I can't imagine how this must be for you. I know she was really special to you. I remember commenting on you guys at the big church picnic." He was being very methodical and to the point. "Becky isn't dead. She's a fighter. It's what you boys liked so much about her."

He gave David a little shake to try to boost his spirits. "I don't know exactly what her status is, but she was taken to the hospital. Her mom was really shaken up as you can imagine. I can't see her allowing any visitors that aren't family." He rubbed David's back and promised he'd give the boys any more details if he could. He politely asked them to go home, and he nodded to Dusty and Gary silently to look after David, who still had his head down, facing the ground.

They all picked David up and watched Becky's stepdad get driven away. "At least he admitted to everything," Officer Smith said with a cold demeanor. "Son of a bitch was read his rights and then spilled his guts out. None of you will have to worry about seeing him around here for a long time." He again patted David, hoping that anything could lift his spirits. As Dusty and Gary helped escort their broken friend back to his car, Officer Smith went and rejoined the remaining officers who were working the scene.

Gary did, in fact, have to be at work; so once David was back on his feet, he gave him a hug and took off for work. David could only imagine his boss's reaction when Gary told him why he was coming in late. Dusty put his arm around his friend as they made their way back to his trailer. The boys didn't say much on that walk; there wasn't much to say. They saw a few local news station vans come barreling down the side streets on their way to Becky's house.

When they entered the short driveway to Dusty's trailer, Bonnie came out crying to give David a big hug. It broke her heart to see David covered in dirt and grass stains as she knew it was a sign of how difficult the news had been for David to take. She sat around the trailer, trying to console the boys, but nothing really seemed to lift their spirits. Even when they turned on the TV to try to get a little sense of normalcy, the first thing they were greeted with was a story about Becky on the local late morning news. In typical fashion, the only time Riverview made the news was to report some crime or horrible story.

Not long after that, David's mom arrived to pick up her broken son. She and Bonnie cried together before she took David home. She cried the entire way, but David didn't have any more tears to give, so he tried to comfort her a bit.

This was the kind of crime that rocked the entire community. David grew angry that, suddenly, everyone had a story about Becky that they wanted to share with the news or the press. They didn't know her or love her like he did. It shook David's mom so badly that she asked if David cared if his dad came and spent the night. He couldn't blame her for wanting someone to hold on to.

That night, David met back up with Dusty. They walked the streets together and talked. David thanked Dusty for everything he had done for him, just like he had planned to do earlier in the morning. Dusty admitted that he was a bit jealous, but being the true friend that he was, he told David how happy and proud he was for him. He told him that he would always be David's friend and have his back, even after he left town. David told him that he was going to make a change in his community somehow someday. The boys were again comforted by each other and knew that they were in this game of life together forever. Things might keep changing, but they knew they would always be friends.

Eventually, they wound their way back around to the field. They had been trying to avoid it in their meandering stroll around town, but as they walked the street that formed the left field boundary, they stopped and looked at the field. Dusty looked at David to see what he was thinking before they both started moving across the grass and clover. The crime scene tape and media trucks had disappeared from earlier in the night. The house was completely dark, and pretty soon, Becky's story would be forgotten as other crimes from the city would soon be grabbing headlines. They made their way to the pitcher's mound area and sat down facing the school.

"How the hell did we end up in the same reading group?" Dusty chuckled, remembering the moment in elementary school that initiated their great friendship. Both boys looked at each other and laughed.

They picked at the dirt a bit before David began speaking. "This is where my life changed, right here." He paused and searched for his next words. "It all changed here because of you and my friends who believed in me when I didn't." They both thought back to when the challenge had been issued at the Dairy Barn. David was trying to hold back his tears as he continued, "And I don't think I'll ever be able to play here again." He was shaking his head and looking down at the ground. Dusty put his arm around him and knew that he wasn't saying that because he thought he was too good or didn't want to be with his friends anymore.

"I just don't think I can come down here ever again," he said, trailing off and breaking up.

Dusty knew he was talking about Becky. "She's a fighter," he began, trying to lift his friend. "She'll be back here soon enough, just like Ricky. We didn't think he'd be back, but—"

"Stop," David interrupted. "I don't want to compare Becky to Ricky." He gave a fleeting smile to let Dusty know that he appreciated what he was trying to say and do.

"I kind of just want to sit here for a while and soak things in one more time, if that's okay?" David asked.

"Sure, anything you want, man," Dusty replied. "Lots of good times here, lots of good memories." They boys sat there for a long time and talked about those memories and stories. They longed for the days when things were a lot more innocent and playing on that field was the highlight of their summers.

Eventually, Dusty's dad found them and took David home. He was comforted to hear his parents talking to each other in the living room, and it made him happy to see his dad holding his mom in his arms on the couch. He smiled at them both and went to his room to collapse from exhaustion.

The following day, Dusty's grandpa came down to visit and talk with David. Along with his mom, they took David out to lunch in town. As expected, they hadn't heard much news from Becky's mom, and she wasn't allowing visitors. She wasn't anything like her daughter personality wise. She was quiet and hard to read. She looked somewhat frail to begin with, and this experience was enough to break any parent. Her parents had both died when she was in high school due to medical issues, which probably explained why she worked in a senior center as a medical assistant and had horrible taste in men. Her mom's only other immediate family was a sister who lived across the state. Dusty's mom and grandpa had both tried to reach out to her and explain how close they had all gotten to Becky, but she just hung up the phone on them, thinking they were members of the press trying to get more details on her condition and story.

It broke David not to even be able to know how she was doing. The person he had grown accustomed to telling everything to couldn't even hear him say that he loved her. His mom and grandpa knew how much she meant to him, and they were struggling to keep his spirits up. Knowing his grandson, his grandpa suggested that, after lunch, they leave him alone for a while. David nodded in agreement and told them that he would see them at home later in the day.

David wasn't certain where he wanted to go but found himself heading toward the city park where he had seen Becky alone on that swing earlier in the summer. When he reached the park, there were young kids there running around and playing without a care in the world. David was jealous with envy as he continued walking to the creek embankment where he and his friends had shared beers that same night. He stood at the top of the embankment and looked toward the city. He couldn't see the hospital, but he knew Becky was there somewhere, alone and fighting for her life.

Trying not to let his mind drift too far, David suddenly heard the blare of a police horn from across the park. Even at that distance, it made him jump and snap to attention. He turned and saw Officer Smith standing outside his patrol car and motioning him over. David was suddenly anxious again because he figured that he was going to update David about Becky, and news this soon likely meant she had taken a turn for the worse or her fight was over.

With his stomach entrenched in his throat, he made the trip across the open field and past the joyous families to the patrol car. Officer Smith's body language gave David no clues about what to expect. "Somebody told me they saw you walking down here," he began without changing his cop demeanor. "So I'm glad I found you. I have something I want to give you, but it might be tough."

David tried to swallow as he prepared for the worst.

Officer Smith reached into the back seat of his squad car, pulled out a medium-sized cloth bag, and handed it to David. He looked at the officer with confusion and fear in his eyes. Extending the bag out toward David, Officer Smith sympathetically said, "We finished up with the crime scene yesterday, so I took another look around Becky's room."

David was opening the bag while Officer Smith went on, "There was an unfinished note that I found on the floor next to the stuffed animal. She mentioned you in the note and referenced the stuffed animal, so I thought you might like to keep them. With a full confession, we really didn't need to keep them as evidence." He raised his lower lip and chin, trying to show toughness and thoughtfulness at the same time.

David saw a notepad with Becky's writing on it and the stuffed lion he had won for her, the one that she said would keep her safe and always remind her of him. He pictured her smiling and waving the lion back and forth after his first big game she had come to watch him pitch in where he impressed so many people. David thanked Officer Smith and accepted his offer for a ride home while closing the bag up.

When he arrived home, he walked halfway up his steps and sat down to read the note. He grabbed the stuffed lion and noticed a smattering of blood across its mane. He squeezed it tightly out of love and anguish. As he pulled the notepad out of the bag, he caught a whiff of Becky's perfume and looked to the city skyline again, wishing he could hold her.

Slowly and gently, he placed the notepad on his lap. The light blue penmanship was rushed and not her familiar spectacular cursive, but it was unmistakably her writing:

David,

I am so scared right now. I've tried calling a few times, but the line is busy. My stepdad is drunk and screaming at the top of his lungs to me. I have my door locked, but I don't think that will stop him. He's mad at my mom about something. I love you so much! I have your lion here with me. If he comes through that door, he's going to find out that I'm much stronger than the last time because of you. I won't let him have his way with me. You mean the world to me, and together, I think we can

It stopped at that point, undoubtedly when he had broken down the door. David cringed as he thought about her trying to fight him off and the horrible beating and abuse she must have taken.

He read the note over and over again, and each time he did, he felt more and more blame and guilt. Why hadn't his mom put the phone back on the hook? If she had, he would have been able to call the police and save her. Why did she think that stupid lion would give her the strength to fight him off? If it wasn't for that lion, she wouldn't be in the hospital fighting for her life. David picked up the lion again violently, this time squeezing it around the neck and hoping to choke the life out of it. He pictured his face in place of the lion's as he let out an anguished roar. When he had squeezed so hard that his arm started to seize up on him, he dropped the lion to the ground. Quickly, he picked it back up and threw it as hard as he could into the bushes in front of his house, went inside, and sobbed.

The last few weeks of summer slipped away quietly. As much as anybody tried, Becky's mom wasn't sharing any information about her or her condition. David decided to ask for more hours at work to help out his mom with the bills and keep his mind occupied. His mom and dad were taking things very slowly, but things were improving. They even went out to dinner one night as a family, and his father asked David all about his baseball experiences throughout the summer. He seemed happy and supportive.

The boys didn't play at the field anymore that summer. Gary enrolled early at the junior college and was taking his studies and athletics seriously for once. Ricky was still recovering, so he spent most of his time at home, letting his body heal, while Joey decided to stay on with the landscaping company. Dusty continued working part time at the restaurant and tavern not too far from the high school at the other end of town. He and David got together whenever they could. David even took him to a few events with his new friends from his summer ball team. While it was a bit awkward at first, Dusty found his niche like he always did with anybody he hung out with.

David called Becky's house and left messages on the machine, but nobody ever picked up or responded. Eventually, the phone number was disconnected. He thought about her every day but had no way of getting in touch with her. He decided he would write her letters and mail them to her. It sounded crazy at first since she lived in town, but it helped David deal with things and made him feel like he was talking to her.

When school started back up, he had to listen to all the people in the Riverview cafeteria talk about Becky and come up with wild stories about her and her stepfather. Becky had been right about how mean girls really can be to one another. David struggled to focus in his classes, but ironically, Dusty helped him keep on track. He even went with David to the track and weight room a few times a week to help keep him motivated and working on his body like he had been instructed to do by the college coaches. He told David he was just doing it so he had more room for Bonnie's cooking, but David knew why he was there and really appreciated it. They really didn't talk much about Becky, but Dusty knew she was always on David's mind.

It was late September when he was spending the night at Dusty's that they heard on the news that Becky had been released from the hospital, almost two months after the assault. They reported that she still had a long recovery ahead and that her step-ad's court date had been set for the spring. They didn't show any pictures of her or mention her condition specifically. Next thing he knew, they were talking about a carjacking on one of the interstates. Just like that, she had flashed back into his life and was gone again.

Her house had been up for sale since mid-August and sold surprisingly fast. David had no idea where she was moving, but he hoped that he might see her in school one day. Nobody at school or in town had any clue where they had moved. He continued writing his letters to her, but he stopped when they were returned because no forwarding address had been left with the post office.

The holidays came and went, and things were about as good as David could have hoped for at home. His parents were back living together, and they were happy. His dad got a new job managing a retail shop, and his mom went to work for him. He didn't seem nearly as stressed or as miserable as he had been while working at the steel mill. They were both home at the same time, except for when she was gone taking her classes in the evenings.

David and his dad started to build a relationship while watching hockey and basketball games on TV together. It gave them something to talk about without having to get too deep into any issues. David enjoyed not watching the games in silence anymore and appreciated how much his dad was willing to change and grow. David knew he would never be extremely close with his father, but he was happy that they were finding common ground.

Sometime around Valentine's Day, a letter arrived for David. It had no return address but was postmarked in a city about five hours away. He took it to his room and opened it, and as soon as he saw the handwriting, there was no mistaking who it was from. Becky had written him to let him know that she received all his letters and that she loved him and missed him more than ever. Her mom had moved them to her sister's place across the state and forbidden her from having any communication with anyone back home. She said the psychologists recommended she cut off any ties to her past to try to avoid any further emotional trauma, and she said her mom checked the phone records to make sure Becky was abiding by their rules. She never thought it would be difficult to not think about Riverview or anyone in it until she was told she couldn't talk to David anymore. Even though her asshole stepdad had gotten her out of Riverview, he was still managing to punish her every day.

She was recovering and expected to be fine eventually, but she still had some cognitive issues, so she wasn't able to enroll in school yet because she had to meet with therapists and specialists multiple days a week until everything was back to normal. She was glad she was young for her class because she would be able enroll in school next year and still graduate in a traditional school. She said her mom would kill her if she knew she was sending this letter, but her aunt loved hearing stories about him, so she promised to sneak this one in the mail without telling.

She said she was in tears thinking about him and how she didn't know if she'd ever see him again. A few words had been smudged to show that she wasn't joking as she had literally cried over the letter she was writing. She promised that she would try to write or call when she got away from her mother but said this would probably be the only thing he would hear for a while. She would understand if he found another girlfriend because who wouldn't want to date the hottest guy in school who was a superstar pitcher? She told him that he wouldn't have to worry about her dating anybody else for a while because her body was still swollen in some areas, and even in her new town, people were whispering about what had happened to her. She figured when she got back to school, it wouldn't be much different from before with girls, but she didn't regret fighting back. She was glad that she finally stood up to him with all her might, and the only thing that she regretted was that it caused her to not be able to see David.

Again, she reminded him that she loved him and said that she missed her stuffed lion. She hadn't been able to pack up her room, so she figured her mom must have thrown it away. She hoped to see him again someday, but if not, she would cherish their time together for the rest of her life and wished she had the lion to remind her of him.

When David finished reading the letter, a teardrop of his own fell and smudged some of the ink. He panicked and tried to dry it as quickly as possible. He wanted to preserve that letter for as long as he lived. He read the letter again a few times and then had a wave of panic come over him. He had thrown the lion into the bushes outside his house months ago after he read the desperate note that Becky was writing him right before her stepdad assaulted her.

He instantly jumped up and ran out into the cold where he had thrown the lion. He practically tore up the bushes, desperately trying to find the one thing that Becky said she missed and wanted. After a few minutes without any luck, he dropped to his knees, crying. Again, he had been selfish and only thought about himself. He felt like he had failed Becky one last time.

Behind him on the porch, his mom and dad had come out to see what had caused him to rush out into the cold without a coat. They found him on his knees, crying, and his mom rushed over to help him out. She asked what he was so upset about, and when David told her he was looking for a stuffed lion, instead of withdrawing in confusion, she looked back at her husband standing on the porch. He nodded and went inside as she helped her son up and slowly gathered him into her arms. As she eased him up the stairs and into the front hallway, David could hear his dad walking down the hallway toward them.

When he turned the corner, David saw his dad holding the stuffed lion in his hands. David just stared at him in stunned disbelief. It was a bit tattered, but it was Becky's lion nonetheless. He just looked at his dad but couldn't say anything. His father innocently shrugged as he said, "I found this when I was picking up the leaves around the house. It seemed so out of place that it didn't make sense, so I showed it to your mom. She said it belonged to Becky, but she wasn't sure if you were ready to have it back yet. She said she brought it to the first game they came and watched you pitch. She told me to put it in our closet to give to you later. I guess we just forgot. I'm sorry." He extended his hand with the lion.

David looked at his mom for affirmation, and she just nodded to confirm that everything her father had said was true. Instinctively, without thinking, David went over to his father and gave him a huge hug. Unsure of exactly what to do or how to handle things, he stood there with his arms at his side as David squeezed him. He then locked eyes with his wife, who gave him a slight gesture with her head to tell him it was okay to hug his son back.

"Thank you, Dad," David said, still clutching him. "Thank you!" David gently accepted the lion from his dad's hand and went off to his bedroom. His mother just looked at her husband with an approving smile to suggest how happy she was with him for not throwing the lion away without mentioning it to her.

That spring, David made sure he brought that lion with him to every baseball game. He put it with his equipment and made sure he could always see it when he was pitching. His teammates laughed and gave him a hard time, but Dusty took care of them for David. Plus, they didn't give him too hard of a time as he led them to a sectional championship, beating Fox Creek 1–0. It was only the second time in school history Riverview had won a sectional, and the fact that it was over Fox Creek made it even more special for the people involved.

His senior year seemed to go by in a flash. It was relatively uneventful. He signed his letter of intent with the state school in November and prepared throughout the winter for his senior season. That year, he went out and pitched them to another sectional championship over Fox Creek. Riverview even managed to get all the way to the state semifinals before falling 1–0 to the eventual state champion, farther than any other team in the history of the school had made it. In the process, David overtook every single one of Randy Black's school records, and Becky's lion was there to watch every game. His dad didn't miss a single game, and his grandpa was there in the stands with him for each one. He thought about Becky every day and didn't have any interest in the girls who came up to him after games, even though they had plenty of interest in him. He checked the mailbox each day when he got home, hoping that he might find a surprise letter from her in there, but he never did.

David had dreamed of moving away for many years growing up, and without Becky around, it wasn't as difficult to leave Riverview as he had thought it might be a couple of summers earlier. Since they stopped playing at the school baseball field since Becky's assault, David didn't really see guys like Ricky, Joey, or Gary very often. Gary had done well enough at the local junior college that not only did he earn a spot on the roster but he also was going to finish out his baseball career at a division 2 school a few states away. Joey had really taken to his work with the landscaping company, so by the time David was leaving for college, he was working close to sixty hours a week to save up for his own equipment to eventually start up his own business. Ricky had slipped back into his old ways without Gary and Joey to keep an eye on him. David barely saw him anymore, but he had heard plenty of stories about his ventures back into the world of selling drugs and running with shady company.

Dusty was the most difficult person for David to say goodbye to. As their older friends had moved forward with their paths in life, David and Dusty grew even closer. Dusty had gotten a serious girlfriend his senior year, but David hung out with them as much as possible. Their friendship had solidified that summer of '91, but it flourished in the following years. They both shed some tears after their final baseball game, knowing it was the last time that they would work as a battery on the field.

Dusty decided to enroll in the local junior college to take some business classes. He was still working in the kitchen at the same restaurant and tavern in Riverview, but the owner told him that if he took some college business classes, he would groom him to take over the place one day. The final days leading up to his departure, David and Dusty talked about how they vowed to remain friends for life. David couldn't promise how often he would be home, but Dusty inspired him to study business in college as well. David told him that, one day, he hoped to come back to Riverview and do something that would make a difference in the community. Bonnie cried like it was her own son leaving when David visited one last time before going off to school.

David's parents both helped him move into his dorm. While he and his dad still didn't always have the most to talk about, his mom was happy, so that made David happy. He was glad to have his dad around, and instead of talking about his own playing days, his dad would now go around in Riverview bragging about his son. David was glad that Randy Black's stories would finally have some competition in the local bars. They were proud to see their son pursuing his dream, and he was proud of them for becoming a real family that he was proud of and missed while he was at school.

The fall of his freshman year was a bit overwhelming at times. The classes were a bit more advanced than he had expected, and while he had long dreamed of living in a city, the size of campus was a bit daunting at first. On top of that, he was a freshman at a major college baseball program. Just like what Gary had done to him back in Riverview when he was an underclassman, he was back to carrying bags and equipment for the older guys. He was extremely relieved to have his summer teammate and friend Ryan Harding as his roommate. Just like he had back home, Ryan took David under his wing and made him feel welcome at school and within the baseball program. They would always walk from their dorm to fall workouts together and back.

David was struggling to find his groove on the team. Most of the upperclassmen had been hitting him pretty hard in the fall workouts. It was a pretty normal occurrence within any good baseball program for the older guys to have their way with the younger ones, but David was struggling and getting down on himself. Ryan would always try to pick him up and tell him how awful he was last season when he was a freshman, but David was starting to have doubts about whether he belonged. He brought Becky's stuffed lion with him but was too scared to actually bring it to the fall workouts.

He started to convince himself that he was just a small-town kid who didn't belong with the big boys. All the familiar doubts and fears he had growing up started to come out that fall as he thought about how embarrassing it would be to have to come back home at Christmas and tell everyone that he probably wasn't even going to be on the team's traveling roster in the spring, not what everyone would want to hear after he left town as a local hero. After a while, Ryan's pep talks became more routine than getting up at five in the morning to go lift with the team.

The fall scrimmages that closed out their fall semester workouts were coming up that Saturday, and David was desperate for anything to feel good about heading into the winter. He decided that he was going to bring Becky's stuffed lion and place it in the pocket of his baseball backpack. When he pitched, he was going to make sure it was in sight within the dugout, and he wasn't going to care what anybody said.

The fall scrimmages were open to the public. The scrimmages were a doubleheader on Saturday that allowed each pitcher on staff to go out and throw a couple of innings. Typically, the more established older guys would pitch the first game, and then the guys hoping to make a name for themselves would get their chance the second game. The younger hitters played the first game and the older ones the second. It was the coach's way of making sure his top hitters and pitchers went into the winter feeling good about themselves.

Fans came out in big numbers since the weather was decent that day. Most were there to watch the first game and get autographs. The stands were so full that the guys in the bullpen were having a hard time finding their girlfriends in the crowd. The single girls on campus who were interested in baseball, and more importantly the players, knew to show up for the second game. It was their chance to see the new baseball players up close and do a little scouting of their own. Plus, when the second game was over, they were free to mingle with the players as they left the complex.

David spent the first game watching from the bullpen. His right leg felt like it was on a trampoline all by itself as he couldn't keep it from nervously bouncing up and down. There were more people there than he anticipated, and the way he'd been throwing the ball lately, he figured he was going to give the fans a lot of confidence in the team's offense in the spring.

The other younger pitchers were also struggling out there, so that helped calm David's nerves slightly as he figured he couldn't do much worse. The only problem was the team was going through arms, and they hoped to play a certain number of innings without running out of pitchers. David's heart flipped when the pitching coach came down in the fourth inning and told him to warm up. "We need you to cover at least two innings, Collins," he said in the typical rugged coach's voice. "Three would be better. We've been out here all day, and I'm tired of coming down here to warm somebody up." With that, he swiftly went back to the dugout.

David had dreamed of wearing the jersey of his state school, but now his heart was pounding as he was warming up before his first appearance in that jersey before fans. As much as he tried, he couldn't settle his heartbeat. He hadn't felt like this since he first pitched for the Fox Creek Legion team in front of Becky and his family. Suddenly, he thought about Becky, wishing she could see him in his uniform. His heartbeat began to slow as he could feel the competitive fire inside him build. No matter where she was, he wasn't going to let her down today. He took the stuffed lion out of his bag and placed it in a side pocket of his equipment bag where he could see it.

"Are you freaking serious, Collins?" the catcher warming him up said.

"Sure am," David replied with a swagger he hadn't had since the first team workout.

"Whatever," the kid said as he shook his head and fired the ball back to David. "This isn't freaking Disney World, kid."

David just blocked him out and told himself that whatever he did, he wasn't going to be afraid. He wasn't going back to Riverview as a failure. He hadn't come this far to lie down in front of his teammates. In fact, it was pitching well against older kids that first got him noticed by his coach in the first place.

When David came in to take the mound, there weren't more people there than a typical high school game. There were the diehards who wanted to see as many players as possible, but most of the remaining crowd were family members and local parents still enjoying one of the last nice days of the fall with their kids who were hoping to snag a few more autographs. He placed his bag with the stuffed lion at the end of the dugout. As he was getting ready to jog out to take the ball, he saw a couple of upperclassmen playing with his bag and messing with the animal. David came back across the foul line and yelled at them to stop messing with his stuff. It was a bold move for an underclassman, but whether it was his tone or the glare from their coach, the boys left his bag alone, and David was on the mound with the fire back in his belly. The guys in the dugout looked at his roommate, Ryan, who had seen the lion in his bag the last summer they played Legion ball with Fox Creek but had no idea why it was so important to him.

David went out there to face the first batter and let the ball rip. There wasn't a radar gun posted in the stadium, but David was throwing hard enough that the diehards began flipping vigorously through their programs to see who this new kid on the mound was. After each out, David glared into the dugout to make sure nobody was messing with his bag. The more outs he got, the farther people got away from his stuff. Before he knew it, David had gone out and thrown three perfect innings. He was the only pitcher on the entire staff to throw multiple perfect innings. The coaches were all raving about him afterward and talked about how they were waiting to see that from him all fall. David had to admit he felt pretty good about himself, and suddenly, he didn't mind the older guys wanting to rub his stuffed lion for good vibes as they were about to have a nice break from baseball until after Christmas break.

Being a freshman, David had to stick around and help do maintenance on the field with the other kids in his class. He could see a few girls hanging around the concourse and talking with some of his older teammates along with a few players and their families, but by the time he walked out of the gate, there were only a few autograph seekers left and a smattering of people. The girls had all left. He noticed it was starting to get much cooler, and the leaves on the trees beyond the left field fence were falling as the breeze picked up slightly. He made sure to sign every autograph for any kid who wanted one because he told himself that if he ever became an athlete, he would do that for kids. He was exhausted and hungry, but he tried to keep up a good face.

Finally, when everyone had gotten what they wanted, he bent over to pick up his bag. The stuffed lion was peeking out, and David just put his lips together tightly before he silently mouthed "thank you" in its direction. It was as he started to rise back that he heard a voice behind him that jolted him.

"Hey, got time for one more autograph?" It was a female voice that sounded familiar but couldn't be possible.

He didn't want to get his hopes up, so he turned slowly with his guard up. When he turned around and saw the face behind the voice, he breathed in so deeply through his nose that his entire body rose. He looked around to see if any upperclassmen were around, playing a joke on him. He was so distracted and unnerved that his voice eluded him.

"Oh, I see. You can sign autographs for complete strangers but not for an old friend?" Again, the girl smiled as she tapped her foot anxiously on the concrete, proud of her use of sarcasm and element of surprise.

"Becky?" David stumbled to get out. "Is . . . it . . ."

She just stood there nodding and trying not to smile, watching David fumble all over himself. "Wow, I thought a guy who was the star of the game wouldn't be this shy. Guess old habits die hard, huh?"

Still in disbelief of who was standing in front of him, he walked over and put his hands on her hips to make sure she was really standing there in front of him. He was still at a loss for words, but the tears running down his cheeks told Becky everything she needed to know about the young man she had loved. She looked at him as he still had his hands gently on her hips and approved of his touch. With that, David pulled her closer to his body than he can ever remember. "I missed you so much, Becky." He just stood there holding her with his eyes until he heard someone passing by them on the concourse.

"I missed you too, David," she said, finally breaking character and allowing the tears to form in her eyes as well. They embraced again for what seemed like forever, both working their hands up and down the other's familiar body. The only thing that separated them was the sound of a young family walking down the concourse to exit the stadium behind the third baseline.

"I see you've got my lion," Becky said, lifting David's bag and running her hand over the animal's face.

David started to pull it out of the pocket, but Becky stopped him. "Keep it. He's ours." To hear her say the word *ours* filled David with a joy he hadn't experienced in more than two years. He knew how special that lion had been to her and how much it meant to him during the time they had been separated.

Once the reality of her actual presence set in, David was able to start putting together thoughts and sentences. "So do you go here? How did you know I'd be here? Why didn't you call me if you knew I was here? How come—"

"Whoa, whoa, whoa, lover boy." She giggled, putting her hand over his mouth to slow him down. "I haven't seen you in two years, so I guess you haven't spoken to anyone since then?" She had always liked giving him a hard time, and her sarcasm helped calm her nerves and steady her heart in the presence of her love. "I'll get to your questions. We've obviously got a lot to catch up on," she said, raising an eyebrow in the way she had so many times to draw a boy in. "That is, if you're interested." She kicked her feet together and nervously looked down.

David took a step back to take her in. Everything had happened so quickly that he didn't even notice what she was wearing, nice jeans with a college sweatshirt. Her hair was cut shorter, but her skin was still the perfect color of bronze to bring out her eyes and smile more than the typical girl. "You bet I'm interested," he excitedly said back to her. "I'm starving. Let's go somewhere. What sounds good?"

She paused and thought for a second before blurting out, "Ice cream?" David smiled and nodded that ice cream with her indeed sounded good.

That evening, they ended up spending the entire night together. She explained that when he signed his letter of intent to come to the state school, her aunt saw the clipping in their local paper and gave it to her. From that moment on, she knew she was going to come here. She had always wanted to go to school here to begin with, so when she saw he was coming, she knew it was destiny, but she wasn't sure how to find him or if he still thought about her. She told him that she was so nervous to even come to the scrimmage because she didn't want him to see her and possibly get upset or lose his concentration, so she sat down the line opposite the bullpen he was in with some friends. When they left early, she went behind the stands and was going to leave too, but then she saw him walking in from the bullpen with her lion hanging out of the pocket and knew that she had to talk to him. She was so nervous and scared that she hid the last three innings and after the game. David laughed to himself that he could make her nervous.

David told her about everything that had been going on back home in Riverview and how his dad had actually saved the lion. He talked about how he had missed her and never gotten over her but how she was still with him for all the games he had pitched. She cried and wished that she could have been there but promised she would never miss another one of his games. They laughed and cried together for hours that night, talking about the great memories and the painful ones.

Becky explained how her mom had a breakdown not long after they moved away, so between that and her own issues, she decided to major in social work and psychology. It broke her to not be able to call him and hear his voice while she was gone, but she just kept counting down the days until they would be on campus together. Then when she got here and saw all the beautiful girls and how they fawned over the athletes, she persuaded herself to give up on him and let him go. She felt so ashamed of what had happened to her, and she didn't think she'd ever be any good for a man.

David told her again that he had never stopped thinking about her and that she would always be more than good enough for her, and even when his family and friends told him to move on, he couldn't. People told him it was crazy because they had only been together for a month, but he told them that they had really been together most of their lives; they just didn't realize it. She was still the most beautiful woman he had ever seen, and he couldn't believe that someone like her could think that other girls had something she didn't. David reaffirmed his dreams to get a business degree and use it to somehow improve their hometown. They both wanted to help people, but the best help in the world was sitting right across from them at that booth. Two best friends had been united, and if it wasn't for a stuffed lion sticking out of a backpack, it may never have happened.

They dived back into their friendship, and the romance came along with it. The time apart had driven them together instead of apart, and it made each of them appreciate the other even more. Becky had transformed David and made him a better man a few years ago, and now he was there to help her as she struggled to put all the evils of her past behind her. She felt confident that she could never trust another man, except David, and she was relieved that she would never have to.

20 CHAPTER

"Hey, are you down there?" David heard the call, but it didn't register at first. "Babe, we've got to get going." The calls were getting more urgent as the voice was descending down the stairs. "Hey, you've been down here for over ten minutes. Is everything okay?"

David turned to see the voice behind him. It was his beautiful wife, Becky. She was focused as always and oblivious to the fact that he had tears in his eyes. "The kids and I have been patiently waiting in the car, but Jake is starting to get really anxious," she announced to him.

David had forgotten all about them. He looked at Becky and then back to the stuffed lion in his hands, the prize that he had won for her so many years ago, that same lion that gave her the courage to go and speak to her love in college, the lion that had gotten David through tough moments when he was a kid, when Becky wasn't around, when he didn't feel like he was good enough during his playing career, and through the rehabs after surgeries when his career was in doubt, yet the real prize stood before him in the doorway to his storage room. It was a prize that he would cherish his entire lifetime.

Through it all, Becky had stood by him while he pursued his dreams. She never once wavered or asked him to give up baseball. She lived in so many outrageous apartments with him and other guys in even more outrageous places, but she never complained. She was by David's side when he was a two-time all-conference pitcher in college and when he signed his professional contract with the Orioles. She was also there by his side when he had surgery on his elbow and then on his shoulder. She was there when he was twenty-eight years old and told that nobody believed in him and his ability to pitch anymore. None of the highs and lows had caused her love for him to waver.

She helped him battle through his depression and was the most beautiful bride he had ever seen. He remembered the first permanent house they bought together on the west side of Fox Creek. She had long stood by her position of not returning back home, but she saw how much it meant to David to be close to his family, so she learned how to conquer the horrors of her childhood while he stood by her side. He remembered how proud he was when she started working with and mentoring young girls in Riverview. He remembered how special it was for them when they moved into this house together, their dream home, a few years ago. It was almost as special as the birth of their two children. Because of what her stepfather had done years ago, it was uncertain and unlikely if she'd ever be able to conceive a child; so when Jake came along after years of trying, they believed it was a miracle. Lauren was another one.

How do you tell the person who is your entire world "thank you"? The person who helped make you a man and was there to hold your world together when you didn't feel like one? David just sat there, fumbling with the stuffed animal, looking at his wife. She still had her youthful face, and those eyes and smile still popped. As always, David's head was in the clouds, while hers was focused on the task at hand. He was speechless by both her beauty and her love.

"David, we've got to go," she urged again. "Your parents are going to wonder where we are, not to mention all the kids on the team who—"

He quietly put his finger over his mouth as he stared at the woman he loved. He got up slowly and walked over to her. Just before he got to her, he did the same little dance with the lion in his hands that she had done years ago after she watched him pitch his first game.

She just laughed at him and said, "Jake is going to love getting that from you." She loved that man with her entire heart. She was so proud of the investment he was making to coach kids from Riverview in baseball and build them great fields in town. She knew the time and money he had put into it and how important it was for him to improve the experiences for struggling kids in his hometown.

"Not nearly as much as I love thinking about you and the stories behind this guy," he replied as he put her in his arms, like he had done so many times before, and kissed her like he did that first night on the merry-go-round. She smiled and then put her head on his shoulder, whispering that she loved him. He said it back to her and then burst out, "Now let's go watch our son win a championship."

David quickly turned off the light, and he and Becky flew up the stairs, giggling like they were kids as they rushed past all the beautiful pictures of their family that lined the walls along the way. They both got into the car, and David triumphantly presented the lion to Jake while his younger daughter, Lauren, laughed in her booster seat. "What's so funny, Ms. Lauren?" David said as he made a fake growl and moved the lion closer to her face.

Jake looked a little dejected and underwhelmed with what his dad had spent so long looking for. "This is supposed to help me?" he said, again losing what little confidence he had. He rotated the tattered stuffed lion around in his hands. He was examining it, trying desperately to figure out how this dusty stuffed animal meant so much to his dad and was supposed to help him with the game he was about to pitch.

"Absolutely," David replied briskly while fastening his seat belt. "This guy was with me for every game I pitched since I was fifteen years old. That's why he's so beat up. Every time I got scared, I'd just look over at him, and he'd make everything better."

"Really?" Jake replied with a hint of doubt still in his voice.

"Really," David jumped back at his son. "And people used to make fun of me for carrying him around with me, but I didn't care, and neither did they when they saw how well he made me pitch."

Jake smiled at the lion and studied it thoroughly before asking, "Why a lion?"

David just looked over at his wife, who was smiling in the passenger seat and told Jake that that was a long story for another time. He put his hand on Becky's thigh, and they both turned to look at their perfect family together. "Are we ready?" David asked in his coach's voice.

"Ready," Jake replied with a confident big smile. "But, Dad, can we go to Uncle Dusty's place and then get ice cream at the Dairy Barn after the game?"

Becky and David just looked at each other and smiled. "Of course," Becky replied, tapping his little knee.

"Don't forget," Lauren chimed in.

"Don't worry, sweetie, I'll never forget," David replied as he smiled once again at his perfectly beautiful wife while starting to back the car out of the driveway. "I promise you I'll never forget."

Made in the USA
Monee, IL
01 April 2021

64394734R00146